Contemporary northwest writing

A COLLECTION OF
POETRY & FICTION

Contemporary northwest writing

EDITED BY ROY CARLSON

OREGON STATE UNIVERSITY PRESS
Corvallis

Library of Congress Cataloging in Publication Data

Main entry under title:

Contemporary Northwest writing.

1. American literature—Northwest, Pacific
2. American literature—20th century. I. Carlson, Roy, 1927-
PS570.C64   810'   .8'09795   79-10120
ISBN 0-87071-324-8
ISBN 0-87071-323-X pbk.

CREDITS

Theodore Roethke "The Waking," copyright © 1953 by Theodore Roethke; "The Lady and the Bear," copyright © 1951 by Theodore Roethke; "The Waking," copyright © 1948 by Theodore Roethke; "The Manifestation," copyright © 1959 by Beatrice Roethke, Administratrix of the Estate of Theodore Roethke; "Meditation at Oyster River," copyright © 1960 by Beatrice Roethke, Administratrix of the Estate of Theodore Roethke; "The Long Waters," copyright © 1962 by Beatrice Roethke, Administratrix of the Estate of Theodore Roethke; "Elegy for Jane," copyright © 1950 by Theodore Roethke; "I Knew a Woman," copyright © 1954 by Theodore Roethke; "The Sensualists," copyright © 1958 by Theodore Roethke from the book *The Collected Poems of Theodore Roethke.* Reprinted by permission of Doubleday & Company, Inc.

William Stafford From *Stories That Could Be True* by William Stafford: "A Bridge Begins in the Trees," copyright © 1970 by William Stafford; "At Cove at Crooked River," "Vocation," "Traveling Through the Dark," copyright © 1960 by William Stafford; "The Tillamook Burn," "Deer Stolen," copyright © 1958 by William Stafford; "Sleeping on Sisters Land," copyright © 1972 by William Stafford; "My Party the Rain," copyright © 1977 by William Stafford. Reprinted by permission of Harper & Row, Publishers, Inc. First published in *Northwest Review:* "Late August at the Game Refuge," copyright © 1974 by William Stafford; "In Oregon," copyright 1974 by William Stafford; "Finding Sky Ranch," copyright © 1974 by William Stafford. Reprinted by permission of the author.

Madeline DeFrees From *When the Sky Lets Go: Poems by Madeline DeFrees:* "Indian Autobiographies," "Peninsular," "Beach Cliff Graffiti," "Domesticating Two Landscapes," "Psalm for a New Nun," "With a Bottle of Blue Nun to All My Friends," "Letter to an Absent Son," "Barometer," "The Odd Woman," copyright © 1978 by Madeline DeFrees. Reprinted by permission of the publisher, George Braziller, Inc. From *Imaginary Ancestors* by Madeline DeFrees: "Grandmother Grant," copyright © 1977 by Madeline DeFrees. Reprinted with permission of the author.

Richard Hugo "Letter to Kathy from Wisdom," reprinted from *31 Letters and 13 Dreams,* Poems by Richard Hugo, with the permission of the author and the publisher, W. W. Norton & Company, Inc. Copyright © 1977 by W. W. Norton & Company, Inc. "Where Mission Creek Runs Hard for Joy," reprinted from *The Lady in Kicking Horse Reservoir,* Poems by Richard Hugo, with the permission of the author and W. W. Norton & Company, Inc. Copyright © 1973 by Richard Hugo. "Again, Kapowsin," reprinted from *What Thou Lovest Well Remains American,*

Foreword

Someone makes a bouquet, maybe just native plants, from the ditch, missed by the mower's blade. Gathering what is there, looking around for what else might serve, wondering whether chance has allowed a useful cluster, the gatherer sorts out pieces and puts them before us, hopefully, trustingly. It's an anthology. It comes from a place. It is part of what that place is.

Should you spare it a glance?

Yes. Listen: historians and other scholars will tell us about places and events, and the actors in them. And people are convinced. They say, "If I can learn enough history, enough background, it may help me understand a place, a life, and the art and literature there." As a plant from the place of this anthology, I want to try out this reversal:—

Suppose historians are talking. One says, "I don't understand this place." And another one says, "If you knew the art and the literature, you might be more able to make sense of the life: you might understand the history."

You historians, and you guides, and all our betters: from us native plants (weeds? maybe?), this little bouquet, not *about* our area, not *about* what happened—but little pieces of life that escaped, and keep on escaping, from what happened to happen.

William Stafford

Preface

Editing a collection of writing is both an enjoyable and a painful experience. The pleasure has come in discovering how many excellent writers, particularly poets, there are in the Pacific Northwest. The pain is the result of this same discovery plus the financial limitations of a project of this kind.

In spite of the generous help of the Oregon State University Foundation, we have realized from the beginning that we would be limited in the number of pages we could print and that our permissions budget would not be large. The result is that we haven't been able to publish the work of some very good writers.

If this volume is a success, we hope we will be able to remedy our oversights and our mistakes in a second collection. We are well aware that there is exciting work being done by people in the region who have not yet gained national prominence but who undoubtedly will in the future.

The people we have included have earned national recognition. They have published in widely circulated magazines, influential journals, and with highly respected publishing houses. Among them they have won virtually all of the prizes and awards given to writers. They have read their work, given lectures, and participated in workshops at universities throughout the world.

In putting this book together, we did not choose these writers, they were chosen for us. Next time we promise to be more adventurous.

This book is dedicated to all of my fellow "Sub-Subs" everywhere and for all time.

Acknowledgments

I would like to thank Rita Miles for her help in getting this project accepted, and John Irving, of the Oregon State University Foundation, for his efforts in getting it funded. Jeff Grass of the OSU Press guided the book to its completion.

I am also indebted to Pat Brandt of the OSU Library and Nancy Pryor of the Washington State Library for pointing me in the right direction and helping me discover materials that I otherwise would not have found. Rosemary Morrison's assistance added greatly to the accuracy of the biographical and bibliographical sections. Susan Irish contributed the design of the book and its cover.

Bill Stafford and Bob Frank have offered advice and encouragement throughout the project which has been greatly appreciated.

However, my deepest appreciation must go to Jean Patterson Udall, who is not only a skillful editor but a patient and understanding friend.

Roy Carlson
Corvallis, Oregon

Contents

Introduction 1

POETRY

Theodore Roethke

Meditation at Oyster River 10
The Manifestation 12
The Waking 12
The Waking 13
The Sensualists 13
Elegy for Jane 14
The Long Waters 15
The Lady and the Bear 17
I Knew a Woman 18

William Stafford

A Bridge Begins in the Trees 20
At Cove at Crooked River 20
Vocation 21
The Tillamook Burn 21
Deer Stolen 22
Sleeping on the Sisters Land 22
My Party the Rain 23
Late August at the Game Refuge 23
In Oregon 24
Finding Sky Ranch 24
Traveling through the Dark 25

Madeline DeFrees

Grandmother Grant 26
Indian Autobiographies 27
Peninsular 28
Beach Cliff Graffiti 28
Domesticating Two Landscapes 29
Psalm for a New Nun 30
With a Bottle of Blue Nun to All My Friends 31
Letter to an Absent Son 32
Barometer 33
The Odd Woman 33

Richard Hugo

Bay of Resolve 35
Ocean on Monday 35
At the Cabin 36
Again, Kapowsin 37

Port Townsend, 1974 _____ 38
Where Mission Creek Runs Hard for Joy _____ 39
Duwamish _____ 40
Assumptions _____ 41
Letter to Kathy from Wisdom _____ 46

Robert Huff
An Old High Walk _____ 47
Now _____ 48
On the Death of Theodore Roethke _____ 48
On Hearing of the Death of Bernard Strempek _____ 49
Codicil _____ 49
Girl Watching At Grant's Pass _____ 50
Porcupines _____ 51
The Smoker _____ 52
Getting Drunk with Daughter _____ 52

Carolyn Kizer
Amusing Our Daughters _____ 54
By the Riverside _____ 55
Running Away from Home _____ 56
A Widow in Wintertime _____ 60
Children _____ 61

David Wagoner
Talking to the Forest _____ 64
Revival _____ 65
Riverbed _____ 66
A Guide to Dungeness Spit _____ 67
Song for the Soul Going Away _____ 68
Song for the Soul Returning _____ 68
Report from a Forest Logged by the Weyerhaeuser Company _____ 69
Elegy for a Forest Clear-Cut by the Weyerhaeuser Company _____ 70
The Fisherman's Wife _____ 71
The Osprey's Nest _____ 72

Beth Bentley
The House on the Barge _____ 73
This Time a Tree Turns Into a Woman _____ 74
Kennel _____ 75
You Again _____ 76
At the Confluence of the Soleduck, the Bogachiel and the Quillayute _____ 77
Mothers _____ 77
Holding (After the Nez Perce) _____ 78
Drowning Girl _____ 79

John Haines

The Stone Harp 80
If the Owl Calls Again 80
Fairbanks Under the Solstice 81
Skagway 82
The Incurable Home 83
The Mirror 84
Willa 85
To My Father 85
Choosing a Stone 86
The Whale in the Blue Washing Machine 87

Gary Snyder

Hay for the Horses 88
Mid-August at Sourdough Mountain Lookout 88
By Frazier Creek Falls 89
The Dead by the Side of the Road 89
The Late Snow & Lumber Strike of the Summer of Fifty-Four 90
Avocado 91
The Way West, Underground 92
This Poem is for Bear 93
Milton by Firelight 95

Sandra McPherson

Selling the House 96
The Mouse 97
Elegies for the Hot Season 98
His Body 99
In the Columbia River Gorge, After a Death 100
Balm 101
The Bittern 101
Triolet 102
Sentience 103
The Plant 103

Olga Broumas

Sometimes, as a Child 104
Sleeping Beauty 105
Five Interior Landscapes 106
Landscsapes without Touch 109
Oregon Landscape with Lost Lover 109
Landscape with Next of Kin 110
Landscape with Poets 111
Landscape with Leaves and Figures 112

FICTION

Vardis Fisher

from *Mountain Man* 116

H. L. Davis

Open Winter 125

Ursula K. Le Guin

Gwilan's Harp 142

Don Berry

from *To Build a Ship* 147

Ken Kesey

from *One Flew Over the Cuckoo's Nest* 157

Tom Robbins

from *Another Roadside Attraction* 178

Notes on Contributors 182

Selected Bibliography 196

Introduction

It is customary for the editor of a collection of regional writing to announce that the literature of the area has finally come of age, that here we have a harvest of some of the finest fiction and poetry in the United States. I certainly feel this is true of the work included in this book. But anyone who sets out to edit a collection and takes the time to search out regional anthologies published during the last one hundred years will find the literary survival rate of the writers included disappointing. Upon realizing this, there is an urge to take stock of oneself and agree with Herman Melville when in the "Extracts" section of *Moby Dick* he said:

> Thou belongest to that hopeless, sallow tribe which no wine of this world will ever warm; and for whom even Pale Sherry would be too rosy-strong; but with whom one sometimes loves to sit, and feel poor-devilish, too; and grow convivial upon tears; and say to them bluntly, with full eyes and empty glasses and in not altogether unpleasant sadness—Give it up, Sub-Subs! For by how much the more pains ye for ever go Thankless!

Putting together a regional collection is to a large extent the thankless job of trying, in a small way, to assure the literary immortality of a group of writers whose work one values. Melville is a good writer to consider in this regard, not only because by identifying with the "poor devil of a Sub-Sub" the editor assumes the appropriate perspective, but because of the ironic ups and downs in the esteem in which Melville's writing has been held over the years. It is impossible for anyone to predict which of our contemporary writers will be read fifty years from now. One can only say the work of these people is valuable to us now.

For instance, none of the poets included in May Wentworth's *Poetry of the Pacific*, published in 1867, is still read today. Unfortunately, this is also true of all of the Northwest poets who published before the first World War. The one exception is Joaquin Miller, whose work was included in the major anthologies of American literature thirty years ago. But today his work too has been universally dropped, and perhaps this is as it should be. The truth is that when compared with the writers of the nineteenth century whose work continues to be read, Miller, in spite of his appeal as a literary personality, does not measure up. The conclusion one is forced to draw is that our Northwest literary past has not been as rich as we would like it to be.

Writing in 1902 John B. Horner said in the Preface to his anthology *Oregon Literature*, "the men and women who made Oregon have already produced more genuine literature than did the Thirteen Colonies prior to the American Revolution." One can't help but admire Horner's pride in the accomplishments of what was still a frontier society. However, of the more than seventy writers he included in his book, only three or four would be recognized today by anyone other than a specialist in the literature of the region. These are Joaquin

1

Miller, his wife Minnie Myrtle Miller, Ella Higginson, and the cartoonist Homer Davenport. For all of fellow "Sub-Sub" Horner's good intentions, this is not a rich harvest.

In 1934 James Stevens and H. C. Davis, in their pamphlet "Status Rerum," assessed the Northwest literary situation:

> The present condition of literature in the Northwest has been mentioned apologetically too long. Something is wrong with Northwest literature. It is time people were bestirring themselves to find out what it is.
>
> Other sections of the United States can mention their literature as a body with respect. New England, the Middle West, New Mexico and the Southwest, California—each of these has produced a body of literature of which it can be proud. The Northwest—Oregon, Washington, Idaho, Montana—has produced a vast quantity of bilge, so vast, indeed, that the few books which are entitled to respect are totally lost in the general and seemingly interminable avalanche of tripe.

In this caustic vein, Stevens and Davis ripped into the magazines of the area, the writing teachers of the various universities, writers' clubs, and poetry societies for their part in corrupting the literature of the Northwest. There is no question that they overstated their case, but unfortunately they weren't too far off the mark.

At one point in their diatribe they asked if it might not be something "about the climate, or the soil, which inspires people to write tripe?" This is an interesting question in that far more serious critics than Stevens and Davis have pondered the influence of the environment on Northwest writers.

There are two basic schools of thought: the first is that a country filled with so much natural beauty would have to inspire an equally glorious literature, while the second holds that all that rain and subsequent lack of bright clear sunny days would have to warp a person's mind and produce a literature of despair. There is evidence to support both points of view, but when one considers the personal lives as well as the product of the more prominent writers, one is inclined to accept the rain as the dominant element.

Entry after entry in the *Journals of Lewis and Clark* begins by describing the Northwest rain:

> The fog so thick this morning that we could not see a man 50 steps off . . . Rained all the after part of last night, rain continues this morning. . . . A cool wet raney morning. . . . A cloudy foggey morning. Some rain . . . . rained very hard the greater part of last night & continues this morning . . . . A hard rain all last night . . . .

During the winter at Fort Clatsop, Clark recorded that there had been only twelve days without rain and only six with sunshine. A wet beginning for the literature of the white man in the Pacific Northwest, but a very good beginning. The *Journals* are the workmanlike, often crude, account of the exploration of this wet, heavily wooded, wild country. They are a description of the journey in terms of the hardships and pleasures as well as an attempt at scientific observation of the land and its plants and animals. The result is a marvelous document, as impressive as anything that has been produced since.

Another fascinating book of this kind is James Swan's *Northwest Coast or, Three Years' Residence in Washington Territory*, the first book written in what is now Washington state. Published in 1857 it is a description of life at Shoal-Water Bay, now called Willapa Bay, among the oyster pickers who, using Indian labor, loaded California schooners with shell fish to be sold in San Francisco.

Norman H. Clark, in his introduction to the University of Washington Press edition of this book, described Swan as "a moral refugee disguised as a businessman when, in 1852, he found shelter and solace in the wilderness of the Northwest Coast." At the age of thirty-four he had used the gold rush as an excuse to escape from wife, family, and business in Boston to reshape his life in the West.

Swan's scholarship, adventuring, and ability to accept and be accepted by the Indians produced the unique character of this book. Swan is not only an accurate, painstaking observer but a good storyteller. His is a charming book, filled with fine description of the rugged Northwest country and a good humored desire to enjoy it as well as survive it.

The territory south of the Columbia was not so fortunate in terms of the first books written in the region. While the intent of these works was clearly literary, the results were not as satisfactory as *The Northwest Coast*.

The first of these was a novel, *Prairie Flower*, probably written by S. W. Moss but possibly written by J. Emerson Bennett or Overton Johnson. While there is controversy over its author, there is none about its merit. It is universally seen as a relatively popular but bad novel. It is a sentimental romance made more interesting by an unusual setting.

The first book both written and printed in Oregon was a spelling book. The second was a political satire written by an ex-minister turned schoolteacher named William L. Adams, who published his work, *A Melodrama entitled "Treason, Stratagems, and Spoils,"* under the pseudonym Breakspear. First appearing in the *Weekly Oregonian* in 1852, it was later reprinted as a book. It dealt with the political ramifications of moving the capitol from Oregon City to Salem. Herbert Nelson was entirely correct in his monograph *The Literary Impulse in Pioneer Oregon* when he wrote, "Like hundreds of political satires produced throughout the United States, it is now dead literature, without interest except as the earliest literary effort produced entirely in Oregon."

Another interesting failure is *The Grains, Or Passages in the Life of Ruth Rover, with Occasional Pictures of Oregon Natural and Moral* by Margaret Jewett Bailey. Published in 1854 in Portland, this early novel is pure soap opera. It is clear that Mrs. Bailey is writing about her own unhappy life with Dr. William J. Bailey. It is the story of what happens when a pious missionary lady marries a hot tempered drunkard with a passion for Indian women. When the

Baileys were finally divorced she was outraged by the fact that the judge only gave her one hundred dollars as a settlement, and she revenged herself by writing a novel. Given her material it might have been a dandy if she had been a better novelist, but as it stands it is interesting only because of the place and time when it was written.

The first important literary figure in the Northwest, and in many ways one of its most outrageous, was Joaquin Miller; however, it wasn't until he went to London in his flamboyant Western clothes that he was discovered as a poet. A combination of Buffalo Bill and Lord Byron, he was accused by some critics of being a fraud, but Cincinnatus Hiner Miller was no phony frontiersman. He had lived the Western pioneer life.

Born in 1841 in Indiana, Miller came to Oregon with his family in a covered wagon in 1854. When he was fifteen he went to northern California to work in the mines. He lived with the Indians and took one for his wife. Returning to Oregon, he enrolled at Columbia College, where he became class valedictorian. Later he practiced law, tried his hand at mining again, rode for the Pony Express, edited newspapers, became a judge, took a herd of cattle from the Willamette Valley to eastern Oregon, fought the Indians, and planted the first orchard in the Canyon City area. With those credentials it is no wonder that the English accepted him as the real thing.

Songs of the Sierras, which was published in London in 1871, made him an immediate success. The reviews were outstanding and he became a celebrity throughout Europe.

Meanwhile, back at the ranch, the reaction was a mixture of disbelief and hostility. A writer for the Albany *Democrat* was one of the most outspoken:

> C. H. Miller, ex-editor of the Eugene Register, and ex-County Judge of Grant County, has published a book of poems and become a man of fame in London. The fact makes us think no more of Miller, but much less of Londoners.

Also participating in the attack was Miller's ex-wife Minnie Myrtle Miller, a poet whose work was well accepted locally. She hired a hall and gave lectures on "Joaquin Miller, the Poet and the Man." A bright lady with a gift for satire, she was able to keep her audiences laughing from beginning to end. She undoubtedly knew things about Miller that the Londoners did not. For instance, the fact that he had deserted his Indian wife and child and had left Minnie Myrtle with three children to support did not go over well in Oregon.

For reasons of this kind, it was very difficult for the people of the Northwest to make an objective judgement about the value of Joaquin Miller's writing. This is still true today but for different reasons. The particular style of poetry written by many poets during the nineteenth century, even Henry Wadsworth Longfellow, is no longer appreciated. Poetic diction, heavy use of rhyme, and the kind of emphasis on alliteration that would cause Theresa Dyer to change her name to Minnie Myrtle do not appeal to the contemporary reader. Joaquin Miller has been dropped from the American literature texts. Longfellow is still included but seldom taught. Even taking literary fashion into consideration, Miller is not in the same league with Longfellow and certainly no competition for the poet he most admired, Byron, but given the circumstances of his life, his achievement is remarkable. And seen in this context, the achievement of Minnie Myrtle, who many felt was his equal as a poet, is even more remarkable.

To a certain degree Joaquin Miller must be recognized as the creation of an ambitious publisher out to exploit a sophisticated public's interest in the uneducated, intuitive poet of the Western frontier. An even more dramatic example of this fascination with the child of nature was the short but internationally known career of Opal Whiteley.

In 1919, under the editorship of Ellery Sedgewick, *The Atlantic Monthly* published *The Story of Opal: The Journal of an Understanding Heart*. This supposedly is the diary of a six or seven year old child written while living in the Oregon woods. In it she tells her thoughts to Michael Angelo Sanzio Raphael, a 250 foot fir tree. Her companions are Lars Porsena of Clusium a crow, Thomas Chatterton Jupiter Zeus, a wood rat, Peter Paul Rubens, a pig, and other animal friends with equally classical names. Through the use of a series of acrostics in French the story reveals that Opal is really the daughter of Henri d'Orleans and that there has been the usual switching of babies that occurs in melodrama. Elbert Bede, the leading authority on Opal, feels that the book is both hoax and plagiarism, but he also points out that Opal was able to get a letter of introduction from the Secretary of State, that she was accepted by the mother of d'Orleans, and that she was accepted at least for a time as an Indian princess in the household of the Maharana of Adaipur. Hoax or not, this is a significant fulfillment of ones fantasies.

Unfortunately, *The Story of Opal* is not great literature. It is simply evidence of the zany character of part of the Northwest literary tradition. Lewis and Clark probably would have blamed this weird streak on the rain.

Fortunately, there is also a sunny side to early Northwest literature. A fine example of this strain is the work of Ella Higginson, who was brought to Oregon by her parents in the 1860's but spent most of her adult life in Bellingham, Washington, and eventually was named poet laureate of that state. She wrote short stories for such magazines as *McClure's* and *Collier's* and published one novel, but her best work was poetry in praise of the Pacific Northwest.

At times Higginson is perhaps too lyrical and romantic for today's readers in her descriptions of the land and rivers of the region. Yet she had a fine mastery of phrase and brought freshness and a unique clarity to her observation of the commonplace.

In 1931 Harold Merriam published an anthology called *Northwest Verse*. The poetry included in it was, almost without exception, very good, which is surprising in that he included the work of seventy-eight people. However, of that number only a half dozen names are still remembered today, and two of them, H. C. Davis and Vardis Fisher, are better known for their novels.

The others, Howard McKinley Corning, Ethel Romig Fuller, Ben Hur Lampman, and C. E. S. Wood, are all accomplished poets whose work deserves a wider audience than it has had in recent years. While I suppose the odds are against it, it seems possible that one of them might still be accepted as a poet of lasting national prominence.

Along with Davis and Fisher, the region has had a succession of fiction writers who have addressed themselves to Northwest themes. Among them are Ernest Haycox, James Stevens, Robert Cantwell, Anita Pettibone, Max Brand (Frederick Faust), James Stevens, Nard Jones, Clara Weatherwax, Archie Binns, and Sheba Hargreaves. None of these writers achieved the national recognition of Davis or Fisher, but it must be considered that they were writing at a time when the novel was flourishing in America and the competition was tough.

Unfortunately, in my judgment, fiction writing today is not what it once was in the Northwest. The exception is science-fiction. Led by Ursula K. LeGuin and Frank Herbert, this genre is prospering.

Whether the decline of conventional fiction is part of a national trend or the result of the impact of television and film, I have no idea. I can only say it is my impression that more and better poetry is being written in the Northwest today than at any time before, but this is not true of fiction.

While it is generally accepted that Ken Kesey and Tom Robbins are major novelists, they have each built their literary reputations on just two novels. But both are relatively young men who will undoubtedly continue to produce outstanding fiction. Don Berry is also a fine writer, but his last novel was published in 1963 and among his other activities he is writing poetry. David Wagoner has nine novels to his credit, but in my judgment he is a better poet than novelist. Davis and Fisher, who also wrote poetry, are carryovers from a previous generation and have been added to the collection to increase the number of first-rate established writers.

Such addition has not been necessary with the poets. While this is not a particularly young group of poets, only one, Theodore Roethke, seems to stand at that man-made dividing line where the past meets the present. His importance to Northwest literature is such that he not only constitutes our past and our present, but, perhaps more than the others, our future as well.

Carolyn Kizer, David Wagoner, Richard Hugo, Robert Huff, Madeline DeFrees and Beth Bentley have all been influenced by Roethke in one way or another, usually because of having been associated with him at the University of Washington. The sense of community that results from this focus on a gifted individual could be defined as regionalism.

Ironically, ten of Roethke's poems appeared in 1940 in a regional anthology called *New Michigan Verse*. Roethke's biographer, Allan Seager, tells us that Roethke was flattered to be included, but had "a few misgivings also because he did not want to be considered a regional poet."

While in many ways Roethke seems to be the most representative Northwest poet, it was late in his career that he began to make full use of Northwest imagery. We claim him as a poet of our region because he spent the major portion of his last sixteen years in Seattle, partially out of choice and partially because of circumstances. Had he been able to make the right academic connection, he very likely would have moved to a warmer, dryer climate because of his arthritis.

William Stafford is another case of mixed regional loyalties. His early work speaks of Kansas as unmistakably as his later poetry is grounded in the Northwest. Region is important to him, but his writing has not been inspired solely by the characteristics of one part of the country.

Robert Huff's work also has been included in an anthology of Midwestern poetry, and I'm sure that other contributors to this volume have been claimed by more than one region as well. This is not surprising in a country and, for that matter, a world in which the population is as mobile as it is today.

Perhaps Olga Broumas is the best example of this kind of mobility. Born in Greece on the Cyclodes island of Syros, she was nine years old when she was brought to the United States but returned to Greece at twelve. At eighteen she came again to this country and spent three years in Philadelphia. The next seven years, she lived in Eugene, Oregon, and even the casual reader of her poetry, I am sure, will be impressed with the way this Oregon experience permeates her work at this stage in her life.

Next year she will be in Vermont and perhaps New England will become a dominant influence in her writing.

I am not arguing that environment is always the key to the origin or meaning of literature. I think more often than not regionalism is simply a convenient way for an editor or critic to give a sense of organization and unity to the work of an extremely diverse group of writers.

However, there is more to it than that. When I asked Sandra McPherson if she would like to be included in this collection, she responded in somewhat the same way Roethke must have in Michigan. She said, "I hope the book isn't going to be full of clams and salmon and all of that." The answer, of course, is that it is. McPherson herself has supplied a fair share of unmistakable Northwest plants and creatures, both dead and alive, and they enrich her work.

The fiction writers are even more deeply preoccupied with region than the poets. The exception is Ursula K. LeGuin who lives in Portland but is as little confined by region as anyone I have read. Vardis Fisher, H. L. Davis, Don Berry, and Ken Kesey are all deeply concerned with the land and the relationship of their people to it. Tom Robbins, at least in *Another Roadside Attraction,* is preoccupied with the rain. But the rain is part of the beauty of the place and along with the clams and the salmon and the sagebrush and the blue heron, it deserves its poet too.

In making our selection, quality rather than equal representation of each of the Northwest states has been our consideration. Even so, the collection does provide a sense of the diversity of Washington, Oregon, Idaho, Montana, and Alaska.

In any case, I trust that another "Sub-Sub" someplace down the line will painstakingly assess the wisdom of our choices in putting this collection together and assume the thankless task of cataloguing our future once it has become our past.

poetry

Theodore Roethke

MEDITATION AT OYSTER RIVER

1

Over the low, barnacled, elephant-colored rocks,
Come the first tide-ripples, moving, almost without sound, toward me,
Running along the narrow furrows of the shore, the rows of dead clam shells;
Then a runnel behind me, creeping closer,
Alive with tiny striped fish, and young crabs climbing in and out of the water.

No sound from the bay. No violence.
Even the gulls quiet on the far rocks,
Silent, in the deepening light,
Their cat-mewing over,
Their child-whimpering.

At last one long undulant ripple,
Blue-black from where I am sitting,
Makes almost a wave over a barrier of small stones,
Slapping lightly against a sunken log.
I dabble my toes in the brackish foam sliding forward,
Then retire to a rock higher up on the cliff-side.
The wind slackens, light as a moth fanning a stone:
A twilight wind, light as a child's breath
Turning not a leaf, not a ripple.
The dew revives on the beach-grass;
The salt-soaked wood of a fire crackles;
A fish raven turns on its perch (a dead tree in the rivermouth),
Its wings catching a last glint of the reflected sunlight.

2

The self persists like a dying star,
In sleep, afraid. Death's face rises afresh,
Among the shy beasts, the deer at the salt-lick,
The doe with its sloped shoulders loping across the highway,
The young snake, poised in green leaves, waiting for its fly,
The hummingbird, whirring from quince-blossom to morning-glory—
With these I would be.
And with water: the waves coming forward, without cessation,
The waves, altered by sand-bars, beds of kelp, miscellaneous driftwood,

Topped by cross-winds, tugged at by sinuous undercurrents
The tide rustling in, sliding between the ridges of stone,
The tongues of water, creeping in, quietly.

3

In this hour,
In this first heaven of knowing,
The flesh takes on the pure poise of the spirit,
Acquires, for a time, the sandpiper's insouciance,
The hummingbird's surety, the kingfisher's cunning—
I shift on my rock, and I think:
Of the first trembling of a Michigan brook in April,
Over a lip of stone, the tiny rivulet;
And that wrist-thick cascade tumbling from a cleft rock,
Its spray holding a double rain-bow in early morning,
Small enough to be taken in, embraced, by two arms,—
Or the Tittebawasee, in the time between winter and spring,
When the ice melts along the edges in early afternoon.
And the midchannel begins cracking and heaving from the pressure beneath,
The ice piling high against the iron-bound spiles,
Gleaming, freezing hard again, creaking at midnight—
And I long for the blast of dynamite,
The sudden sucking roar as the culvert loosens its debris of branches and sticks,
Welter of tin cans, old bird nests, a child's shoe riding a log,
As the piled ice breaks away from the battered spiles,
And the whole river begins to move forward, its bridges shaking.

4

Now, in this waning of light,
I rock with the motion of morning;
In the cradle of all that is,
I'm lulled into half-sleep
By the lapping of water,
Cries of the sandpiper.

Water's my will, and my way,
And the spirit runs, intermittently,
In and out of the small waves,
Runs with the intrepid shorebirds—
How graceful the small before danger!

In the first of the moon,
All's a scattering,
A shining.

THE MANIFESTATION

Many arrivals make us live: the tree becoming
Green, a bird tipping the topmost bough,
A seed pushing itself beyond itself,
The mole making its way through darkest ground,
The worm, intrepid scholar of the soil—
Do these analogies perplex? A sky with clouds,
The motion of the moon, and waves at play,
A sea-wind pausing in a summer tree.

What does what it should do needs nothing more.
The body moves, though slowly, toward desire.
We come to something without knowing why.

THE WAKING

I wake to sleep, and take my waking slow.
I feel my fate in what I cannot fear.
I learn by going where I have to go.

We think by feeling. What is there to know?
I hear my being dance from ear to ear.
I wake to sleep, and take my waking slow.

Of those so close beside me, which are you?
God bless the Ground! I shall walk softly there,
And learn by going where I have to go.

Light takes the Tree; but who can tell us how?
The lowly worm climbs up a winding stair;
I wake to sleep, and take my waking slow.

Great Nature has another thing to do
To you and me; so take the lively air,
And, lovely, learn by going where to go.

This shaking keeps me steady. I should know.
What falls away is always. And is near.
I wake to sleep, and take my waking slow.
I learn by going where I have to go.

THE WAKING

I strolled across
An open field;
The sun was out;
Heat was happy.

This way! This way!
The wren's throat shimmered,
Either to other,
The blosoms sang.

The stones sang,
The little ones did,
And flowers jumped
Like small goats.

A ragged fringe
Of daisies waved;
I wasn't alone
In a grove of apples.

Far in the wood
A nestling sighed;
The dew loosened
Its morning smells.

I came where the river
Ran over stones:
My ears knew
An early joy.

And all the waters
Of all the streams
Sang in my veins
That summer day.

THE SENSUALISTS

"There is no place to turn," she said,
    "You have me pinned so close;

My hair's all tangled on your head,
   My back is just one bruise;
I feel we're breathing with the dead;
   O angel, let me loose!"

And she was right, for there beside
   The gin and cigarettes,
A woman stood, pure as a bride,
   Affrighted from her wits,
And breathing hard, as that man rode
   Between those lovely tits.

"My shoulder's bitten from your teeth;
   What's that peculiar smell?
No matter which one is beneath,
   Each is an animal,"—
The ghostly figure sucked its breath,
   And shuddered toward the wall;
Wrapped in the tattered robe of death,
   It tiptoed down the hall.

"The bed itself begins to quake,
   I hate this sensual pen;
My neck, if not my heart, will break
   If we do this again,"—
Then each fell back, limp as a sack,
   Into the world of men.

ELEGY FOR JANE

My Student, Thrown by a Horse

I remember the neckcurls, limp and damp as tendrils;
And her quick look, a sidelong pickerel smile;
And how, once startled into talk, the light syllables leaped for her,
And she balanced in the delight of her thought,
A wren, happy, tail into the wind,
Her song trembling the twigs and small branches.
The shade sang with her;
The leaves, their whispers turned to kissing;
And the mold sang in the bleached valleys under the rose.

Oh, when she was sad, she cast herself down into such a pure depth,
Even a father could not find her:
Scraping her cheek against straw;
Stirring the clearest water.

My sparrow, you are not here,
Waiting like a fern, making a spiny shadow.
The sides of wet stones cannot console me,
Nor the moss, wound with the last light.

If only I could nudge you from this sleep,
My maimed darling, my skittery pigeon.
Over this damp grave I speak the words of my love:
I, with no rights in this matter,
Neither father nor lover.

THE LONG WATERS

1

Whether the bees have thoughts, we cannot say,
But the hind part of the worm wiggles the most,
Minnows can hear, and butterflies, yellow and blue,
Rejoice in the language of smells and dancing.
Therefore I reject the world of the dog
Though he hear a note higher than C
And the thrush stopped in the middle of his song.

And I acknowledge my foolishness with God,
My desire for the peaks, the black ravines, the rolling mists
Changing with every twist of wind,
The unsinging fields where no lungs breathe,
Where light is stone.
I return where fire has been,
To the charred edge of the sea
Where the yellowish prongs of grass poke through the blackened ash,
And the bunched logs peel in the afternoon sunlight,
Where the fresh and salt waters meet,
Where the sea-winds move through the pine trees,
A country of bays and inlets, and small streams flowing seaward.

2

Mnetha, Mother of Har, protect me
From the worm's advance and retreat, from the butterfly's havoc,
From the slow sinking of the island peninsula, the coral efflorescence,
The dubious sea-change, the heaving sands, and my tentacled sea-cousins.

But what of her?—
Who magnifies the morning with her eyes,
That star winking beyond itself,
The cricket-voice deep in the midnight field,
The blue jay rasping from the stunted pine.

How slowly pleasure dies!—
The dry bloom splitting in the wrinkled vale,
The first snow of the year in the dark fir.
Feeling, I still delight in my last fall.

3

In time when the trout and young salmon leap for the low-flying insects,
And the ivy-branch, cast to the ground, puts down roots into the sawdust,
And the pine, whole with its roots, sinks into the estuary,
Where it leans, tilted east, a perch for the osprey,
And a fisherman dawdles over a wooden bridge,
These waves, in the sun, remind me of flowers:
The lily's piercing white,
The mottled tiger, best in the corner of a damp place,
The heliotrope, veined like a fish, the persistent morning-glory,
And the bronze of a dead burdock at the edge of a prairie lake,
Down by the muck shrinking to the alkaline center.

I have come here without courting silence,
Blessed by the lips of a low wind,
To a rich desolation of wind and water,
To a landlocked bay, where the salt water is freshened
By small streams running down under fallen fir trees.

4

In the vaporous grey of early morning,
Over the thin, feathery ripples breaking lightly against the irregular shoreline—
Feathers of the long swell, burnished, almost oily—
A single wave comes in like the neck of a great swan
Swimming slowly, its back ruffled by the light cross-winds,
To a tree lying flat, its crown half broken.

I remember a stone breaking the eddying current,
Neither white nor red, in the dead middle way,
Where impulse no longer dictates, nor the darkening shadow,
A vulnerable place,
Surrounded by sand, broken shells, the wreckage of water.

5

As light reflects from a lake, in late evening,
When bats fly, close to slightly tilting brownish water,
And the low ripples run over a pebbly shoreline,
As a fire, seemingly long dead, flares up from a downdraft of air in a chimney,
Or a breeze moves over the knees from a low hill,
So the sea wind wakes desire.
My body shimmers with a light flame.

I see in the advancing and retreating waters
The shape that came from my sleep, weeping:
The eternal one, the child, the swaying vine branch,
The numinous ring around the opening flower,
The friend that runs before me on the windy headlands,
Neither voice nor vision.

I, who came back from the depths laughing too loudly,
Become another thing;
My eyes extend beyond the farthest bloom of the waves;
I lose and find myself in the long water;
I am gathered together once more;
I embrace the world.

THE LADY AND THE BEAR

A Lady came to a Bear by a Stream.
"Oh why are you fishing that way?
Tell me, dear Bear there by the Stream,
Why are you fishing that way?"

"I am what is known as a Biddly Bear,—
That's why I'm fishing this way.
We Biddly's are Pee-culiar Bears.
And so,—I'm fishing this way.

"And besides, it seems there's a Law:
A most, most exactious Law
Says a Bear
Doesn't dare
Doesn't dare
Doesn't DARE
Use a Hook or a Line,
Or an old piece of Twine,
Not even the end of his Claw, Claw, Claw,
Not even the end of his Claw.
Yes, a Bear has to fish with his Paw, Paw, Paw.
A Bear has to fish with his Paw."

"O it's Wonderful how with a flick of your Wrist,
You can fish out a fish, out a fish, out a fish,
If *I* were a fish I just couldn't resist
You, when you are fishing that way, that way,
When you are fishing that way."

And at that the Lady slipped from the Bank
And fell in the Stream still clutching a Plank,
But the Bear just sat there until she Sank;
As he went on fishing his way, his way,
As he went on fishing his way.

I KNEW A WOMAN

I knew a woman, lovely in her bones,
When small birds sighed, she would sigh back at them;
Ah, when she moved, she moved more ways than one:
The shapes a bright container can contain!
Of her choice virtues only gods should speak,
Or English poets who grew up on Greek
(I'd have them sing in chorus, cheek to cheek).

How well her wishes went! She stroked my chin,
She taught me Turn, and Counter-turn, and Stand;
She taught me Touch, that undulant white skin;
I nibbled meekly from her proffered hand;
She was the sickle; I, poor I, the rake,
Coming behind her for her pretty sake
(But what prodigious mowing we did make).

Love likes a gander, and adores a goose:
Her full lips pursed, the errant note to seize;
She played it quick, she played it light and loose;
My eyes, they dazzled at her flowing knees;
Her several parts could keep a pure repose,
Or one hip quiver with a mobile nose
(She moved in circles, and those circles moved).

Let seed be grass, and grass turn into hay:
I'm martyr to a motion not my own;
What's freedom for? To know eternity.
I swear she cast a shadow white as stone.
But who would count eternity in days?
These old bones live to learn her wanton ways:
(I measure time by how a body sways).

William Stafford

A BRIDGE BEGINS IN THE TREES

In an owl cry, night became real night;
from that owl cry night came
on the nerve. I felt the shock
and rolled into the dark upon my feet
listening. There was no wind.

Among the firs my fire was almost out;
I heard the lake shore tapping, then
what was no wind, a cry
within the owl cry, behind the cross
of dark the mountain made.

"Honest love will come near fire," I cried,
"and counts all partway friendship a despair."
(For that night sound had struck a nerve,
a crazybone; or some old crag had lapsed,
or just the fire had died.)

My voice went echoing, inventing response
around the world for all of our greatest need,
the longest arc, toward Friend, from All Alone.
For that brief tenure my old faith
sang again along the bone.

AT COVE ON THE CROOKED RIVER

At Cove at our camp in the open canyon
it was the kind of place where you might look out
some evening and see trouble walking away.

And the river there meant something
always coming from snow and flashing around boulders
after shadow-fish lurking below the mesa.

We stood with wet towels over our heads for shade,
looking past the Indian picture rock and the kind of trees
that act out whatever has happened to them.

Oh civilization, I want to carve you like this,
decisively outward the way evening comes
over that kind of twist in the scenery

When people cramp into their station wagons
and roll up the windows, and drive away.

VOCATION

This dream the world is having about itself
includes a trace on the plains of the Oregon trail,
a groove in the grass my father showed us all
one day while meadowlarks were trying to tell
something better about to happen.

I dreamed the trace to the mountains, over the hills,
and there a girl who belonged wherever she was.
But then my mother called us back to the car:
she was afraid; she always blamed the place,
the time, anything my father planned.

Now both of my parents, the long line through the plain,
the meadowlarks, the sky, the world's whole dream
remain, and I hear him say while I stand between the two,
helpless, both of them part of me:
"Your job is to find what the world is trying to be."

THE TILLAMOOK BURN

These mountains have heard God;
they burned for weeks. He spoke
in a tongue of flame from sawmill trash
and you can read His word down to the rock.

In milky rivers the steelhead
butt upstream to spawn
and find a world with depth again,
starting from stillness and water across gray stone.

Inland along the canyons
all night weather smokes
past the deer and the widow-makers—
trees too dead to fall till again He speaks,

Mowing the criss-cross trees and the listening peaks.

DEER STOLEN

Deer have stood around our house
at night so still nobody knew,
and waited with ears baling air.
I hunt the still deer everywhere.

For what they heard and took away,
stepping through the chaparral,
was the sound of Then; now it's Now,
and those small deer far in the wild

Are whispers of our former life.
The last print of some small deer's foot
might hold the way, might be a start
that means in ways beyond our ken

Important things. I follow them
through all the hush of long ago
to listen for what small deer know.

SLEEPING ON THE SISTERS LAND

Rain touches your face just at daylight.
No sky in the west: you turn your head
and the world revolves into gray so bright
that a glance like love falls deep
    toward the dreams that you left.

What lands are these, forever near?
They are great gray islands that come for us,
where the new dreams are, far as the sky
and the light, and sudden as rain
    that touches your face.

MY PARTY THE RAIN

Loves upturned faces, laves everybody,
applauds tennis courts, pavements; its fingers
ache and march through the forest numbering
limbs, animals, Boy Scouts; it recognizes
every face, the blind, the criminal
beggar or millionaire, despairing child,
minister cloaked; it finds all the dead
by their stones or mounds, or their deeper listening
for the help of such rain, a census that cares
as much as any party, neutral in politics.

It proposes your health, Governor, at the Capitol;
licks every stone, likes the shape of our state.
Let wind in high snow this year
legislate its own mystery: our lower winter
rain feathers in over miles of trees
to explore. A cold, cellophane layer,
silver wet, it believes what it touches,
and goes on, persuading one thing at a time,
fair, clear, honest kind—
a long session, Governor. Who knows the end?

LATE AUGUST AT THE GAME REFUGE

Out on the wide marsh at Malheur
the wind opens its mouth.

Cloud signals over the mountains
hang for hours, once they are spoken.

Birds in the grass are simmering, never
quite ready for thunder.

Shivering for miles, the reeds bow.
A big brown animal thrashes off in the rain—

Summer, getting away.

IN OREGON

Old barns let in the rain that always
tried, and the sun that waited. Shadows
cluster there, with sunlight buttons.
After a farm has failed, barns last
on, their walls laced wih patches
of field and grove. This country has a cast
of thousands, many scattered and unseen.
The floors go first, but serve on where
they can. Everyone they ever
knew comes back—ripe wheat, ripe wheat.

In the hills they are there,
courted by blackberry vines, and
apple trees that know the wind.
You walk the vacant country, give
a look to anything that holds on.
Down a fence row your eyes come
to rest, far—a post, a post,
a tree, an old barn, rain.

FINDING SKY RANCH

There beyond Hay Creek turn at
the red barn. You can cross
the ford unless beaver have flooded
it again. Then the hills
receive you, eyes alive with wonder.
The road on old arrowheads hunts
through upland pasture till it finds
the Kibby place, ambushed by Indian
paintbrush and wild apple trees.
You can walk there all day and look back.

Don't worry—old Oregon:
blackberry vines won't let it fall.

TRAVELING THROUGH THE DARK

Traveling through the dark I found a deer
dead on the edge of the Wilson River road.
It is usually best to roll them into the canyon:
that road is narrow; to swerve might make more dead.

By glow of the tail-light I stumbled back of the car
and stood by the heap, a doe, a recent killing;
she had stiffened already, almost cold.
I dragged her off; she was large in the belly.

My fingers touching her side brought me the reason—
her side was warm; her fawn lay there waiting,
alive, still, never to be born.
Beside that mountain road I hesitated.

The car aimed ahead its lowered parking lights;
under the hood purred the steady engine.
I stood in the glare of the warm exhaust turning red;
around our group I could hear the wilderness listen.

I thought hard for us all—my only swerving—,
then pushed her over the edge into the river.

Madeline DeFrees

GRANDMOTHER GRANT

Not the rejected lies of the New York Foundling
home, not the adoptive widow of two names,
one of devious spelling,
not the dogtag pinned to the plaid dress
for the train ride to Missouri, but the surname
worn like a shoulder brand
on the skin of the natural mother,
Grandmother Grant.

When I went in my black robes through the hot
streets of the city, a young nun
pale as the star I followed
led to the desk of a three-faced guardian. One
face called me Sister to my face. One was
motherly: "O my dear, I can't risk the wrong
information." One, older than the order, nervous,
bit the sentence off
on a fragment of Irish history.

I couldn't get past the gate. I recognized
the road I was on
led to heaven or hell. Either was barred,
date too early for the name.
A Closed File. I should tell my mother to come.
Back home in Oregon, sixty-nine, wanting to know,
not wanting to know, she waited.
I crossed the continent angry, three thousand
miles of featureless plain.

Mother, now that you've gone, I'm the same,
swaddled no more in the habit.
Whatever it is that drives us—bad blood,
the face in the unlighted window,
I'm bound to get it straight. If he knocked her down
in the stinking hold of a ship and raped her,
if she followed him out of the church
into the oldest garden under moonstone limbs

of the sycamore, it's too late
to cover her tracks.

Whoever she was, whatever ties,
here is my claim. I need to come into my own.

INDIAN AUTOBIOGRAPHIES

For Gary Kimble

I have no way of knowing how you tracked me here.
Maybe a dry branch cracked in the forest heart.
A puff of smoke twisted to begin its lazy climb.
We did not move. The night was ours. I watched a maple leaf
turn over in your face and die. Clues we dropped
along the way were just a game for tourists.
Cigar-store Indians and those cute, concentric nuns.
We wound them up and let them take the stage
and watched each other from the eyes behind our eyes.

How many cigarettes to bring me peace?
You let me wander the ground over and over
When you knew every pore in the moss,
the shadow a bird makes, the river of dew
in a leaf's concave, you said
some terrible gentle word that sent me back
to the place it all began. We learned
to keep still in dialects so old our trust
restored the language. Collectors dug up scraps
of dirty blankets, framed them, amazed
at their design. Where sun can't penetrate
there may be time to use cold shade for cover,
prove the race is human.

Late fall again outside.
Half-breeds remember. We tie a scarlet rag
on the tamarack and sink our lightweight steps
in the looked-for snow.

PENINSULAR

My own voice brings you back
over the dark night waves
wide as the sea's arms and the wind's
enclosure, lapping the disparate shores
with a somber echo or breaking on bone-
white sand with a thundering nearness.

Your face moves under the fractured
waters, always and never the same
in the deep green light. And the cry
of wheeling seasons lengthens across
your shadow, lost in the wavering image
my eyes refract.

        Child or grandfather
god in the seaweed silence, wrapped
in the streaming bands or the bearded surge:
I drown you in each new day, but the body
rises to float, face down,
on the crest of a quartered moon.

I cannot call over the roiling tide;
my ears drum with a hollow, dumb containment,
and my voice comes back, back, like a message
in a bottle, sealed in the universal vessel,
home to the harbor's continental drift
to break its narrow neck on the structured rock.

BEACH CLIFF GRAFFITI

Already your name is worn on the rock—
gouge and scar—
sandstone kiss of knife against cliff,
the silica glare.
I take them into the circular track of the sea
under the picture-window stare
of brick and wood.

Sunstruck bodies litter the sand.
A windy bird

stretches the sky to its frame.
Slow gain of the sea
on land. I feel you moving in
with the singing surf.
My voice rides a heady wind
lost on the sea floor. Whose echo rings
off that lighthouse rock,
washes small life into tidepools?

I tunnel under the long roar
to that far cove where your hands gather
the moody night. Whose image?
Whose inscription? Impartial sun
looks into particular marks,
the unlettered code of climbers
the crude moon leaves in shadow. Now

I touch your sign
with earth-moving fingers
the world slides from under
the shifting slope near dune grass

my legend, line, in tune
with the salty racetrack and marine bodies,
with the maned waves.

DOMESTICATING TWO LANDSCAPES

Where I wait, huge sea rhythms roll. Winds
cover chimes, flow on anonymous errands
to mornings after. Forgotten toast still burning,

I try to remember who it was that went down.
One of the crew? No use. "Walk on water," he said.
If somebody answers today I'll know I was afraid.

I can't hold my head above the laundry.
Every day out there, hulls and shells and ruined bodies
wash ashore. Women lament. Comb the beach

for signs or souvenirs, foam slapping at ankles,
faces tight. For years I watched them from the ridge.
Waves held me upright. That was earlier, somewhere

I can't go back to. Salt rises in my closed throat,
waves follow everywhere I run. The mountain
tells me I'll be crushed. Sea flushes

out of my ears. Bulk bears me down, rears
above the surface spitting rock. When an island saves
you from drowning it burns you out. Centuries to come

monastery bells may shimmer through sea-green silence
in lyric washes; stones melt on an unsuspecting town
hot from a friendly mountain to cast the skiing neighbors

in ceramic postures. The fluted empty cup
of a blueberry muffin, warm from the oven, stiffens
besides your plate. The cycle run, I go to join the washing,

hang it all on the line. Temperature at normal,
the frigidaire hums grace. Our bones follow, but
we keep them in their chairs. After the meal

you will know that the soft word from a cold tap
or the electric range, echoes uneasy
under snow and terrified of being heard.

PSALM FOR A NEW NUN

My life was rescued like a bird from the fowler's snare.
It comes back singing tonight in my loosened hair

as I bend to the mirror in this contracted room
lit by the electric music of the comb.

With hair cropped close as a boy's, contained in a coif,
the years made me forget what I had cut off.

Now the glass cannot compass my dark halo
and the frame censors the dense life it cannot follow.

Like strength restored in the temple this sweetness wells
quietly into tissues of abandoned cells;

better by as much as it is better to be
a woman, I feel this gradual urgency

till the comb snaps, the mirror widens, and the walls recede.
With head uncovered I am no longer afraid.

Broken is the snare and I am freed.
My help is in the name of the Lord who made
heaven and earth. Yes, earth.

WITH A BOTTLE OF BLUE NUN
TO ALL MY FRIENDS

1

Sisters,
The Blue Nun has eloped with one
of the Christian Brothers. They are living
in a B&B Motel just out of
Sacramento.

2

The Blue Nun works the late shift
in Denver. Her pierced ears
drip rubies
like the Sixth Wound.

3

This is to inform you
that the Blue Nun
will become Mayor of Missoula
in the new dispensation.
At fifty-eight she threw her starched coif
into the ring and was off to a late win
over Stetson and deerstalker,
Homburg and humbug,
Church and State.

4

When you receive this you will know
that the Blue Nun
has blacked out
in a sleazy dive
outside San Francisco.
They remember her in Harlem.
She still carried her needle case
according to the ancient custom.

5

You may have noticed
how the walls lean towards the river
where a veil of fog hides a sky diver's
pale descent. The parachute
surrounds her like a wimple.
That's what happens when Blue Nuns
bail out.
It's that simple.

LETTER TO AN ABSENT SON

It's right to call you son. That cursing alcoholic
is the god I married early before I really knew him:
spiked to his crossbeam bed, I've lasted thirty years.
Nails are my habit now. Without them I'm afraid.

At night I spider up the wall to hide in crevices
deeper than guilt. His hot breath smokes me out.
I fall and fall into the arms I bargained for,
sifting them cool as rain. A flower touch could tame me.
Bring me down that giant beam to lie submissive
in his fumbling clutch. One touch. Bad weather
moves indoors: a cyclone takes me.

How shall I find a shelter in the clouds, driven by
gods, gold breaking out of them everywhere?
Nothing is what it pretends. It gathers to a loss
of leaves and graves. Winter in the breath.
Your father looked like you, his dying proportioned
oddly to my breast. I boxed him in my plain pine
arms and let him take his ease just for a minute.

BAROMETER

Over the wreck of winter another season
crashes on this unprotected coast, cryptic
with April flotsam and the dried lavender tears
of wisteria. All through a cold spring
it has been snowing somewhere at the back
of my mind. Sleet covers a hulk dredged
from weeds to bleach on salt islands. Ashore,
ivy quickens on brick faces; over
the seawall forsythia in sunlight
flares, and cherry in white mounds chastens
the drowning eye.

           Hollow with the tug and slap
of far tides in a strict cove, I swallow
the whole ocean at one look
and in the shadow of a rock, breathe in
the drift of the sand.

THE ODD WOMAN

At parties I want to get even,
my pocket calculator rounds everything off,
taught to remember. I'm not so good
at numbers, feel awkward
as an upper plate without a partner.
Matched pairs float from the drawing board
into the drawing room, ears touched
with the right scent,
teeth and mouth perfect.

The cougar jaw yawns on the sofa back,
his molars an art-object.
The old and strange collect around me,
names I refuse pitched at my head
like haloes. This one is a dead-ringer.
It rings dead. I pat the head of the beagle
nosing in my crotch and try to appear
grateful. A witch
would mount the nearest broom

and leave by the chimney. At ten I plot
my exit: gradual shift to the left,
a lunge toward the bourbon. The expert hunters
are gutting a deer
for the guest of honor. Soft eyes
accuse my headlights. I mention early
morning rituals. A colleague
offers to show me the door I've watched
for the last hour.

We come to my coat laid out
in the master bedroom, warm hands curled
in the pocket. I know
how a woman who leaves her purse behind
wants to be seduced. I hang mine
from the shoulder I cry on.
Say goodnight to the Burmese buddha,
hunters in the snow,
and leave for the long river drive to town.

Richard Hugo

BAY OF RESOLVE

Think how we touch each other when we sight land
after two years at sea. How we say, "It's still there."
The gulls weren't lying who came to pilot us home.
No matter what happens inside them, the houses climb
lovingly tight to hills, and the smoke rising
above the houses takes the sea chill out of our bones.
When we make out women, the form of them certain
against the white seawall, we stand on the rail and wave.

What holds us back? The shore boats are waiting.
We sit glum in our quarters and sweat. The mate
yells, "going ashore" and the pink girls in the corner
with wild lemon hair cry "farewell," our bite marks
still clear on their necks. How they fought for our kisses
south of Australia. What dishes they cooked.
Can we ever leave them? Those bright days they flew
ahead on the bow singing "on," every red inch
of their bodies stung by the shark spray, their faces
shining alive with our love under the pulsing sky.
Our first kiss on land is cold. We turn away.

This bay never gets wild. The harbor is ideal. We need
not anchor our boat. Three months of summer
the water lies flatter than dawn. In this calm weather
we have no reason to mock the captain or sneak
back of the bilge pump to study worn photos of girls.
Long ago, didn't we read how all journeys end?
The man in that story, his name lost now, came home
tired from the raw world of dragon and flame
and developed a coin, still in use, a salmon on one side
under the words "Good As Water." On the other
a woman firm in silver relief.

OCEAN ON MONDAY

Here at last is ending
Where gray coordinates with nothing
the horizon wrinkles in the wind.

These will end: shrimp a mile
below, blue shark, sole
rocks alive as crabs in shifting green.

patent bathers, barnacles, kelp that lies
in wilting whips, jelly-
fish that open lonely as a hand,

space that drives into expanse
boredom banging in your face
the horizon stiff with strain.

AT THE CABIN

We ripple aspen the way we move out
in the morning meadow wind. Stay close
through the buffalo willow's manic perfume
across the field of lupin where the fresh track
of a cougar gives us the direction not to go.
We climb high lichen and below us
farther than our first dream of the void
the north fork of the Teton cannot move.
We are frozen deep in hunger.
If we tumble coupled down the rock side
bouncing from the last ledge out in sky
in final isolation like the eagle, like the bones
of Crees, we'll shatter on the valley floor
separate as stars. Love's the best way
to feel safe. Love on moss. Love on springy bed
of juniper. And there must be definite ways
of telling how the mate remaining, widower Mallard
or warrior Cree who killed his wife by mistake
doubles his grief every storm.

Pale letter from home: "We hope you return
someday. We love you still." The pages
ride thermals like white spastic birds
across the canyon to Uninhabited Mountain.
More than letter disappears. More than past.
The red hawk stumbles, catches himself and climbs.
The cougar, spurred by rumor of a spacious cave,
turns south to Ear Mountain and a hoped for role:
I am good enough to own a home.

We come back tired. Ways of hating the past
sour inside us. We bore ourselves remembering
children in ruin, too many tears at the pass.
If the Teton falters, move the rocks.
No matter how water jitters, water
has no nerves. Rivers flow because the first law
of all land is slant. The second, desire to ride.
We ripple aspen the way we move back
to the cabin baking in motionless noon.
And the aspen ring. The river loosens at its pools
and takes off shooting wildly at the sky
like some drunk cowboy, his first night back in town
after centuries of good work done.

AGAIN, KAPOWSIN

That goose died in opaque dream.
I was trolling in fog when the blurred
hunter stood to aim. The chill gray
that blurred him amplified the shot
and the bird scream. The bird was vague form
and he fell as a plane would fall on a town,
unreal. The frantic thrashing was real.
The hunter clubbed him dead with an oar—
crude *coup de grâce*. Today, bright sky
and the shimmering glint of cloud on black water.
I'm twenty years older and no longer row
for that elusive wisdom I was certain
would come from constant replay of harm.
Countless shades of green erupted up the hill.
I didn't see them. They erupt today, loud
banner and horn. Kingdoms come through for man
for the first time.

This is the end of wrong hunger. I no longer
troll for big trout or grab for that infantile pride
I knew was firm when my hand ran over
the violet slash on their flanks. My dreams include
wives and stoves. A perch that fries white in the pan
is more important than his green vermiculations,
his stark orange pelvic fin. And whatever

I wave goodbye to, a crane waves back
slow as twenty years of lifting fog. For the first time
the lake is clear of hemlock. From now on
bars will not be homes.

Again, Kapowsin. Now the magic is how
distances change as clouds constantly alter
the light. Lives that never altered here are done.
Whatever I said I did, I lied. I did not claw
each cloud that poured above me nude.
I didn't cast a plug so perfectly in pads
bass could not resist and mean faces of women
shattered in the splash. Again, Kapowsin.
The man who claimed he owned it is a stranger.
He died loud in fog and his name won't come.

PORT TOWNSEND, 1974

On this dishonored, this perverted globe
we go back to the sea and the sea opens for us.
It spreads a comforting green we knew when children—
celery—Wesson Oil can—through islands. It flares
fresh immediate blue beyond the world's edge
where dreams turn back defeated and the child weeps
replaying some initial loss. Whatever it does for us
it is resolute, even when it imitates sad grasses
on the inland plains and gulls are vultures overhead
hidden in the bewildering glare.
Aches of what we wanted to be and reluctantly are
play out in the wash, wash up the sand and die
and slip back placid to the crashing source.
The sea releases our rage. Logs fly over
the seawall and crush the homes of mean neighbors.
Our home, too. The sea makes fun of what we are
and we laugh beside our fire, seeing our worst selves
amplified in space and wave. We are absurd.
And sea comes knocking again in six hours. The sea
comes knocking again. Out there, salmon batter
candlefish senseless for dinner. The troller flashes
his dodger through the salmon school. The sky widens
in answer to claustrophobic prayer. The sea believes us
when we sing: we knew no wrong high back in the mountains

where lost men shed their clothes the last days
of delirium and die from white exposure. We found one
sitting erect, his back against the stars, and even dead
he begged us to take him west to the shore of the sea.

WHERE MISSION CREEK RUNS HARD FOR JOY

Rapids shake the low hung limbs like hair.
In your wine old fields of wheat replay
gold promises of what a kiss would be. In your face
a horse still flogs your face. Whatever is odd,
the Indian without a tribe who dresses mad
in kilts, the cloud that snaps at mountains,
means, to you, life at normal, no rest
from the weird. My obsessions too
ugly out in air and down the driving
water to the dam. We rest easy in these pines.
This run-off, lives or water, leaves us mute.

I fight the sudden cold diminished light
with flashbacks of a blonde, somewhere
outside Bremerton, her face my first sun
and I never knew her name. Was it you
across this table now, all centuries of what
all men find lovely, Mongolian and Serb,
invested in your face still pink from
the wind's slap and that sadistic wheat?
Money's in the creek. Gold stones magnify
to giant coins, and you poise gold alone
on rock above the wealthy water
and the slow swamp of some early bitter scene.

Kiss my wine and pour it down my tongue.
Pour it twisted down my hair. Protective armour
fragments in the creek's road. You are right
to say the trees here grow too straight.
I am right to bring back all the harsh
bizarre beginning of the dirt, the long beat
of each sun across the cabbage, and the hate
that comes from nowhere, that's accounted for
in photos of ourselves we took and still sneak

looks at late at night. And we are right—
the coins are real, the low hung limbs are hair
and Mission Creek, this wild high run-off
in our mouths is clearly on its way.

for Joy Tweten

DUWAMISH

Midwestern in the heat, this river's
curves are slow and sick. Water knocks
at mills and concrete plants, and crud
compounds the gray. On the out-tide,
water, half salt water from the sea,
rambles by a barrel of molded nails,
gray lumber piles, moss on ovens
in the brickyard no one owns.
Boys are snapping tom cod spines
and jeering at the Greek who bribes
the river with his sailing coins.

Because the name is Indian, Indians
ignore the river as it cruises
past the tavern. Gulls are diving crazy
where boys nail porgies to the pile.
No Indian would interrupt his beer
to tell the story of the snipe
who dove to steal the nailed girl
late one autumn, with the final salmon in.

This river colors day. On bright days
here, the sun is always setting or obscured
by one cloud. Or the shade extended
to the far bank just before you came.
And what should flare, the Chinese red
of a searun's fin, the futile roses,
unkept cherry trees in spring, is muted.
For the river, there is late November
only, and the color of a slow winter.

On the short days, looking for a word,
knowing the smoke from the small homes
turns me colder than wind from

the cold river, knowing this poverty
is not a lack of money but of friends.
I come here to be cold. Not silver cold
like ice, for ice has glitter. Gray
cold like the river. Cold like 4 P.M.
on Sunday. Cold like a decaying porgy.

But cold is a word. There is no word along
this river I can understand or say.
Not Greek threats to a fishless moon
nor Slavic chants. All words are Indian.
Love is Indian for water, and madness
means, to Redmen, I am going home.

ASSUMPTIONS

When I feel a northwest town may trigger a poem, before I start writing I assume one or more of the following—

The name of the town is significant and must appear in the title.

The inhabitants are natives and have lived there forever. I am the only stranger.

I have lived there all my life and should have left long ago but couldn't.

Although I am playing roles, on the surface I appear normal to the townspeople.

I am an outcast returned. Years ago the police told me to never come back but after all this time I assume that either I'll be forgiven or that I will not be recognized.

At best, relationships are marginal. The inhabitants have little relation with each other and none with me.

The town is closely knit and the community is pleasant. I am not a part of it but am a happy observer.

A hermit lives on the outskirts in a one room shack. He eats mostly fried potatoes. He spends hours looking at old faded photos. He has not spoken to anyone in years. Passing children often taunt him with songs and jokes.

41

Each Sunday, a little after 4 p.m., the sky turns a depressing gray and the air becomes chilly.

I run a hardware store and business is slow.

I run a bar and business is fair and constant.

I work in a warehouse on second shift. I am the only one in town on second shift.

I am the town humorist and people are glad to see me because they know I'll have some good new jokes and will tell them well.

The churches are always empty.

A few people attend church and the sermons are boring.

Everybody but me goes to church and the sermons are inspiring.

On Saturday nights everyone has fun but me. I sit home alone and listen to the radio. I wish I could join the others though I enjoy feeling left out.

All beautiful young girls move away right after high school and never return, or if they return, are rich and disdainful of those who stayed on.

I am on friendly terms with all couples, but because I live alone and have no girlfriend, I am of constant concern to them. I am an 11 year old orphan.

I am 89 and grumpy but with enormous presence and wisdom.

Terrible things once happened here and as a result the town became sad and humane.

The population does not vary.

The population decreases slightly each year.

The graveyard is carefully maintained and the dead are honored one day each year.

The graveyard is ignored and overrun with weeds.

No one dies, makes love or ages.

No music.

Lots of excellent music coming from far off. People never see or know who is playing.

The farmer's market is alive with shoppers, good vegetables and fruit. Prices are fixed. Bargaining is punishable by death.

The movie house is run by a kind man who lets children in free when no one is looking.

The movie house has been closed for years.

Once the town was booming but fell on hard times around 1910.

At least one person is insane. He or she is accepted as part of the community.

The annual picnic is a failure. No one has a good time.

The annual picnic is a huge success but the only fun people have all year.

The grain elevator is silver.

The water tower is gray and the paint is peeling.

The mayor is so beloved and kind elections are no longer held.

The newspaper, a weekly, has an excellent gossip column but little or no news from outside.

No crime.

A series of brutal murders took place years ago. The murderer was never caught and is assumed still living in the town.

One man is a social misfit. He is thrown out of bars and not allowed in church. He shuffles about the streets unable to find work and is subjected to insults and disdainful remarks by beautiful girls. He tries to make friends but can't.

A man takes menial jobs for which he is paid very little. He is grateful for what little work he can find and is always cheerful. In any encounter with others he assumes he is wrong and backs down. His place in the town social structure is assured.

Two whores are kind to everyone but each other.

The only whore in town rejected a proposal of marriage years ago. The man left town and later became wealthy and famous in New York.

Cats are fed by a sympathetic but cranky old woman.

Dogs roam the streets.

The schoolhouse is a huge frame building with only one teacher who is old but never ages. She is a spinster and everyone in town was once in her class.

Until I found it, no outsider had ever seen it.

It is not on any map.

It is on a map but no roads to it are shown.

The next town is many miles away. It is much classier, has a nice new movie house, sprarkling drive-ins and better looking girls. The locals in my town dream of moving to the next town but never do.

The town doctor is corrupt and incompetent.

The town druggist is an alcoholic.

The town was once supported by mining, commercial fishing or farming. No one knows what supports it now.

One girl in the town is so ugly she knows she will never marry or have a lover. She lives in fantasies and involves herself in social activities of the church trying to keep alive her hopes which she secretly knows are futile.

Wind blows hard through the town except on Sunday afternoons a little after four when the air becomes still.

The air is still all week except on Sunday afternoon when the wind blows.

Once in awhile an unlikely animal wanders into town, a grizzly bear or cougar or wolverine.

People stay married forever. No divorce. Widows and widowers never remarry.

No snow.

Lots of rain.

Birds never stop. They fly over, usually too high to be identified.

The grocer is kind. He gives candy to children. He is a widower and his children live in Paris and never write.

People who hated it and left long ago are wealthy and living in South America.

Wild sexual relationships. A lot of adultery to ward off boredom.

The jail is always empty.

There is one prisoner in jail, always the same prisoner. No one is certain why he is there. He doesn't want to get out. People have forgotten his name.

Young men are filled with hate and often fight.

I am welcome in bars. People are happy to see me and buy me drinks.

As far as one can see, the surrounding country is uninhabited.

The ballpark is poorly maintained and only a few people attend the games.

The ballpark is well kept and the entire town supports the team.

The team is in last place every year.

People sit a lot on their porches.

There is always a body of water, a sea just out of sight beyond the hill or a river running through the town. Outside of town a few miles is a lake that has been the scene of both romance and violence.

David Wagoner has seen the town, assessed it realistically and decided it is a good place to stay clear of.

Carolyn Kizer would feel hopelessly out of place.

Kenneth Hanson hates it and may have lived there once but won't tell anybody.

William Stafford has never seen it.

William Stafford saw it once briefly but didn't write a poem.

LETTER TO KATHY FROM WISDOM

My dearest Kathy: When I heard your tears and those of your
mother over the phone from Moore, from the farm
I've never seen and see again and again under the most
uncaring of skies, I thought of this town I'm writing from,
where we came lovers years ago to fish. How odd
we seemed to them here, a lovely young girl and a fat
middle 40's man they mistook for father and daughter
before the sucker lights in their eyes flashed on. That was
when we kissed their petty scorn to dust. Now, I eat alone
in the cafe we ate in then, thinking of your demons, the sad
days you've seen, the hospitals, doctors, the agonizing
breakdowns that left you ashamed. All my other letter
poems I've sent to poets. But you, your soft round form
beside me in our bed at Jackson, you were a poet then,
curving lines I love against my groin. Oh, my tenderest
racoon, odd animal from nowhere scratching for a home,
please believe I want to plant whatever poem will grow
inside you like a decent life. And when the wheat you've known
forever sours in the wrong wind and you smell it
dying in those acres where you played, please know
old towns we loved in matter, lovers matter, playmates, toys,
and we take from our lives those days when everything moved,
tree, cloud, water, sun, blue between two clouds, and moon,
days that danced, vibrating days, chance poem. I want one
who's wondrous and kind to you. I want him sensitive
to wheat and how wheat bends in cloud shade without wind.
Kathy, this is the worst time of day, nearing five, gloom
ubiquitous as harm, work shifts changing. And our lives
are on the line. Until we die our lives are on the mend.
I'll drive home when I finish this, over the pass that's closed
to all but a few, that to us was always open, good days
years ago when our bodies were in motion and the road rolled out
below us like our days. Call me again when the tears build
big inside you, because you were my lover and you matter,
because I send this letter with my hope, my warm love. Dick.

Robert Huff

AN OLD HIGH WALK

(In Memory of My Father)

Leading poor Delmore's bear up here
on this tight line, Dad, may I say
thanks for the gift of balance once again.
Practice, you said, without a net,
makes things look really peaceful down below:
caged lions, tigers, and the man
with the revolver (Clyde), chair, rings,
the barebacks, top- hat- master, clowns,
even the whips. I'm troubled yet
about that other animal featured
as being more than we can take—
performers, simple circus folk—
fixed on his fat banana, mute
as petroglyphs in current. Those pig eyes
seem to be going mad as mine
for lack of privacy. Still, it's a job.
I mean I think that old gorilla knows
why I'm high-wired and who's leading whom.
He's got his tire and I've got
the bear. No easier this being
good in worlds away from home: far
people gape, waiting the toe's slip,
pause, dive, sawdust that turns out
colorful after all, heartless
and red as hardwoods in the fall.
But, Father, keep in mind, I mean
we like the way we're managing
these high tricks therapeutic here.
The guys are taut, the tent is up,
and I believe the world below
would be serene, will really miss
all three of us off balance when
the ape breaks loose and we're not happening.

NOW

Imagine coastal spray, far movement, marsh,
And birdcall—not the little ones—
Cocked in the rock, reeds winnowing, just dawn,
Flocks in the sea like negatives of stars.
Picture the loving distance waking there—
Our blood infatuated with old bones—
Whacked grass impatient, wind glued on the gull,
And all the idiotic diving birds,
The weed-whipped, grain-grabbed, dipping dears,
Ready to rise. And there you are and I . . .

ON THE DEATH OF THEODORE ROETHKE

August 1963

Hard I must listen now
For motion among stones,
Watch light along bleached bones,
Lean toward a brackish glow,
Because I'm not all here.
Death worked too long this year.
Most of me says: You know,
It isn't just for birds
About the afterwords
But frequency is low.
A living spirit shares
Some romping with the bears
You said somewhere, although
I've also heard a mouse
Hides in an open house,
And I must take it slow
Near porcupines and pike,
Peregrines and the like,
Birch bark, robbed rat, and roe—
In water and in air
Recall the spirit spare,
Listening as I go
To down of green-winged teal
When the blue martens steal,
By moonlight, speckled snow,
For any afternote

Natural to your throat
That finds me in its flow
Or happens to the stones
Under my falling bones,
Because the earth is so.

ON HEARING OF THE DEATH
OF BERNARD STREMPEK

It is Thanksgiving, 1964,
The San Juans fogging in, the Cascade's jaw
Numb in its cloudy swell of Novocain,
Dim-witted, moon-eyed fish less and less near.
I'm reading that last night the sleek *Shalom's*
Bow blundered through a tanker off New Jersey—
Some twenty lives now well accounted for—
When, caught and sliced and on the telephone,
Denying Mayday from almost that far,
A voice that couldn't be identified
Says: "Killed . . . He's dead . . . accident in Ohio."

What does this vaingloriousness down here?

A favorite line of his . . . Like Hardy's head,
My friend's, I think, come now to terms at last,
Apart from heart forever, with his body.
How to give thanks for that to seven birds
Whose flight below this fog bank, unlike gulls',
Tells me mine must remember his dear heart
Because a new migration is arriving . . .

CODICIL

No wake, please,
service or
funeral.
The ashes
at all cost
are to be
delivered

directly
into the
hands of near
survivors
who shall (if
need be) bribe
morticians
until what
was so loud
is partly
toward its still
patch of deep
sound beside
a stream in
the Union
Creek District
of the green
Rogue River
National
Forest, tucked
below one
or two clumps
of daisies—
which ought to
take—or if
not, any
fern that thrives
in shady
light will do
the trick at
least as well
or better.

GIRL-WATCHING AT GRANT'S PASS

(To Ellwood Johnson)

Imagine time's like changing neighborhoods.
Done, let's pretend those water skis are shells,
This wide bend really an old-fashioned sea,
Gill-netter's' floats now airy, bobbing bells,
And every engine not the enemy.
This way, we manage turnpikes, swampy woods,

Overcast, open water, dim stars lost,
Reefs, tilted compass, rain, fog, smashed wrist watch—
Everything but those everlasting beams
Mast-lashed Odysseus' ears were bound to catch.
Imagine this girl moves because she means
Her legs do not feel lovely when they're crossed,

Tumbles herself aglitter and, replete
With river water's flowing lechery,
Becomes for us earth-shaking amber thighs . . .
Contained behind the raucous Mercury
Roaring that roped-in rattle to the skies
As if the rooster tail adorned her feet.

PORCUPINES

   I knew that porcupines liked to eat trees,
woodsheds, wood piles, cabins, and anything anybody
touched long enough to leave salt on; that they were
rodents who waddled around their food, making a hog-
like noise; and that their spines were always hurting
dogs, whose curiosity about bushes urges their noses
close to those that move.

   I had been told about their priceless teeth,
which in midlife are deep yellow, inlaid in old age
with intricate brown designs. The Indians, I read,
brought to the quills an artful skill which fashioned
heraldry. And everyone said porcupines were slow
to die. Shoot off half that neckless, faceless
lump around the eyes, yet moves the porcupine.

   What keeps them moving I was left to learn by
moonlight on a butte they seemed to own. They came
in squads, ate up the ladder rungs, ax handles, boxes;
everything more base than they themselves was theirs
to feed upon. And so they chewed until I murdered
them and saw the product of their alchemy.

   Rich as their teeth, much madder than their
spines, their entrails are the millers of their being.
There the enormous task of their lives is all the

time going on. I loosed it in one who went dragging
his intestines up a lava slope. His ghost gnaws hard
now at my dignity. Tenacious, dull, drab animal—
turned inside out, he headed for the dark, lugging
his precious golden chemistry, which glittered in the
darkness like the overflow of Henry Morgan's hold.

THE SMOKER

Sitting down near him in the shade,
I watch him strike a match on his white cane.
He burns his finger but displays no pain.
This smiling blind man with a hearing aid

Smokes by the hour. Now he's blowing rings.
He measures in the smoke and takes much care
To shape his mouth for pumping circled air.
He fathers hundreds of round hoverings.

I offer: It's too warm; it ought to rain.
His only comment is a smiling cough.
Maybe he's got his hearing aid turned off
To keep such interference from his brain,

Or can't hear through the haze, or won't let sound
Disturb his gentle passion. Who can tell
What he envisions with his sense of smell
Heaving my presence at him by the pound?

I never blame him when he comes in dreams
A slow smile smoking, circled to the thighs,
And screws both of his thumbs into my eyes
And will not stop to listen to my screams.

GETTING DRUNK WITH DAUGHTER

Caught without wife and mother, child,
We squat close, scratching gibberish in the sand,
Inspect your castle, peek into the pail
Where shells await your signal to attack

The stick gate, strike down squads of stones,
And storm the tower of the Feather Queen,
When, perchspine arrow in his head,
Lord Cork falls dead, his bride carted away.
And my pailful of ice is melting down
Around what will be two dead soldiers soon.

Odors remind me your cheeks reeked with kisses:
Whiskey, tobacco, dentures—sourdough—
When Father found you on the trail he misses.
Too bad the old man had to see you grow
Into my blonde wag with your woman's wishes,
Playing pretend wife, Daughter . . . even though
He threw himself to rags and knows his bliss is
Walking the sweaty mares he can't let go.

Precocious runt. Noting our shapely neighbor
Is amber from toenails to Brillo hair,
Has rolled, and drops her top and props her cleavage,
You grin above your army. Dear, her spine's
Not likely to compete with you or bourbon
Since you're your mother's small ape from behind.
Oh, I know you know I know love likes beaches—
For blood outruns the heart, no doubt,
But mine runs to your lordship's mortal splinter.
I've one cork left. So let the spearmen start.

Tomorrow's going to come. We'll be together.
The sun will bake us, and we'll let our bones
Fly with wastrel gulls, who love this weather,
Enlisting stronger sticks, more stalwart stones.
Your mother's got a feather where she itches.
Your daddy's got a fishbone in his brain.
The world lies down and waits in all its ditches.
But you and I aren't going to let it rain.

Carolyn Kizer

AMUSING OUR DAUGHTERS

for Robert Creeley

We don't lack people here on the Northern coast,
But they are people one meets, not people one cares for.
So I bundle my daughters into the car
And with my brother poets, go to visit you, brother.

Here come your guests! A swarm of strangers and children;
But the strangers write verses, the children are daughters like yours.
We bed down on mattresses, cots, roll up on the floor:
Outside, burly old fruit trees in mist and rain;
In every room, bundles asleep like larvae.

We waken and count our daughters. Otherwise, nothing happens.
You feed them sweet rolls and melon, drive them all to the zoo;
Patiently, patiently, ever the father, you answer their questions.
Later we eat again, drink, listen to poems.
Nothing occurs, though we are aware you have three daughters
Who last year had four. But even death becomes part of our ease:
Poems, parenthood, sorrow, all we have learned
From these, of tenderness, holds us together
In the center of life, entertaining daughters
By firelight, with cake and songs.

You, my brother, are a good and violent drinker,
Good at reciting short-line or long-line poems.
In time we will lose all our daughters, you and I,
Be temperate, venerable, content to stay in one place,
Sending our messages over the mountains and waters.

BY THE RIVERSIDE

Do not call from memory—
all numbers have changed.
From the cover of the telephone directory

Once I lived at a Riverside
1-3-7-5, by a real stream, Hangman's Creek,
Named from an old pine, down the hill
On which three Indians died. As a child,
I modeled the Crucifixion on that tree
Because I'd heard two Indians were thieves
Strung up by soldiers from Fort Wright in early days,
But no one remembered who the third one was.

Once, in winter, I saw an old Indian wade,
Breaking the thin ice with his thighs.
His squaw crouched modestly in the water,
But he stood up tall, buck-naked. "Cold!" he said,
Proud of his iron flesh, the color of rust,
And his bold manhood, roused by the shock of ice.
He grinned as he spoke, struck his hard chest a blow
Once, with his fist. . . .So I call, from memory,
That tall old Indian, standing in the water.

And I am not put off by an operator
Saying, "Sor-ree, the lion is busy. . . ."
Then, I would tremble, seeing a real lion
Trammeled in endless, golden coils of wire,
Pawing a switchboard in some mysterious
Central office, where animals ran the world,
As I knew they did. To the brave belonged the power.
Christ was a brave, beneath the gauzy clout.

I whispered to the corners of my room, where lions
Crowded at night, blotting the walls with shadows,
As the wind tore at a gutter beneath the eaves,
Moaned with the power of quiet animals
And the old pine, down the hill,

                       where Indians hung:
Telling my prayers, not on a pale-faced Sunday
Nor a red God, who could walk on water
When winter hardened, and the ice grew stronger.
Now I call up god-head and manhood, both,
As they emerged for a child by the Riverside.
But they are all dead Indians now. They answer
Only to me. The numbers have not changed.

55

RUNNING AWAY FROM HOME

Most people from Idaho are crazed rednecks
Grown stunted in ugly shadows of brick spires,
Corrupted by fat priests in puberty,
High from the dry altitudes of Catholic towns.

Spooked by plaster madonnas, switched by sadistic nuns,
Given sex instruction by dirty old men in skirts,
Recoiling from flesh-colored calendars, bloody gods,
Still we run off at the mouth, we keep on running.

Like those rattling roadsters with vomit-stained back seats,
Used condoms tucked beneath floor-mats,
That careened down hairpin turns through the blinding rain
Just in time to hit early mass in Coeur d'Alene!

Dear Phil, Dear Jack, Dear Tom, Dear Jim,
Whose car had a detachable steering-wheel:
He'd hand it to his scared, protesting girl
Saying, "Okay, *you* drive"—steering with his knees;

Jim drove Daddy's Buick over the railroad tracks,
Piss-drunk, just ahead of the Great Northern freight
Barrelling its way thru the dawn, straight for Spokane.
O the great times in Wallace & Kellogg, the good clean fun!

Dear Sally, Dear Beth, Dear Patsy, Dear Eileen,
Pale, faceless girls, my best friends at thirteen,
Knelt on cold stone, with chilblained knees, to pray,
"Dear God, Dear Christ! Don't let him go All the Way."

O the black Cadillacs skidding around corners
With their freight of drunken Jesuit businessmen!
Beautiful daughters of lumber-kings avoided the giant
Nuptial Mass at St. Joseph's, and fled to nunneries.

The rest live at home: bad girls who survived abortions,
Used Protestant diaphragms, or refused the sacred obligation
Of the marriage bed, scolded by beat-off priests,
After five in five years, by Bill, or Dick, or Ted.

I know your secrets: you turn up drunk by 10 a.m.
At the Beauty Shoppe, kids sent breakfastless to school.
You knew that you were doomed by seventeen.
Why should your innocent daughters fare better than you?

Young, you live on in me: even the blessed dead:
Tom, slammed into a fire hydrant on his Indian Chief
And died castrated; Jim, fool, fell 4 stories from the roof
Of his jock fraternity at Ag & Tech.;

And the pure losers, cracked up in training planes
In Utah; or shot by a nervous rookie at Fort Lewis;
At least they cheated the white-coiffed ambulance chasers
And death-bed bedevillers, and died in war in peace.

Some people from Oregon are mad orphans
who claim to hail from Stratford-upon-Sodom.
They speak fake B.B.C.; they are Unitarian fairies,
In the Yang group or the Yin group, no Middle Way.

Some stay Catholic junkies, incense sniffers who
Scrawl JESUS SAVES on urinal walls, between engagements;
Or white disciples of Black Muslims; balding blonds
Who shave their pubic hair, or heads, for Buddha.

I find you in second-hand bookstores or dirty movies,
Bent halos like fedoras, pulled well down,
Bogarts of buggery. We can't resist the furtive questions:
Are you a writer too? How did you get out?

We still carry those Rosary scars, more like a *herpes
Simplex* than a stigmata: give us a nice long fit
Of depression; give us a good bout of self-hate;
Give us enough Pope, we pun, and we'll hang.

Hung, well hung, or hungover, in the world's most durable
Morning after, we'd sooner keep the mote and lose the eye.
Move over, Tonio Kröger; you never attended
Our Lady of Sorrows, or Northwestern High!

Some people from Washington State are great poetasters,
Inbibers of anything, so long as it makes us sick
Enough to forget our sickness, and carry on
From the Carry Out: Hostess Winkies and Wild Duck.

We "relate," as they say, to Indians, bravest of cowards
Furtively cadging drinks with a shit-faced grin:
Outcasts who carry our past like a 90 lb. calcified foetus
We park in the bus-station locker, and run like sin.

Boozers and bounders, cracked-up crackerbarrel jockeys,
We frequent greasy bistros: Piraeus and Marseilles,
As we wait for our rip-off pimps, we scribble on napkins
Deathful verse we trust executors to descry.

Wills. We are willess. As we have breath, we are wilful
And wishful, trusting that Great Archangel who Still Cares,
Who presides at the table set up for celestial Bingo.
We try to focus our eyes, and fill in the squares.

Some people from Spokane are insane salesmen
Peddling encyclopedias from door to door,
Trying to earn enough to flee to the happy farm
Before they jump from the Bridge, or murder Mom;

Or cut up their children with sanctified bread-knives
Screaming, "You are Isaac, and I am Abraham!"
But it's too late. They are the salutary failures
Who keep God from getting a swelled head.

Some shoot themselves in hotel rooms, after gazing
At chromos of the Scenic Route through the Cascades
Via Northern Pacific, or the old Milwaukee & St. Paul;
Those trains that won't stop rattling in our skulls!

First they construct crude crosses out of Band-Aids
And stick them to the mirror; then rip pages
From the Gideon Bible, roll that giant final joint,
A roach from *Revelations,* as they lie dying.

Bang! It's all over. Race through Purgatory
At last unencumbered by desperate manuscripts
In the salesman's sample-case, along with the dirty shirts.
After Spokane, what horrors lurk in Hell?

I think continually of those who are truly crazy:
Some people from Montana are put away;
They shake their manacles in a broken dance
With eyes blue-rimmed as a Picasso clown's.

Still chaste, but nude, hands shield their organs
Like the original Mom & Dad, after the Fall;
Or they dabble brown frescoes on the walls
Of solitary: their Ajanta and Lascaux.

While the ones that got away display giant kidneys
At the spiral skating-rink of Frank Lloyd Wright,
Or framed vermin in the flammable Museum
Of Modern Mart. But they're still Missoula

In their craft and sullen ebbing, Great Falls & Butte.
Meanwhile, Mondrian O'Leary squints at the light
Staining the white radiance of his well-barred cell,
Till ferocious blurs bump each other in dodgem cars.

O that broken-down fun-house in Natatorium Park
Held the only fun the boy Mondrian ever knew!
Now seven-humped, mutated radioactive Chinook salmon
Taint the white radiance of O'Leary's brain.

O mad Medical Lake, I hear you have reformed:
No longer, Sunday afternoon, the tripper's joy.
Watch the nuts weep! or endlessly nibble fingers.
Funny, huh? The white ruin of muscular men.

Twisting bars like Gargantua; lewd Carusos,
Maimed Chanticleers, running off at the scars.
They hoot their arias through the rhythmic clashing
Of garbage-can lids that serve as dinner trays;

Inmates are slopped, while fascinated on-
Lookers watch Mrs. Hurley, somebody's grandma,
Eating gravy with her bare hands. Just animals, Rosetta.
She's not *your* mother. Don't let it get you.

Suddenly, Mr. Vincente, who with his eleven brothers
Built roads through the Spokane Valley
Where Italians moved like dreams of Martha Graham
As they laid asphalt over subterranean rivers,

Spots a distant cousin, Leonard, an architect,
Until seventh grade, who seems to know him:
Leonard displays, by way of greeting,
His only piece of personal adornment:

How the tourists squeal! Watch them fumble at coat, and fly!
Girdled and ginghamed relatives disperse
Back to the touring car, the picnic basket
With its home-made grappa in giraffe-necked bottles.

As sun-scarred men urge olive children on,
Grandma Hurley, who thought the treat was for her,
Shyly waves her gravy-dappled fingers,
Couple-colored as her old brindled cat.

Enough of this madness! It's already in the past.
Now they are stabbed full of sopers, numbed & lobotomised
In the privacy of their own heads. It's easier for the chaplain:
They're nodding. If you consent to be saved, just nod for God.

It's never over, old church of our claustrophobia!
Church of the barren towns, the vast unbearable sky,
Church of the Western plains, our first glimpse of brilliance,
Church of our innocent incense, there is no goodbye.

Church of the coloring-book, crude crayon of childhood,
Thank God at last you seem to be splitting apart.
But you live for at least as long as our maimed generation
Lives to curse your blessed plaster bleeding heart.

A WIDOW IN WINTERTIME

Last night a baby gargled in the throes
Of a fatal spasm. My children are all grown
Past infant strangles; so, reassured, I knew
Some other baby perished in the snow.
But no. The cat was making love again.

Later, I went down and let her in.
She hung her tail, flagging from her sins.
Though she'd eaten, I forked out another dinner,
Being myself hungry all ways, and thin
From metaphysic famines she knows nothing of,

The feckless beast! Even so, resemblances
Were on my mind: female and feline, though
She preens herself from satisfaction, and does
Not mind lying even in snow. She is
Lofty and bedraggled, without need to choose.

As an ex-animal, I look fondly on
Her excesses and simplicities, and would not return
To them; taking no marks for what I have become,
Merely that my nine lives peal in my ears again
And again, ring in these austerities,

These arbitrary disciplines of mine,
Most of them trivial: like covering
The children on my way to bed, and trying
To live well enough alone, and not to dream
Of grappling in the snow, claws plunged in fur,

Or waken in a caterwaul of dying.

CHILDREN

What good are children anyhow?
        They only break your heart.
The one that bore your fondest hopes
        will never amount to anything.
The one you slaved to give the chances you never had
        rejects them with contempt.
They won't take care of you in your old age.
        They don't even write home.
They don't follow in your footsteps.
They don't avoid your mistakes.
It's impossible to save them from pain.
        And of course they never listen.
Remember how you hung on the lips
        of your father or grandfather,
Begging for the old stories:
        "Again! Tell it again!
        What was it like 'in olden times' "?
We have good stories too:
        funny, instructive, pathetic.
Forget it. Write them down for your friends.

Your friends, with whom you have that unspoken pact:
Don't ask me about my children, and I won't inquire of yours.
Remember how we used to exchange infant pictures?
How we boasted of cute sayings? How we . . .
    Forget it.
Put away those scrapbooks, with the rusted flute in the closet,
    with the soiled ballet-slippers.
Tear up the clumsy Valentines.
Tear up every crayoned scrap that says, 'I love you, Mama.'
They don't want us to keep those mementoes;
    they find them embarrassing.
Those relics of dependent love,
That orange crayon that didn't dare write, 'I hate you.'
Forget their birthdays, as they forget yours.
Perhaps because they never finish anything,
    not a book, not a school,
Their politics are cruel and sentimental:
Some monster of depravity
    who destroyed millions with his smile,
Who shadowed our youth with terror,
    is a hero to them.
Now he smiles benignly from their walls.
Because they are historyless, they don't believe in history:
    Stalin wasn't so bad.
    The Holocaust didn't really happen.
    Roosevelt was a phony.
But the worst of it is:
    they don't believe we ever believed;
They don't believe we ever had ideals.
They don't believe that we were ever poor.
They don't believe that we were passionate
    —or that we are passionate today!
Forget it. Don't torture yourself.
    You still have some life to salvage.
Get divorced. Go on a diet.
Take up the career you dropped for them twenty years ago.
Go back to the schools they deserted, and sign up for courses:
Study Tranquillity 101; take Meditation; Enroll for Renewal.

Remember those older friends we used to envy,
    brilliant and glittering with beauty,
Who refused to have children,
    not about to sacrifice their careers;
Who refused the mess, the entrapment

as we toiled over chores and homework,
worried about measles and money . . .
Have you seen them lately?
They no longer converse in sparkling cadenzas.
They are obsessed with their little dog
  who piddles on their Oriental rug,
  who throws up on their bedspreads.
They don't notice his bad breath;
His incessant yapping doesn't seem to disturb them.
To be honest about it,
  the whole apartment smells!
And the way they babble to him in pet names
  instead of talk of Milton, Chaucer, Dante.
The way they caress him makes you fairly ill;
  the way they call him, 'Baby.'

David Wagoner

TALKING TO THE FOREST

"When we can understand animals, we will know the
change is halfway. When we can talk to the forest, we will
know that the change has come."
—Andrew Joe, Skagit Tribe, Washington

We'll notice first they've quit turning their ears
To catch our voices drifting through cage-bars,
The whites of their eyes no longer shining from corners.
And all dumb animals suddenly struck dumb
Will turn away, embarrassed by a change
Among our hoots and catcalls, whistles and snorts
That crowd the air as tightly as ground-mist.

The cassowary pacing the hurricane fence,
The owl on the driftwood, the gorilla with folding arms,
The buffalo aimed all day in one direction,
The bear on his rock—will need no talking to,
Spending their time so deeply wrapped in time
(Where words lie down like the lion and the lamb)
Not even their own language could reach them.

And so, we'll have to get out of the zoo
To the forest, rain or shine, whichever comes
Dropping its downright shafts before our eyes,
And think of something to say, using new words
That won't turn back bewildered, lost or scattered
Or panicked, curling under the first bush
To wait for a loud voice to hunt them out,

Not words that fall from the skin looking like water
And running together, meaning anything,
Then disappearing into the forest floor
Through gray-green moss and ferns rotting in shade,
Not words like crown-fire overhead, but words
Like old trees felled by themselves in the wilderness,
Making no noise unless someone is listening.

REVIVAL

for Richard Hugo

When Brother Jessen showed the tawny spot
On the carpet where a man threw up a demon,
He had another man by the ear
Beside the rose-covered plastic cross. He shouted
Into that ear a dozen times in a row,
"I curse you, Demon, in the name of Jesus!"
Some of his flock clapped hands. He knelt and sweated.
"They can try skating and wienie roasts," he said,
"But that don't keep the kids out of lovers' lane."
He pointed at me, "You don't believe in demons."

Next door, they were chasing some with double shots,
And the wind was up, and it was one of those nights
When it's hard to breathe
And you can't sit or talk, when your eyes focus
On all disjointed scraps shoved into corners,
And something's going to happen. People feel fine,
Brother Jessen says, if they can lose their demons.
They wash in showers of everlasting dew
Which is the sweat of angels sick for men.

The demon has names, he told me, like Rebellion,
And it won't submit, it wants a cup of coffee,
Wants to go for a walk, and like as not
Turns up in Hell. Hugo, if you and I,
Having been cursed by some tough guy like Jesus,
Were to lose that wild, squat, bloody, grinning demon
Locked in the pit of our respective guts,
Whose fork has pitched us, flattened us to walls,
Left us in alleys where the moon smells dead,
Or jerked us out of the arms of our wives to write
Something like this, we'd sprawl flat on the floor,
A couple of tame spots at a revival.

Let's save a little sweat for the bad guys
Who can't keep out of lovers' lane for a minute,
Who, when they trip, will lie there in the rut
For old time's sake, rebellious as all Hell,
Croaking forever, loving the hard way.

RIVERBED

1

Through the salt mouth of the river
They come past the dangling mesh of gillnets
And the purse-mouthed seines, past the fishermen's last strands
By quarter-light where the beheaded herring
Spiral against the tide, seeing the shadowy others
Hold still, then slash, then rise to the surface, racked
And disappearing—now deepening slowly
In the flat mercurial calm of the pulp mills, groping
Half clear at last and rising like the stones below them
Through swifter and swifter water, the salmon returning
By night or morning in the white rush from the mountains,
Hunting, in the thresh and welter of creek mouths
And shifting channels, the one true holding place.

Out of our smoke and clangor, these miles uphill,
We come back to find them, to wait at their nesting hollows
With the same unreasoning hope.

2

We walk on round stones, all flawlessly bedded,
Where water drags the cracked dome of the sky
Downstream a foot at a glance, to falter there
Like caught leaves, quivering over the sprint
Of the current, the dashing of surfaces.

In a month of rain, the water will rise above
Where we stand on a curving shelf below an island—
The blue daylight scattered and the leaves
All castaways like us for a season.
The river turns its stones like a nesting bird
From hollow to hollow. Now gulls and ravens
Turn to the salmon stranded among branches.

They lie in the clear shallows, the barely dead,
While some still beat their flanks white for the spawning,
And we lie down all day beside them.

A GUIDE TO DUNGENESS SPIT

Out of wild roses down from the switching road between pools
We step to an arm of land washed from the sea.
On the windward shore
The combers come from the strait, from narrows and shoals
Far below sight. To leeward, floating on trees
In a blue cove, the cormorants
Stretch to a point above us, their wings held out like skysails.
Where shall we walk? First, put your prints to the sea,
Fill them, and pause there:
Seven miles to the lighthouse, curved yellow-and-grey miles
Tossed among kelp, abandoned with bleaching rooftrees,
Past reaches and currents;
And we must go afoot at a time when the tide is heeling.
Those whistling overhead are Canada geese;
Some on the waves are loons,
And more on the sand are pipers. There, Bonaparte's gulls
Settle a single perch. Those are sponges.
Those are the ends of bones.
If we cross to the inner shore, the grebes and goldeneyes
Rear themselves and plunge through the still surface,
Fishing below the dunes
And rising alarmed, higher than waves. Those are cockleshells.
And these are the dead. I said we would come to these.
Stoop to the stones.
Overturn one: the grey-and-white, inch-long crabs come pulsing
And clambering from their hollows, tiptoeing sideways.
They lift their pincers
To defend the dark. Let us step this way. Follow me closely
Past snowy plovers bustling among sand-fleas.
The air grows dense.
You must decide now whether we shall walk for miles and miles
And whether all birds are the young of other creatures
Or their own young ones,
Or simply their old selves because they die. One falls,
And the others touch him webfoot or with claws,
Treading him for the ocean.
This is called sanctuary. Those are feathers and scales.
We both go into mist, and it hooks behind us.
Those are foghorns.
Wait, and the bird on the high root is a snowy owl
Facing the sea. Its flashing yellow eyes
Turn past us and return;
And turning from the calm shore to the breakers, utterly still,

They lead us by the bay and through the shallows,
Buoy us into the wind.
Those are tears. Those are called houses, and those are people.
Here is a stairway past the whites of our eyes.
All our distance
Has ended in the light. We climb to the light in spirals,
And look, between us we have come all the way,
And it never ends
In the ocean, the spit and image of our guided travels.
Those are called ships. We are called lovers.
There lie the mountains.

SONG FOR THE SOUL GOING AWAY

I have wakened and found you gone
On a day torn loose from its moon, uprooted
And wilting. How can I call you back with dust in my mouth?
My words lie dead on the ground like leaves. Night speech,
Water speech, the speech of rushes and brambles
Have thinned to muttering and a vague crackle,
And the bird in my ribcage has turned black and silent.
Where a man would stand, I sit; where a man would sit,
I lie down burning; where a man would speak,
My voice shrinks backward into its dark hovel.
The dragonfly has taken his glitter from the pool,
Birds' eggs are stones, all berries wither.
Without you, my eyes make nothing of light and shadow,
And the cup of each eyelid has run dry.
I go as aimless as my feet among sticks and stones,
Thinking of you on your mad, bodiless journey.

SONG FOR THE SOUL RETURNING

Without singing, without the binding of midnight,
Without leaping or rattling, you have come back
To lodge yourself in the deep fibres under my heart,
More closely woven than a salmonberry thicket.
I had struck the rocks in your name, but no one answered;
Left empty under the broken wings of the sun,
I had tasted and learned nothing. Now the creek no longer

Falters from stone to stone with a dead fishtailing
But bursts like the ledges of dawn, the east and west winds
Meet on the hillside, and the softening earth
Spreads wide for my feet where they have never dared to go.
Out of the silent holts of willow and hazel, the wild horses,
Ears forward, come toward us, hearing your voice rise
    from my mouth.
My hands, whose craft had disappeared, search out each other
To shelter the warm world returning between them.

REPORT FROM A FOREST LOGGED BY THE
WEYERHAEUSER COMPANY

Three square miles clear-cut.
Now only the facts matter:
The heaps of gray-splintered rubble,
The churned-up duff, the roots, the bulldozed slash,
The silence,

And beyond the ninth hummock
(All of them pitched sideways like wrecked houses)
A creek still running somewhere, bridged and dammed
By cracked branches.
No birdsong. Not one note.

And this is April, a sunlit morning.
Nothing but facts. Wedges like halfmoons
Fallen where saws cut over and under them
Bear ninety or more rings.
A trillium gapes at so much light.

Among the living: a bent huckleberry,
A patch of salal, a wasp,
And now, making a mistake about me,
Two brown-and-black butterflies landing
For a moment on my boot.

Among the dead: thousands of fir seedlings
A foot high, planted ten feet apart,
Parched brown for lack of the usual free rain,
Two buckshot beercans, and overhead,
A vulture big as an eagle.

Selective logging, they say, we'll take three miles,
It's good for the bears and deer, they say,
More brush and berries sooner or later,
We're thinking about the future—if you're in it
With us, they say. It's a comfort to say

Like *Dividend* or *Forest Management* or *Keep Out.*
They've managed this to a fare-thee-well.
In Chicago, hogs think about hog futures.
But staying with the facts, the facts,
I mourn with my back against a stump.

ELEGY FOR A FOREST CLEAR-CUT BY THE
WEYERHAEUSER COMPANY

Five months after your death, I come like the others
Among the slash and stumps, across the cratered
Three square miles of your graveyard:
Nettles and groundsel first out of the jumble,
Then fireweed and bracken
Have come to light where you, for ninety years,
Had kept your shadows.

The creek has gone as thin as my wrist, nearly dead
To the world at the dead end of summer,
Guttering to a pool where the tracks of an earth-mover
Showed it the way to falter underground.
Now pearly everlasting
Has grown to honor the deep dead cast of your roots
For a bitter season.

Those water- and earth-led roots decay for winter
Below my feet, below the fir seedlings
Planted in your place (one out of ten alive
In the summer drought),
Below the small green struggle of the weeds
For their own ends, below grasshoppers,
The only singers now.

The chains and cables and steel teeth have left
Nothing of what you were:
I hold my hands over a stump and remember

A hundred and fifty feet above me branches
No longer holding sway. In the pitched battle
You fell and fell again and went on falling
And falling and always falling.

Out in the open where nothing was left standing
(The immortal equivalent of a forest fire),
I sit with my anger. The creek will move again,
Come rain and snow, gnawing at raw defiles,
Clear-cutting its own gullies.
As selective as reapers stalking through wheatfields,
Selective loggers go where the roots go.

THE FISHERMAN'S WIFE

When she said, "No,"
I freed the hook, holding the two-foot rainbow
With both hands over the dock-side in the water.
Its mouth would scarcely move
Though I scooped it, belly down, below the surface
Again and again to rouse it.
Hoping too soon, I let it go. It tilted,
Beginning to slide out of sight, its tailfin stiff.

Again, she said, "No." Before I could take her place,
She had stepped casually in her summer dress
Into the lake and under, catching the trout
And coming upward, cradling it in her arms.
Then breathing less than it, not shutting her eyes,
She settled slowly under water, her face
As calm as that water deep below the cedars.

I caught her by the hair, bringing her back
Alive. The trout slid loose, its red-and-silver side
Flashing beyond her, down into the dark.
I saw the tail flick once before it faded.

I helped her up. She stared at me, then the water.
We sat on edge till the moon came out, but nothing
Rose, belly up, to mock it at our feet.

THE OSPREY'S NEST

The osprey's nest has dropped of its own weight
After years, breaking everything under it, collapsing
Out of the sky like the wreckage of the moon,
Having killed its branch and rotted its lodgepole:
A flying cloud of fishbones tall as a man,
A shambles of dead storms ten feet across.

Uncertain what holds anything together,
Ospreys try everything—fishnets and broomsticks,
Welcome-mats and pieces of scarecrows,
Sheep bones, shells, the folded wings of mallards—
And heap up generations till they topple.

In the nest the young ones, calling fish to fly
Over the water toward them in old talons,
Thought only of hunger diving down their throats
To the heart, not letting go—(not letting go,
Ospreys have washed ashore, ruffled and calm
But drowned, their claws embedded in salmon).
They saw the world was bones and curtain-rods,
Hay-wire and cornstalks—rubble put to bed
And glued into meaning by large appetites.
Living on top of everything that mattered,
The fledglings held it in the air with their eyes,
With awkward claws groping the ghosts of fish.

Last night they slapped themselves into the wind
And cried across the rain, flopping for comfort
Against the nearest branches, baffled by leaves
And the blank darkness falling below their breasts.
Where have they gone? The nest, now heaped on the
    bank,
Has come to earth smelling as high as heaven.

Beth Bentley

THE HOUSE ON THE BARGE

Tamed by island, breakwater, inlet,
the Sound broods; it's Christmas Day;
my father, husband and I
stroll back and forth, walking
off dinner. No Olympics loom
back of Whidbey, the Sound is warship-grey,
the scene a block print, large forms,
few details, no color.

We watch a barge anchored offshore;
it holds a derelict house
tilted at such an extreme angle
it may slide off any moment
into the water; our eyes keep it steady.
Gulls perch on the roofbeam, wheel
about slatted walls. The dark house
slumps, a weathered barn
on the sea's prairie. I pick up
limpet shells. In my pocket,
my finger wears one like a roof.
My father is telling
one of his long stories.

On a train crossing Montana, he met
another salesman who, it seems,
had known his family in Russia.
They swap memories, names. A half-
century emerges, dripping algae,
sends tendrils to my father's eyes.
I recall someone I met, too,
not long ago, the father of one
of my students. He'd been born
in the same small town as my mother;
his father's store just down the block
from my grandfather's store,
on Concord Street, in South St. Paul.

He hadn't known Aunt Belle or Uncle Al,
but he remembered the store

and the old brown house I loved
as a child: three stories high,
black iron fence, wide porch;
it stood on the main street, next door
to a saloon. I lay in a high-windowed
bedroom summer mornings,
tracing whorls on the maple bedstead,
smelling cantaloup, coffee, fresh bread
drift up the stairs, my grandmother's voice
clear as she bartered with a vendor.

I told him my cousin had sent me
a letter saying the store had just been torn down.
As for the house, it long ago vanished.
Tilting, tilting off the turning planet,
it slid and sank, bottoming the years.
Shored in sand, its brown walls waver
on sunlit floors, where fish drift
in and out its broken windows,
schooling finny broods, dreaming in corners.

THIS TIME A TREE TURNS INTO A WOMAN

That a force surged, pressed to her sides,
and moist warmth trickled, a snail-track,
barely woke her. She'd received
rain and snow, bird-lime, insect droppings,
a mild mortar. But this rain
seeped into her fissures, broke open
her hull. Suddenly shelled,
she felt her tender inner green
split and peel back;
a pulse dizzied her veins.

Circling, a whirlpool, it hauled all her parts
towards its seething center. Her outermost twigs
scrabbled against the sky, small claws;
her roots shuddered and shook off their earth
in a shower of small stones.
Branches cracked and plummeted.

Her first steps were wooden lurches
on thick ankles, flat feet turned in.
Her knees knocked. She walked with a thump.
But as she learned the knack, her long,
hard legs found their stride. Stiff
habits fell. Her body swayed,
itself a limb, easy-boned
under a supple pelt. Behind her,
a flock of birds, her hair,
lifted in glittering layers,
veered in the light.

As for her voice, it eluded hearing;
from willowly lips emerged
a soft rasp, like wind among leaves.
When a mortal, puzzled by that half-familiar
dialect drew near, he was pulled
into her eyes' calm wilderness.
He stumbled, entangled in vines,
dark forest closing over his head,
his last breath stifled
in the damp, sweet smother of moss.

KENNEL

He's howling again, he
who I kept hidden in the shed,
howling for food or attention,
more water, perhaps. He never
pauses in his shrill litany,
not even when I bring out
something special, something ground-up
and rich, or raw and bloody.
His opaque pupils stare
without light into mine, under
his lowering brow, his jaw
pulls back, his pointed teeth
glisten in his dripping maw.

It's all I can do to hand him
his greasy plate, and run;
he makes no move, almost
as if it isn't the food he wants.

I've left the door unlatched
at night, but he doesn't escape:
I can hear his trot trot trot,
back and forth, back and forth,
until my own heart trots
keeping time with his footfall.

Sometimes it seems I've heard
him howling all my life.
If I don't feed him, show him
my presence, he'll do something bad,
something they'll blame me for.

YOU AGAIN

This time I recognize your limp.
You have aged.
The floating cartilage in your knee
makes you favor your left leg.
Your diet has left you pale
though not necessarily thinner.

If there are auras, yours is gray,
for you abhor violence,
and faint at the sight of blood.
No, it is your habit
of turning away that makes
one shoulder higher than the other; denial
creases your lips with distaste.

On the street, I hear close behind me
your uneven step.
Your long shoe crooks between mine;
I trip, curse.

Someday you'll catch up with me,
your mouth at my ear, hissing.

And you will fit yourself into me
as a corpse into its casket.

AT THE CONFLUENCE OF THE SOLEDUCK, THE BOGACHIEL AND THE QUILLAYUTE

Two spotted cows spread out on warm rocks
dappled by dappled alders. Gulls
circle, one eye open for lip
of trout or salmon. Our stick-brown daughters
stir the tortoise-green somnolence,
salt a broth of water that rests
from three journeys, conjoined in the bridge's
shadow at an ancient fork, near home;
the years' crumbs mingle, mealy. Our daughters,
bone-thin, dip and churn, yell,
their bodies shed fingernails, hair, dead skin;
their perfume a *bouquet garni,* leaves
a ring of oil: they slough off childhood.
The leavings sink, join fish-chalk, minerals,
a boil of nourishment to freshen the sea's
cauldron: it floats in a mist of midges
the last five miles, under trees.

MOTHERS

(After a woodcut by Kaethe Köllwitz)

Back to back, old stumps grown together
send along linked shoulders
news some ancient nerve records:

A mouth is near; there's blood on its breath;
slither lurks like smoke; mind the trees.

They are the first cave, fire
at its center; they
are an iron kettle, thick
with burnt-on layers of dread,
love, mystery, fierce tales
sending up steam, a rich stink.

Behind a buttress of thighs,
clutches of young bones sort
into structures, cloudy eyes clear.

Sara, my grandmother's grandmother's grandmother's
mother, I bear your carbon,
a charred shield. My black

flakes onto my daughter's flesh,
a first layer: she slows, darkens;
she hardens

to her place in the circle.

HOLDING (AFTER THE NEZ PERCE)

Have been turning, have been turning
turning slowly, have been slowing

The lake breathes without swimmers
draws toward its pulse, its center
toward, away from, breathing slowly

the weed steadies, sheds its gothics
turns to scaffold, thinning, thinning
curves inside a cave of air

losing speed, turning slowly
slowing down, have been walking
walking toward a place of quiet
changing rhythm, losing speed

each weed arches and springs back
each itself, itself only
untouched, untouching

wintering

I am slowed, I am holding
I am stayed, holding steady
slowly holding, I am changed

holding steady
holding steady

DROWNING GIRL

We swam by where she dangled,
caught in our lives. Her arms,
loose as seaweed, hands folding,
unfolding, hungered towards us.
Our wake turned and turned
the pale stem of her neck.
Our talk waterfalled down
her ears. She hung, suspended,
a question-mark, hair lifting,
falling. We saw her fingers
curl. We didn't hear
her heart burst, a depth-
charge, but watched
her water-lily head
loll in the current, watched
her float upwards, weightless.
She kept her white eyes open.
Through shifting waters, they glare
at us, scoured clean as shells.

John Haines

THE STONE HARP

A road deepening in the north,
strung with steel,
resonant in the winter evening,
as though the earth were a harp
soon to be struck.

As if a spade
rang in a rock chamber:

in the subterranean light,
glittering with mica,
a figure like a tree turning to stone
stands on its charred roots
and tries to sing.

Now there is all this blood
flowing into the west,
ragged holes at the waterline of the sun—
that ship is sinking.

And the only poet is the wind,
a drifter
who walked in from the coast
with empty pockets.

He stands on the road
at evening, making a sound
like a stone harp
strummed
by a handful of leaves . . .

IF THE OWL CALLS AGAIN

at dusk
from the island in the river,
and it's not too cold,

I'll wait for the moon
to rise,
then take wing and glide
to meet him.

We will not speak,
but hooded against the frost
soar above
the alder flats, searching
with tawny eyes.

And then we'll sit
in the shadowy spruce and
pick the bones
of careless mice,

while the long moon drifts
toward Asia
and the river mutters
in its icy bed.

And when morning climbs
the limbs
we'll part without a sound,

fulfilled, floating
homeward as
the cold world awakens.

FAIRBANKS UNDER THE SOLSTICE

Slowly, without sun, the day sinks
toward the close of December.
It is minus sixty degrees.

Over the sleeping houses a dense
fog rises—smoke from banked fires,
and the snowy breath of an abyss
through which the cold town
is perceptibly falling.

As if Death were a voice made visible,
with the power of illumination . . .

Now, in the white shadow
of those streets, ghostly newsboys
make their rounds, delivering
to the homes of those
who have died of the frost
word of the resurrection of Silence.

SKAGWAY

I dreamed that I married
and lived in a house in Skagway.

My wife was a tall, strong girl
from the harbor,
her dark hair smelled of rain,
our children walked to school
against the wind.

Through years piled up like boxcars
at a vacant station, my hammer
echoed on the upper floors,
my axe rang in a yard
where leaves and ladders fall.

By kerosene light I wrote
the history of roundhouse rust,
of stalled engines, and cordwood
sinking by the tracks.
Against the October darkness
I set a row of pale
green bottles in a wall
to see the winter sun.

A snowman knocked at night,
he roamed the lots and whispered
through the graveyard fences.

I met in April an aging pioneer
come back for one more summer.
We listened together as
the last excursion
rumbled toward White Pass.

And slowly that fall the houses
grew blank and silent,
the school door shackled with a chain.
My people on an icy barge
turned south, grey gulls in a mist.

I walked down the littered alleys,
searching the lights of broken windows;
with a weathered shingle
I traced in the gravel of Main Street
a map of my fading country . . .

Until my shoes wore out
and I stood alone
with all the Skagway houses,
a ledger in the wind,
my seventy pages peeling.

THE INCURABLE HOME

Then I came to the house of wood
and knocked with a cold hand.
My bones shone in my flesh
as the ribs in a paper lantern,
the gold ring slipped from my finger.

The door swung open, strong hands
seized me out of the darkness
and laid me in a bed of wood;
it was heavy, weighted with shadows,
lined with cloth woven from wheat straw.

Four posts stood by the corners;
thick candles were lighted upon them,
and the flames floated
in pools of forest water.
The air smelled of damp leaves and ashes.

People whose faces I knew and had forgotten
wound a chain about my hands.

They dipped their fingers in the water,
wrote their names on a clay tablet
and stood aside,
talking in the far country of sleep.

THE MIRROR

I

From the bed where I lay
I saw a tilted mirror
holding together four thin blue
walls and a yellow ceiling.

II

A door turned its white face
inward; I rose and stood before
a rain-streaked window
whose paper curtains whispered
against me in the cloudy light.

III

I went farther and deeper
into that world of glass,
prowling an endless hallway
where lonely coathangers
banged softly together.

IV

Down the turning stairway
under a lamp suddenly dark
I came to an entry, or an exit;
and beyond that I saw the grey
siding of the roominghouse,
a sign blowing and creaking . . .

V

Tarpaper and wind,
a street rolling stones
to the foot of a snowy mountain.

WILLA

The first time I saw Willa
she was combing the spring light
for harebells and stargrass,

this girl with a snowborn child
in her arms,
our sister in life.

Her gaze lighted a furrow
where the dark roots
worked and sang;

like the winter wound in my heart,
the depth was of ice
warmed by the sun in her shadow.

May she grow to be a woman,
beholder of earth and its children,
sheltered by
day lilies taller than men.

TO MY FATHER

Last evening I entered a pool
on the Blackfoot River
and cast to a late rise,
maybe the last of a perishing fall.

Light shone on that water,
the rain-dimple of feeding trout,
and memory,
and the deep stillness of boyhood.

And I remembered, not the name
of the river, nor the hill
in Maryland looming beyond it,
nor the sky, a late rose
burning that eastern summer;

but the long, rock pool that whispered
before us, and your voice
steady and calm beside me:
"Try it here, one more time . . . "

And the fly with its hook floated down,
a small, dim star riding a ripple,
and the bright fish rose
from under its rock, and struck.

Night is on that water.

Last evening I watched a rise
break again on the still current,
quiet as a downed leaf,
its widening circle in the dusk.

CHOOSING A STONE

It grows cold in the forest
of rubble.

There the old hunters survive
and patch their tents with tar.

They light fires in the night
of obsidian—
instead of trees they burn
old bottles and windowpanes.

Instead of axe blows and leaves
falling,
there is always the sound
of moonlight breaking,
of brittle stars ground together.

The talk there is of deadfalls
and pits armed
with splinters of glass,

and of how one chooses a stone.

THE WHALE IN THE
BLUE WASHING MACHINE

There are depths in a household
where a whale can live . . .

His warm bulk swims from room
to room, floating by on the stairway,
searching the drafts, the cold
currents that lap at the sills.

He comes to the surface hungry,
sniffs at the table,
and sinks, his wake rocking the chairs.

His pulsebeat sounds at night
when the washer spins, and the dryer
clanks on stray buttons . . .

Alone in the kitchen darkness,
looking through steamy windows
at the streets draining away in fog;

watching and listening,
for the wail of an unchained buoy,
the steep fall of his wave.

Gary Snyder

HAY FOR THE HORSES

He had driven half the night
From far down San Joaquin
Through Mariposa, up the
Dangerous mountain roads,
And pulled in at eight a.m.
With his big truckload of hay
           behind the barn.
With winch and ropes and hooks
We stacked the bales up clean
To splintery redwood rafters
High in the dark, flecks of alfalfa
Whirling through shingle-cracks of light,
Itch of haydust in the
           sweaty shirt and shoes.
At lunchtime under Black oak
Out in the hot corral,
—The old mare nosing lunchpails,
Grasshoppers crackling in the weeds—
"I'm sixty-eight" he said,
"I first bucked hay when I was seventeen.
I thought, that day I started,
I sure would hate to do this all my life.
And dammit, that's just what
I've gone and done."

MID-AUGUST AT SOURDOUGH MOUNTAIN LOOKOUT

Down valley a smoke haze
Three days heat, after five days rain
Pitch glows on the fir-cones
Across rocks and meadows
Swarms of new flies.

I cannot remember things I once read
A few friends, but they are in cities.
Drinking cold snow-water from a tin cup
Looking down for miles
Through high still air.

BY FRAZIER CREEK FALLS

Standing up on lifted, folded rock
looking out and down—

The creek falls to a far valley.
hills beyond that
facing, half-forested, dry
—clear sky
strong wind in the
stiff glittering needle clusters
of the pine—their brown
round trunk bodies
straight, still;
rustling trembling limbs and twigs

listen.

This living flowing land
is all there is, forever

We *are* it
it sings through us—

We could live on this Earth
without clothes or tools!

THE DEAD BY THE SIDE OF THE ROAD

How did a great Red-tailed Hawk
    come to lie—all stiff and dry—
        on the shoulder of
            Interstate 5?

Her wings for dance fans

Zac skinned a skunk with a crushed head
    washed the pelt in gas; it hangs,
        tanned, in his tent

Fawn stew on Hallowe'en
   hit by a truck on highway forty-nine
     offer cornmeal by the mouth;
        skin it out.

Log trucks run on fossil fuel

I never saw a Ringtail til I found one in the road:
   case-skinned it with the toenails
     footpads, nose, and whiskers on;
       it soaks in salt and water
       sulphuric acid pickle;

she will be a pouch for magic tools.

The Doe was apparently shot
   lengthwise and through the side—
     shoulder and out the flank
       belly full of blood

THE LATE SNOW & LUMBER STRIKE
OF THE SUMMER OF FIFTY-FOUR

Whole towns shut down
        hitching the Coast road, only gypos
Running their beat trucks, no logs on
Gave me rides. Loggers all gone fishing
Chainsaws in a pool of cold oil
On back porches of ten thousand
Split-shake houses, quiet in summer rain.
Hitched north all of Washington
Crossing and re-crossing the passes
Blown like dust, no place to work.

Climbing the steep ridge below Shuksan
    clumps of pine
    float out the fog
No place to think or work
    drifting.

On Mt. Baker, alone
In a gully blazing snow:
Cities down the long valleys west
Thinking of work, but here,
Burning in sun-glare
Below a wet cliff, above a frozen lake,
The whole Northwest on strike
Black burners cold,

The green-chain still,
I must turn and go back:
        caught on a snowpeak
        between heaven and earth
And stand in lines in Seattle.
Looking for work.

AVOCADO

The Dharma is like an Avocado!
Some parts so ripe you can't believe it,
But it's good.
And other places hard and green
Without much flavor,
Pleasing those who like their eggs well-cooked.

And the skin is thin,
The great big round seed
In the middle,
Is your own Original Nature—
Pure and smooth,
Almost nobody ever splits it open
Or ever tries to see
If it will grow.

Hard and slippery,
It looks like
You should plant it—but then
It shoots out thru the
                fingers—
gets away.

THE WAY WEST, UNDERGROUND

The split-cedar
smoked salmon
cloudy days of Oregon,
the thick fir forests.

Black Bear heads uphill in
Plumas county,
round bottom scuttling through willows—

The Bear Wife moves up the coast.

where blackberry brambles
ramble in the burns.

And around the curve of islands
foggy volcanoes
on, to North Japan. The bears
& fish-spears of the Ainu.
Gilyak.
Mushroom-vision healer,
single flat drum,
from long before China.

Women with drums who fly over Tibet.

Following forests west, and
rolling, following grassland,
tracking bears and mushrooms,
eating berries all the way.
In Finland finally took a bath:
like redwood sweatlodge on the Klamath—
all the Finns in moccasins and
pointy hats with dots of white,
netting, trapping, bathing,
singing holding hands, the while

see-sawing on a bench, a look of love—

Karhu—Bjorn—Braun—Bear
[lightning rainbow great cloud tree
dialogs of birds]

Europa. 'The West.'
the bears are gone
                            except Brunhilde?

or elder wilder goddesses reborn—will race
    the streets of France and Spain
                with automatic guns—
            in Spain,
Bears and Bison,
Red Hands with missing fingers,
Red mushroom labyrinths;
lightning-bolt mazes,
Painted in caves,

Underground.

THIS POEM IS FOR BEAR

"As for me I am a child of the god of the mountains."

A bear down under the cliff.
She is eating huckleberries.
They are ripe now
Soon it will snow, and she
Or maybe he, will crawl into a hole
And sleep. You can see
Huckleberries in bearshit if you
Look, this time of year
If I sneak up on the bear
It will grunt and run

The others had all gone down
From the blackberry brambles, but one girl
Spilled her basket, and was picking up her
Berries in the dark.
A tall man stood in the shadow, took her arm,
Led her to his home. He was a bear.
In a house under the mountain
She gave birth to slick dark children
With sharp teeth, and lived in the hollow
Mountain many years.
                snare a bear: call him out:

honey-eater
forest apple
light-foot
Old man in the fur coat, Bear! come out!
Die of your own choice!
Grandfather black-food!
             this girl married a bear
Who rules in the mountains, Bear!
             you have eaten many berries
             you have caught many fish
             you have frightened many people

Twelve species north of Mexico
Sucking their paws in the long winter
Tearing the high-strung caches down
Whining, crying, jacking off
(Odysseus was a bear)

Bear-cubs gnawing the soft tits
Teeth gritted, eyes screwed tight
             but she let them.

Til her brothers found the place
Chased her husband up the gorge
Cornered him in the rocks.
Song of the snared bear:
             "Give me my belt.
             "I am near death.
             "I came from the mountain caves
             "At the headwaters,
             "The small streams there
             "Are all dried up.

—I think I'll go hunt bears.
                   "hunt bears?
Why shit Snyder,
You couldn't hit a bear in the ass
             with a handful of rice!"

MILTON BY FIRELIGHT

Piute Creek, August 1955

"O hell, what do mine eyes
        with grief behold?"
Working with an old
Singlejack miner, who can sense
The vein and cleavage
In the very guts of rock, can
Blast granite, build
Switchbacks that last for years
Under the beat of snow, thaw, mule-hooves.
What use, Milton, a silly story
Of our lost general parents,
        eaters of fruit?

The Indian, the chainsaw boy,
And a string of six mules
Came riding down to camp
Hungry for tomatoes and green apples.
Sleeping in saddle-blankets
Under a bright night-sky
Han River slantwise by morning.
Jays squall
Coffee boils

In ten thousand years the Sierras
Will be dry and dead, home of the scorpion.
Ice-scratched slabs and bent trees.
No paradise, no fall,
Only the weathering land
The wheeling sky,
Man, with his Satan
Scouring the chaos of the mind.
Oh Hell!

Fire down
Too dark to read, miles from a road
The bell-mare clangs in the meadow
That packed dirt for a fill-in
Scrambling through loose rocks
On an old trail
All of a summer's day.

Sandra McPherson

SELLING THE HOUSE

Nothing of ours there now. Nothing to comfort, nothing to break.
The bedrooms stretch and yawn off the dining room. The kitchen
Goes hungry. The bathrooms remain unnecessary complications
In the emptiness.

Everything's clean as a cloud,

But who's fooled? Not the faucets drooping forlorn
As willows over a dry stream bed. Not the dumbwaiter,
Trapped in the basement, a damned soul: dust
The gypsy lives there.

Must have shocked the old place

When we moved in, splashing color on the floor, dropping
Our fat sofas, fat people dropping onto them. We slapped
Pictures on its walls like band-aids. We brought our own light
Like missionaries.

Sold. Sold out. The roof

Will have no more temptation to eavesdrop;
The basement, no reason to sweep back its shadows.
The steps needn't be servants any more:
Sky walks them.

Nobody needs you now, house,

But nobody leaves you alone. Mounted on your
Sunken pedestal, nailed down with marigolds, you'll fall
Against our ears and wishes. We'll see
Our past

For the awkward lumber it is.

Then that goes too.
They say that it's easy,
Merely an erasure,
Quick as tomorrow,

Simple as forgiving.

THE MOUSE

Two have frozen; one—a misfortune—
broke its back; two more ate poison
too soon to reach safety in the live trap;
three were let out in soft yellow weeds.

Bulldozers came. And now this nineteenth
mouse shakes and drums its rhubarb-
spider feet and backs away.
I give it goat cheese and anise cake

to have good memories. "The dark mice
of my past," says Vittorini,
"overran me." And he boarded the long train
to the island of his mother.

Mother's island was a chair, mother's island
was silence inside the plasmic sound
of a mouse. Mother's island had hibiscus,
orange, palm, it was a beautiful place.

And the small meats of their bodies ate seeds—
but not enough so there was any vacant
patch of ground. Up through the space of fear
grew wheat, comb-honey, sunflowers, oaks.

And like the mouse she showed great courage
when she entered the hospital to die
then didn't die and even began to eat.
She thought of heaven, and other scenic places . . .

Now she comes home. The earth is strung and tied
with cold-faded grass. Squirrels flock
and smarten in the short sunlight.
The owl appears by day. She fears forgetting.

ELEGIES FOR THE HOT SEASON

1. *The Killing of the Snails*

Half the year has hot nights, like this,
When gnats fly thick as stars, when the temperature is taken
On the tongues of flowers and lovers,
When the just-dead is buried in warm sod.
The snail-pebbled lawns glimmer with slime trails, and the unworried,
Unhurried snail tucks into his dark knuckle, stockaded
With spears of grass, safe. When I first heard
The sound of his dying, it was like knuckles cracking.

The lightest foot can slay snails. Their shells break
More easily than mirrors. And like bad luck, like
A face in a mirror, they always come back.

Good hunting nights were stuffy as a closed room.
No moon shone but my father's flashlight.
As if it were Jericho, he circled the house,
And I'd hear all evening the thick crunch
Of his marching, the sound of death due
To his size 13 shoe.

In the morning I'd find them, little clots on the grass, pretend
They'd been singed by geranium fire-bursts, asphyxiated by blue
Iris flame, burnt to shadows under the strawberry blossom.
The fuchsias bled for them. White-throated calla lilies
Maintained appearances above the snail slum.

But the slow-brained pests forgave and fragilely claimed the garden
The next hot season, like old friends, or avengers.

2. *The Killing of the Caterpillars*

Today I watch our neighbor celebrating May,
Ringing round the besieged cherry-tree,
His haunted maypole, brandishing his arson's torch
Through the tents of caterpillars. He plays conductor,
Striking his baton for the May music.
And the soft, fingery caterpillars perform,
Snap, crackle, pop.

They plummet through a holiday of leaves like fireworks or
    shooting stars or votive candles
Or buttercups, under the hex of the neighbor's wand, first
    fruits of euthanasia,

Ripe and red before the cherries. And it is over,
Grown cold as a sunset. They lie on the grass
Still and black as those who lie under it.

It is night. Lights burn in the city
Like lamps of a search-party, like the search-beam
Of my father's flashlight, at every swing discovering
Death.

HIS BODY

He doesn't like it, of course—
Others, who don't wear it but see it, do.
He's pale, like a big desert, but you can find flowers.
No, not entirely pale:
Between shin and ankle the twin sun marks;
And where his shirt (now draped from a chair back)
Was, he contrasts with dark hands
And neck/face
Like a rained-on street where a car has just been driven
Away.
Don't picture a beer paunch.
And he is a smooth animal, or soft where he isn't smooth,
Down to his toadskin testicles.
He lies prone on clean bedsheets.
There is a single light in the room.
Now run your hand down his back, its small, and up
The hips and over. Their sheen's like that
On blue metal music boxes made to hold powder.
But the rest of him is sprouted with black down-going hair,
His whiskers in so many foxholes,
Eager to out.
Are they in any order?
Age has so far
Remained locked inside.
I'm not a doctor
And glad not to have a doctor's viewpoint.
I'm glad I haven't the petite,
Overwhelmed sight of an antibody.
And yet I'm not just anybody perusing his body—
I have a reason to like it better than I like other bodies.
Someone else can praise those,
Each lonely and earthly, wanting to be celestial.

IN THE COLUMBIA RIVER GORGE, AFTER A DEATH

These only wait—

Red apples, thronged
Mouths, whole dumb
Choirs of them—

Tall cliffs, blue,
Shadowy,
Haughty chins.

They are the fathers
Of their own
Feet

Wading below,
Taking forever
To be carved.

And then
What can they expect?
This is patient country.

Like the river, I should leave here.
I should be home in sorrow with you.
Yet this landscape

Shows me
How he died, how he became suddenly
No more man

But that unseizeable
Cleaving
Edge the patient expect.

ERRATUM

*The final 28 lines were inadvertantly
omitted from Sandra McPherson's poem,
"In the Columbia River Gorge, After
a Death," which appears on page 100.
Those lines are:*

Even my child,
That first blood shed,
Awake in the hospital nursery,

Born and more
Herself than she will ever be,
Lives only at the mercy

Of cloud and cliff-edge,
Under that weathercock mercy,
My little waterfall.

When I come too close,
Earth shuts up its tongues,
But I hear what it means

In the idling motor, in the note
Child-held until the breath runs out,
In the unwinding

Music of the spawning fish,
Playing against the current
Into some longsuffering water.

Land, if I take you
Into my fist,
There

You'll stay, longer than I can hold you,
So patient you are,
Waiting

At the end of the breadline
For your loaf
Of ash,

Of flesh.

ERRATUM

The final 20 lines were inadvertantly
omitted from Beth Bentley's poem, "Kennel,"
which appears on pages 75 and 76. Those
lines are:

Lately, I've given him bits
of food from my plate to appease him,
pieces of bread and meat, my milk.
He does not grow sleek.
It's I who am getting lean,
hair dry, skin coarse, eyes dull
and sunken. I peer at myself
in the looking glass and growl.

Last night I spent hours in the shed
with him to keep him still.
I could no longer distinguish
his smell from my smell, his panting
from my breaths which came fast.

Hot and rank we lay
in the dark, muzzle to muzzle,
shuddering at the scent
of a passing stranger. When lightning
flared and thunder crashed
we moaned in unison, one voice,
one consubstantial flesh.

BALM

Like a skeleton, the old woman who has kept
Herself in shape suns by the pool. Gray, gouged cat
Hair skids from last evening's spat.
I spring-clean and hem thin
Dresses, flags, alibis. The baby gets away
With what she can.

These hours are such a balm. Our voices ring
Bright, they hold in their rain. Gardening
On a whim, you attack Jack's
Beanstalk weeds with a crowbar. Tap, tap, tap,
The needle tests—a blind man—
For my thumb.

Holy or not, we fatten like lambs
In this city of refuge, this day of rest. The old
Woman occults. Paper
Wasps in the eaves swing their hovering
Hotel, their doors by ours wide open.
—Pax, pax, your skull-bare

Garden smiles, my work's gone underground.

THE BITTERN

Because I have turned my head for years
in order to see the bittern
I won't mind not finding
what I am looking for
as long as I know it could be there,
the cover is right,
it would be natural.

I loved you for what you had seen
and because you took me to see things,

alpine flowers
and your heart under your shirt.

The birds that mate for life
we supposed to be happiest,

my green-eyed,
bitter evergreen.

The bough flies back into the night.

I might be driving by a marsh
and suddenly turn my head—
That's not exactly the way you see them, you say.
So I look from the corners of my eyes
as if cheating in school
or overcoming a shyness.

In the end I see
                    nothing
but how I go blindly on loving
a life from which something is missing.

Clouds rushing across the sun,
gold blowing down on the reeds—

nothings like these . . .

TRIOLET

She was in love with the same danger
everybody is. Dangerous
as it is to love a stranger,
she was in love. With that same danger
an adulteress risks a husband's anger.
Stealthily death enters a house:
she was in love with that danger.
Everybody is dangerous.

SENTIENCE

"The female genital, like the blank page anticipating the poem,
is an absence, a not me, which I occupy.
By occupying absence, I experience myself becoming more
than what I was. The blank page and this genital
are an appeal to being. By being where I was not,
I am no longer self-contained: I experience myself
in the dimensions, contours, textures of my mate.
When she is naked like lava undressed of pine
I not only feel her but see her. She is wrinkled.
I am poor; I will take even the wrinkled.
High country, faceless, rough on the feet, swindling the lungs.
I am poor but igneous landscape asks nothing of me
nor gives me anything I want but myself."

(*Half derived from a student's essay.*)

THE PLANT

If it came to change our lives, it didn't want
Step-forward converts. And if we were
Hamhanded or clayfooted when it came,
We weren't healed. It rode our straight days
On a merry-go-round, chinked our aimless hours

On its keyring. Rarefied, lanky,
Stunning as a man back from the dead,
It drew in birdsongs, housewives' chatter. Dogs howled
Into it; men felt small by it. And all the time its face
Remained unmoved as a psychiatrist's.

Rising from its broad platform leaves,
Face tranced on the moon, mopping the wet wind
In storms, blossoming, its blossoming
A coronation, the plant was not one of us but a gift
Of itself. It suffered our stares until

It died, blurring like a UFO, never geysering
In our air again. The wonder gone,
Our lives shambled apart. We were the audience
After a play, agreeing no more together
What to laugh at, when to cry.

Olga Broumas

SOMETIMES, AS A CHILD

when the Greek sea
was exceptionally calm
the sun not so much a pinnacle
as a perspiration of light, your brow and the sky
meeting on the horizon, sometimes

you'd dive
from the float, the pier, the stone
promontory, through water so startled
it held the shape of your plunge, and there

in the arrested heat of the afternoon
without thought, effortless
as a mantra turning
you'd turn
in the paused wake of your dive, enter
the suck of the parted waters, you'd emerge

clean caesarean, flinging
live rivulets from your hair, your own
breath arrested. Something immaculate, a chance

crucial junction: time, light, water
had occurred, you could feel your bones
glisten
translucent as spinal fins.
                              In rain-
green Oregon now, approaching thirty, sometimes
the same
rare concert of light and spine
resonates in my bones, as glistening
starfish, lover, your fingers
beach up.

SLEEPING BEAUTY

I sleep, I sleep
too long, sheer hours
hound me, out
of bed and into clothes, I wake
still later, breathless, heart
racing, sleep
peeling off like a hairless
glutton, momentarily
slaked.   Cold

water shocks me
back from the dream.   I see
lovebites like fossils: *something*
that did exist

dreamlike, though
dreams have the perfect alibi, no
fingerprints, evidence
that a mirror could float
back in your own face, gleaming
its silver eye.   Lovebites like fossils.   Evidence.
Strewn

round my neck like a ceremonial
necklace, suddenly
snapped apart.

o

Blood.   Tears.   The vital
salt of our body.   Each
other's mouth.
Dreamlike

the taste of you
sharpens my tongue like a thousand shells,
bitter, metallic.   I know

as I sleep
that my blood runs clear
as salt
in your mouth, my eyes.

o

City-center, mid-
traffic, I
wake to your public kiss.   Your name
is Judith, your kiss a sign

to the shocked pedestrians, gathered
beneath the light that means
stop
in our culture
where red is a warning, and men
threaten each other with final violence: *I will drink
your blood.*   Your kiss
is for them

a sign of betrayal, your red
lips suspect, unspeakable
liberties as
we cross the street, kissing
against the light, singing, *This
is the woman I woke from sleep, the woman that woke
me sleeping.*

o

o

FIVE INTERIOR LANDSCAPES

for Stephen

I

It's all right. Things slow down. Some light
shines in the convex mirror. The candle burns.
Someone dictates a poem. The blue
field of the sheet live with wiggling
poppies, lashing their sperm-tail stems.
The special sheet, bought for the double
bed of the sleeping loft, four pillows
at its head and feet. Here
one pillow's enough. Inside the sleeping

bag, red afghan
keeps my feverish body warm
and dry. I'm not prepared for this. How much
I miss you.

II

The pressure falls sometimes so low
in my veins I can't breathe hard enough
to force the double
vocal chords and call. Next room a woman
friend respects my closed door. Like me
and unlike me, is silent. Right side, arm, thigh
shake for an hour in what Leah who massages me
at home calls
fear. But shaking from the central
muscle to the long thin bone, it puts
more fear in me than it lets go. Not only suffering
but that no one knows
how I suffer. I've found
thermometers are useful props
for saying no to calls from poets parties. It lies
by the bed like a dictated song. Later I write
or try to write
from life.

III

Still they decide to have a party.
I do not recognize this life. Drinking and drinking
in noisy halls full of smoke for pleasure. The noise
finds me staring wall to wall, alone, a stranger
to my home-brought treasures. Blue
flowered sheet, red afghan, enamel mirror
shining its scooped-out face. It's all
right. The candle burns. Epiphanies
are only numinous
clichés. Something you've known
the words to all your life undone by Nina
Simone, voice and piano. Be grateful. Stockpile.
Fastidiously keep your body clean. Live
like a poet you'll write
like one.

IV

Baths, showers, water. The padded
well-soaked scrub. Clean hair. Warm water.
Two years since we went
our ways, over and over I
turn to the ample tub, the glass
stall waterfall, the friendly fixtures.
On the road or camping I crave them
like a fix. I remember my life
the way a tourist
back from a Mediterranean
country remembers. I wash and wash. Nothing sloughs
off, nothing cleans windshields, the rear
view. When I shake I remind myself
it always stops, stay quiet, promise
the worn-out limbs
a bath. If someone dictates a poem you have not seen
before, can it seem
a familiar poem?

V

Strange as it is, the only thing familiar is this act.
Writing. Getting stoned
with anyone since you is like bringing home
total strangers. I thought grass cleared
everyone's daily defensive
fog, brought on its kind
of music. The extra gesture. The flower, the odd
piece of silver beside the bowl. Most often now
I like to smoke alone. I try to care
at least as well
for me as I did for you. I didn't know about
such subtle losses. A light pain
that goes on too long gets
forgotten, becomes an agent, you trust
the familiar face till she flashes
a badge and it's you
in the funhouse mirror. In line for lunch, a woman's
voice above the clatter and starch "It has
to grow a scab before you scratch it."

LANDSCAPE WITHOUT TOUCH

She has dreams of wolves it bewilders
her how it started with the skin
she put on totemlike one night
now she dreams whole packs and prowls
she prowls
her eye bright mica on the sidewalk
she prowls on bristling phosphorescent slight
she is somnolent by day
she sleeps in light
she becomes one
one less
one less human
one at home among wolves
one palest pelt
one

OREGON LANDSCAPE WITH LOST LOVER

I take my bike
and ride down to the river
and put my feet into the water
and watch the ten toes play distortions

with the light. I had forgotten all this time
how good it is to sit by water
in sun all day and never have to leave
the river moving

as no lover ever moved
widehipped deadsure and delicate—
after a while I cannot bear
to look. Pleasure dilates me

open as a trellis
free of its green sharp glossy leaves like tongues
made out of mirrors gossipping
in the sun the wind. By which

I mean
somehow
free of the self.
Through all the hungry-eyed

criss-crossing slits along the trellis
finding them leaving them
bare and clean the widehipped delicate
green river flows

voluptuous as any lover anywhere
has been.

LANDSCAPE WITH NEXT OF KIN

Imagine father that you had a brother were
not an orphan singly that you had a twin
who moved away when he got married had
a kid a similar carrer whom you had not seen
but heard from frequently for thirty years
imagine meeting him some evening somewhere
familiar to you both not in the village but by
the sea / perhaps / you have

been talking for hours
and for many days
at ease in the proprietor's
gaze—he is young you are old he could have been
a soldier in your regiment that northern province
not so long ago / perhaps he is / you are

here this evening you and your brother seated at the damp
alloy table rusting in some seaside
Patra of the mind identical sighting
the prow of the ferry from Brindisi / perhaps / a woman

bows out from the throng
of tourists very feminine and very strong
resemblance to this man your brother you have never
married / yourself / tonight
are you sipping

the weak milk of your ouzo
having heard everything / at ease / on the other side
of the customs waiting for his daughter your
first blood kin is there anything
in the love you feel
swimming towards him as you did
nine months one heartbeat

pounding like an engine in those waters / is
there anything you won't forgive
her / him

LANDSCAPE WITH POETS

Leaning
over the footbridge the Willamette
river in thaw you said John Berryman
jumped off a bridge like this your
officemate was there he waved
back thinking *friendly*
fellow John
hand raised still
smiling stradled the rail broke
ice

Below
us water hungry
current so swollen it appeared
intimate inflamed

We looked down
river down to sea
so long I held you feeling
a stranger surfacing than fear an ancient species
decimated in the wild wild singing
its last migration down through ice
floes huge emotional the killer
whale the heart

LANDSCAPE WITH LEAVES AND FIGURE

Passionate Love Is Temporary
Insanity the Chinese
say that day
I walked nine miles in the bowl
the hill makes coming round
and round avoiding
the road in
sane I realized a whole
week later at the time
I sank my crepe
soles in the spread
of leaves grass needles
bedding down the path
I took describing
every tree bush fern each
stone leaf stick
isolate
detail in the mind
one woman / it was icy cold / my nose
froze in the air lichen were dancing
up hundred-footed trees the ivy
dirndling up like glitter
flint I stood
there planted
firmly and I could not feel
the cold
wind rain the ivy glinting
savagely like mirrors on the skirts
the six-armed goddess dancing
a storm / wet / it was wet inside
the forest though no rain
was falling it was
sliding
down and you
meanwhile clear
cross-country from the snow
packs of Vermont two weeks one half
a honeydew papaya moon
were eating
while I rimmed the bowl
the woods make in the penetrating
silence between rains in

Oregon in
sane I realized a whole
week later and I said
since you had not yet
left Because
I love you Yes
you said I know that
day

fiction

Vardis Fisher

from MOUNTAIN MAN

The storm foretold by the doves and owls came in shocking fury when they were still in the foothills of the Bighorn Mountains. The moment the first drops kissed his cheeks, Sam stopped and dismounted and stripped off all his clothes. He knew that this storm would be a champion. Seeing what her man did and knowing the reason, Lotus slipped off her horse and did likewise. The leather garments of both Sam put inside a rainproof pouch. The mountain men told stories of greenhorns dressed in leather and caught in heavy downpours who had then ridden into hot sun, only to find an hour or two later that the leather on them was tighter than their own skins. It had to be cut off. Looking up to study the sky, Sam was sure that this would be one of the Almighty's finest thunder-symphonies.

As they rode along, both completely naked, with the first large raindrops caressing their skins, Sam began to sing, howling into the storm his admiration of the Creator, whose genius had wrought such marvels. Of a storm in Beethoven's pastoral symphony a musician had said that it was more than a storm; it was a cataclysm, a stupendous convulsion of all the powers; but for Sam it was nothing compared to what he had heard in these mountains. Beethoven had hardly done more than whisper among the aspens. Sam's spirit in such hours as this needed stronger music than any Beethoven or Bach or Vivaldi had dreamed of. He shouted his head off, knowing that once the conductor got the hang of things he would open with a prelude that would shake the earth. He thought of Blake's words, that music exults in immortal thoughts; but at its greatest reach, when the heavenly instruments flung down the grandeur of their thunders, music was a lament over what Thomas Browne had called the iniquity of oblivion—the lonely finality of death and the eternal night of the grave. But he was young today, and in love, and his naked bride was close behind him. He strove to improvise his mood, pouring forth wild baritone harmonies that dissolved into the winds. As the lightning's voice roared in awful grandeur, like a gigantic orchestra of drums and percussion, the sheets of fire set whole areas of sky aflame, and Sam became so intent on trying to become a part of it that for a little while he forgot the girl behind him. When he turned to look at her he knew that the storm was sounding the depths of her primitive emotions, for he could tell that she was singing. Lotus could not hear his words, except now and then, but she could see his imperious gestures, like those of a man using a pine tree for a baton; and she knew that he was lost in wild raptures. At first he had been concerned with the blandishments of the early raindrops and with tuning up his throat, but when the first crashing chords came he opened his soul to the sky and sent it forth on wings. If Lotus had had knowledge of whiteman's music she might have thought her man was improvising a rosalia; he was singing, "Rejoice, O My Heart!" climbing from key to key until his voice cracked and he doubled over coughing. He was a handsome figure—a big golden fellow on a black stallion, wet with rain, his hair flowing out into the wind that was rushing over him, his arms gesturing to the horns to come in, or the strings, as in fancy he herded the harmonies into overwhelming crescendo. Bushes and trees along the way were in such convulsions of frenzied joy that now and then one tore its roots free of the earth and went off into the sky and the thunders like a huge shaggy bird. "Hear! Hear!" Sam shouted, drenched now, his hair sopped and matted, the rain moving in a thin cool envelope down over his whole body and over the glossy pelt of his horse. The rain was also stirring the innumerable scents of the sweet earth, so that all the harmonies of rain music were infused with fragrance. It occurred to him that an opera house ought to be drenched with sweet essences, instead of with the bad breath and body odors of a thousand overdressed creatures. Remembering again that his wife was behind him, he turned to look back; and her wet face and hair, her eyes shining like two black jewels, and her lips parted across white teeth were all such a picture of female loveliness that he stopped, slipped down, and went back to kiss her. "It's beautiful!" he cried in her ear, and kissed the wet ear. Then he kissed her wet leg that was next to him, and drawing the wet foot up, he kissed it.

The storm, he thought, was close to the climax of its overture. Lightning was now setting whole patches of sky afire; thunder was crashing in such chords that the earth trembled; but for him all this was only a potpourri of the themes, moving from allegro to vivace. He hoped it was so; no thunderstorm could be too violent for him. He now threw his arms wide, to embrace the whole wet world around him; again kissed his bride's leg and her foot; and bursting again with tempests of song, returned to his horse. His girl-wife, fascinated, soaked, and shivering a little, looked at his broad naked rain-swept back and wondered in her innocent Indian way if he was actually a man, or a spirit. He frightened her but in his presence she felt safe from enemies; for what a fountain of energy and courage he was, bellowing praise to the Great Spirit as he rode on and on in the deepest and darkest and wildest rainstorm his wife had ever known.

They rode on and on in the heavenly music of falling rain, and the whole atmosphere of earth was darkened to night. Lotus knew it was not night. Somewhere ahead the sun would be shining, and indeed it was shining just around and beyond the blue-and-purple belt. After riding for two hours in a downburst that seemed eager to wash all the mountains into the rivers they came to the outriding scarves and skirts of it, with sunlight making jewels of the countless raindrops clinging to trees and grasses. In this wonderland that was half rain mist and half sun glow they rode for another hour, and then were out of it. The storm was behind them, sweeping in a vast gloomy darkness across the Beartooth Pass. When Sam stopped, Lotus was the first to reach the earth. He went back and from the packhorse took their pouch of clothing; but then glanced at his wife, and finding her as supremely lovely as a caltha lily washed

117

by rain and caressed by sun, he set the pouch aside and took her up, one arm under her knees, the other against the small of her back, and set her against his chest, with his lips to her shoulder. Then he held her away, so that she could turn her head to look at him; and for a few moments they looked into one another's eyes, without smiling.

"You know," he said, "I think we should have a feast."

She tried to look round her, for berries and roots.

After kissing over her body he set her down and looked off at the sun; it was an hour and a half high. After putting on his leather clothing he dug into a pack for dry cotton cloth to wipe his weapons. One reason he liked a storm like the one that had just swept over them was that then it was safe for a man to ride unarmed; no brave ever skulked around in such a deluge, but cowered in his miserable leaking tent while the sky raining dogs and cats scared him out of his wits, and every blast of thunder made him shake like a sick dog.

Dressed, they rode again, now in pale golden sunlight, with Sam's nostrils sniffing out the scents. He was as hungry as a wolf in forty-below weather and for his supper wanted buffalo hump and loin, though this was not best buffalo country. He might have to settle for elk steaks, or even antelope or deer. But on entering a grove of aspen he saw the kind of grouse that the trappers called fool hen, for the reason that these chickens seemed to have a little sense of enemies. He dismounted and ran among them with a long stick, knocking their heads off. They were plump and fat. Thinking that they would need at least eight for supper and a half dozen for breakfast, he kept after them, among the trees and up the hillside; and when he returned to the horses he had eleven. He saw that Lotus had hitched the beasts to a tree and gone. Was she after berries? No, she was after mushrooms, and in a few minutes she came in with a gallon of them. "Waugh!" cried Sam, looking at the white fat buttons. What a feast they would have! They would spit the chickens over an aspen or cherry fire; and under them in a kettle he would catch their juices, to use in basting them and to fry the mushrooms. While he was gathering firewood, Lotus, with revolver and knife at her waist, explored the thickets; returned with a quart of large ripe serviceberries; again disappeared, and came back with a dozen ripe red plums, wild onions, and a handful of fungus that she had stripped from a rotted tree stump.

"And what be that?" asked Sam, staring at the mold. He knew that Indians ate just about everything in the plant world, except such poisons as toadstools, larkspurs, and water parsnips. It was a marvel what they did with the common cattail—from spikes to root, they ate most of it. The spikes they boiled in salt water, if they had salt; of the pollen they made flour; of the stalk's core they made a kind of pudding; and the bulb sprouts on the ends of the roots they peeled and simmered.

Lotus was looking at him to see if he was pleased. To show her how pleased he was with such a resourceful wife he put his mouth organ to his lips, an arm round her waist, and began to waltz with her. The elder Johann Strauss's waltzes had been sweeping over Europe like an epidemic for years; in a letter last spring his father had written Sam that the younger Johann was even better, and was the rage of all the capitals. Sam found the three-fourths time just right for him, when in moccasins, with no floor but the leaf depth of an aspen grove. Around and around he went, his right arm controlling his wife, his left hand holding the harp to his lips. "Wall now!" he said, pausing at last; and lifting her as if she were a child, until her face was even with his own, he kissed her. "What a fine supper we'll have."

But the fungus bothered him. He knew that Indian women boiled tree mold and moss with buffalo beef, as white women boiled potatoes and cabbage; but he had found them tough and tasteless. A brave would open the end of a gall bladder and use the bile as a relish on raw liver; and warriors with an overpowering thirst for rum would get drunk by swigging down the contents of as many gall bladders as they could tear out of dead beasts.

Lotus went hunting a third time and returned with a few of the succulent roots that had saved John Colter's life. These Sam tossed among hot embers; later he would peel them and slice them and simmer them in grouse fat. He set on a pot of coffee. When the supper was ready he spread a robe for them to sit on, with their backs against an overhanging precipice of stone. The rifle at his side, revolver and knife at his waist, and his gaze on the only direction from which an enemy could approach, he rinsed his mouth with cold mountain water and began to eat. What more, he asked Lotus, did any fool want in this world? She asked what "fool" meant. "The King of England," he said. "The President of the United States. All fools, because money- or power-mad." They had never tasted such grouse. They never would. The world, he said, before sinking his teeth into half a breast and tearing it off, was full of vanity and vexation of spirit, as the Bible said; as well as of persons who didn't have enough get-up-and-gumption to go find their food, after their mothers had painted their nipples with aloes and tucked their breasts away. Feeding flesh and juices and hot mushrooms into his mouth, he told his staring wife that in no restaurant on earth could such fowl be found, or such mushrooms, or such odors of heaven in a place to eat, or such paintings as the magnificent sunset yonder, with two rainbows through it. Tomorrow they would have buffalo loin basted with boss; mushrooms simmered in marrow and hump fat; hot biscuits covered with crushed wild currants; and they would before long have buffalo tongue and beaver tail, and flapjacks shining with marrow fat like golden platters. Waugh! What a life they would have! It was a fine world, and they would eat and sing and love their way right through the best of it, like Breughel peasants on their way to heaven.

Pulling handfuls of grass to wipe his greasy beard, he turned to see how his wife was doing. He had eaten his third bird and taken up a fourth; she was still with her first. "Good?'" he asked. Her eyes told him that it was good. What, he wondered, watching her, did the red people know about cooking? If hungry, they simply tore a beast open and shoved their heads in, like wolves; and after drinking the pool of blood in the bowl of fat under the kidneys, or burying his famished red face in the liver, as likely as not the Indian would then yank the guts out, and while with one hand he worked the contents of the gut down and away from him, with the other he would feed the gut into his mouth like a gray wet tube, which in fact it was, his eyes bulging ferociously as his ravenous hunger choked it down. As cooks the squaws—or the few he had observed, anyway—were filthy, by white standards. For the Indian nearly every live thing was food, including the flies and spiders and beetles that tumbled into the buffalo broth, or the moths and butterflies and grasshoppers, or even a chunk of meat that a dog had been chewing at. Sam would have said that he was not squeamish, but his appetite was never good when he sat at an Indian feast. After he had paid for his bride his father-in-law had set before him the boiled and roasted flesh of dogs, and though Sam had heard that Meriwether Lewis had preferred dog to elk steak or buffalo loin he had had to gag it down, as though he were eating cat. Well, there were white trappers who thought the cougar, a tough muscular killer, the finest of all meats.

Sam was aware from time to time that his wife was studying him. He did not know why. He did not know that Lotus felt there must be some fatal lack in her, or he would have ordered her to do the cooking and the chores. Among her people the husband was lord and king; he hunted and made war and beat his wife and that was about all that he did. Sam baffled her. At the beginning she had been suspicious of him, and a bit contemptuous, but his extreme gentleness in the intimacies, his thoughtfulness, his daily gathering of flowers for her, his making for her magnificent mantles to hang from her shoulders, his way of touching her and hovering like a colossus over her needs and welfare, had reached down to what was in all women, and found warmth and a home. He had fertilized and nourished in her an emotion that, if not love, was the next thing to it. She had even learned to like his cooking, as she had learned to like his embrace. When he looked at her now, holding his fourth bird, his eyes twinkling, she flashed a smile at him that parted over perfect teeth, wet with fool-hen grease. He ate five of the birds and she ate two, and they ate all the mushrooms and roots and berries, and drank a two-quart pot of coffee. With grass he wiped his beard and said he guessed he ought to shave the damned thing off, and then he filled his pipe.

When she felt round her for grass he watched her. Throughout the journey he had covertly watched her to see if she ate bugs. The Indians of some tribes, notably the Diggers, ate every insect they could find; it was a wonder, whitemen said, that there was a beetle or stinkbug or longlegs left in all the desert of the Humboldt. The Diggers seemed able to exist for weeks, months, even years on nothing but dried ants and their larvae. Sam had seen the miserable starved wretches in their filthy coyote skins plopping live ants, moths, crickets, and caterpillars into their mouths. He had watched squaws build a fire around a hill of big red ants, thrust a stick into the hill, hold a skin pouch at the top of the stick, and catch every ant in the hill, as they crawled up in three or four solid lines to escape from the flames. He had never seen a Flathead eat a bug; their food was chiefly small game, fish, roots, and wild fruits. He also watched his wife for signs of illness. All the trappers had heard the tale of the missionary who had told Indian people that their way of worshipping the Great Spirit was wrong. The Indians then sent four chiefs to St. Louis to learn the right way, and there they had sickened on whiteman's food and died. Lotus looked to Sam like a picture of perfect health, though one morning after drinking a cup of coffee she had slipped into the brush to vomit, and had returned looking faded and foolish.

"Smell it," Sam said, and drew in a long breath. What was it? Besides the odors of food and tobacco and coffee he could smell aspen and its berry bushes and grasses; geranium on the stone ledge above him; catnip in the palm of his left hand; and something that he was not able to identify. Rising, rifle across his arm, he began to prowl in the woods around him Lotus saw him through the trees, sniffing, turning his head this way and that; bending low to peer at something on the ground; and at last falling to his knees and going on all fours like a beast. On returning he said, "Funny I didn't smell it before. Hank says when a man marries he loses half his sense and his enemies soon track him down." He was sniffing at a finger. "Crows," he said. "The Absaroka. This is Crow country. Over there they made a fire and burned some hair in it. That don't look good to this coon."

"Crow," said Lotus.

"A war party," said Sam. He brought his stallion in and staked him as a sentinel only fifty feet from his bed. Then he went east a mile or two over the path the Crows had taken to scout the area. He and his wife had been in Crow country several days; most of the mountain men trusted the Crows but Sam trusted no redman. He was worried but he tried to hide his mood from Lotus.

The next morning at daylight they headed south, and about noon he saw a wolf and suspected that buffalo were not far away. A few minutes later he sat on a hilltop, overlooking a herd. Seeing among the big shaggy beasts some deer and antelope, he knew that packs of wolves had surrounded the herd, to drag down the young, the sick, the wounded, the old, and the stragglers. It was a habit with deer and antelope to seek safety in buffalo herds. This was a large herd, and as Sam studied it he was again impressed by the orderly manner in which a big herd, even a hundred thousand head, moved across the miles. On the other hand, a herd would stampede at no more than a shadow. The old-timers like Bill Williams said the herds put vedettes out, in the way of an army, to give the alarm if enemies approached—four or five young bulls that, on scenting the foe, would rush pell-mell straight for the herd. The cows and calves would then move to the center and the bulls would surround them. In April and May, during calving time, the bulls went round and round the cows, to protect them from the wolves. In old age the bulls became abject victims of terror; all alone on a vast prairie a bull would give a feeble bellow when he saw wolves approaching, and the wolves would answer in concert.

While wondering if he was within rifle sound of Crow warriors it occurred to him that possibly this was the first herd of these beasts Lotus had ever seen. He turned to look at her face. What he saw there so riveted his attention that he could only stare. She was so lost in contemplation of the tens of thousands of beasts, making the prairie black as far as she could see, that she was unaware of him. Well, good Lord, she should see one of the big migrations, when a herd was a full hundred miles across, and extended to such depth that a man could only guess at the number. Williams and Bridger and other mountain men said they had seen herds of at least a million beasts, with ten thousand wolves around the circumference.

Did she like buffalo better than fish and rabbit? Did he dare have tenderloin for supper? It was his favorite meat. Mick Boone was extremely fond of moose, if it was taken in its prime. Bear Paws Meek was a beaver-tail man; he swore that a tail, properly seasoned and expertly basted with wild goose oil, was the only food he would ask for in heaven. Cady preferred elk.

Sam examined his rifle and they rode forward until they were about three hundred yards from the nearest beasts. Again he studied them. He wanted a fat tender one and a swift clean kill. A buffalo, unless shot through the heart or brains or spine, took a lot of time to die. While sitting and watching he told Lotus his favorite story of a greenhorn. An especially choice lubber, callow and green, had fired eight or nine pistol balls into a bull and had then stood, nonplused and bug-eyed, while blood poured from the beast's nostrils. A practical joker had told the numskill to slip up from the rear and hamstring the bull. He could then cut its throat. Accepting the suggestion, the city tenderfoot had crept up behind the bull and stabbed at one of its hams with a knife. In that instant the beast exploded with fury, its nostrils spouting blood and foam for thirty feet. For some inexplicable reason the tenderfoot had seized the bull's short stiff tail, and the bull then whirled round and round at such speed that the man clinging to its tail was flung off his feet and laid out on the air; and round and round he went, his eyes popped out like glazed marbles, his voice begging for help. Then the bull dropped dead. The thing that had scared the daylights out of him, the greenhorn afterward confessed, was his fear that the tail would pull out or break off.

Telling Lotus to be alert, Sam left her and slipped forward, until he was only forty yards from a young barren cow. He shot it through the heart and was cutting its throat when Lotus came forward. Sam rolled the beast over to its belly and pulled the four legs out like broken braces to prop it. He made an incision from the boss to the tail and skinned the heavy hide back both ways. Entering a side, he cut the liver free and drew it out. Laying it across the cow's back, he sliced off several morsels, offered one to Lotus on the point of his knife, and plopped one into his mouth. As Lotus chewed her black eyes smiled at him. When going to a pannier for his hatchet Sam had to kick a coyote out of his path and chase a dozen into the distance. Coyotes were a worse nuisance than flies when a man was butchering. They would come in close, while the wolves, farther out, trotted back and forth, drooling. If you threw a piece of flesh to a coyote the idiot instead of eating it would make off with it, and the wolves would pounce on it and tear the meat from its jaws. It sometimes looked as if the coyote was the half-witted lackey of its larger and more ferocious cousin. Both beasts were also a camp nuisance. They would slink into a camp and chew saddles and bridles and leather clothing, and had been known to eat a part of the moccasins off a sleeping man's feet.

Pausing every few moments to look round him for enemies, Sam chopped the ribs in two along both sides, and the spine in two, back and front, so that he could lift out the choicest portion of the tenderloin. That ought to do them for supper, he said. Lotus had been looking round for edible roots, and came in with an armful of lupine and two dozen mushrooms. Sam looked hard at the lupine. The camas root he had eaten, after it was pounded into flour and mixed with water to make flat dough-cakes, which were then baked over hot stones. The onion bulb, or poh-poh, made into a thick jelly, was even more tasteless than the camas, or the skunk cabbage, mixed with the inner bark of pine or hemlock. He preferred cakes made of sunflower or buffalo and blue grama grass seeds. He had never eaten the lupine root.

Lotus went off again and returned with a quart of the blue-purple choke-cherries. Sam made a face at them, for they puckered the hell out of a person's mouth. Knowing how he prepared mushrooms, Lotus made incisions in their plump bellies, stuffed inside each a blob of marrow fat, and set the buttons on their backs in an inch of hot hump fat. When they were turned to a nice golden brown and the steaks were hot and dripping and the sliced lupine roots were sizzling in a platter of fat and the coffee was steaming Sam looked up at the sky, for this was his way of saying grace before a meal. Every time he feasted he thanked the Giver of the earth's fantastic abundance.

"No taxes," he said. He had uttered these words so many times that Lotus now said, "No taxes."

"No jails."

"No jails."

The steaks were as tender as young Canada goose. The mushrooms melted in his mouth. Even the lupine tasted fine.

"Good?" he asked.

"Good," she said, gravely nodding.

Sam chose a fat golden mushroom and offered it to her on the point of a green stick. She opened her mouth in a pucker, sucked the mushoom in, and closed her eyes. He fed her choice morsels of steak, knowing all the while that she was abashed by these little gallantries. Instead of feeding their wives delicious morsels the red husbands as likely as not kicked them away from the fire and left for them only the scraps of the feast. Still, most of the squaws were fat, and Lotus, it seemed to him, had gained ten pounds since her wedding day.

Sam had cooked the whole tenderloin and half the liver. Raw liver and rose hips, the older mountain men said, were enough to keep any man healthy, if he also had pure water and air and a hard bed. Some of them ate a lot of yarrow, including its white flowers when it was blooming; as well as the onion bulb, the thorn apple, pine nuts, watercress, and viscera besides liver. Sam had watched red women in the Snake River country shake chilled grasshoppers off sagebrush into baskets, in cold September mornings, and roast them in pits and pound them into cakes, as well as crickets, mice, snakes, wood ticks, and ants. He had seen them thicken soup with these things, and through Bill Williams said they were all fine Sam had refused to taste them. Just the same, Bill could outwalk any man in the country, and go for two or three days and nights without food, sleep, or rest.

After they had eaten and Sam had smoked a pipe they both set to work on the buffalo hide. Stretching it flat on the earth, fur side down, with knives and stone chisels they took off every last particle of the flesh and fat. While Lotus boiled this flesh and fat into a thick gelatinous soup, Sam opened the skull and took out the brains. He then turned the task over to his wife, for the reason that no man seemed to have a woman's intuitive skills in making fine leathers and robes of the skins of beasts. Sam sat back, rifle across his arm, and smoked another pipe while drinking another cup of coffee.

What a beautiful evening, and what a wonderful life it was! He hoped he would live to be a hundred years old.

H. L. Davis

OPEN WINTER

The drying east wind, which always brought hard luck to Eastern Oregon at whatever season it blew, had combed down the plateau grasslands through so much of the winter that it was hard to see any sign of grass ever having grown on them. Even though March had come, it still blew, drying the ground deep, shrinking the watercourses, beating back the clouds that might have delivered rain, and grinding coarse dust against the fifty-odd head of work horses that Pop Apling, with young Beech Cartwright helping, had brought down from his homestead to turn back into their home pasture while there was still something left of them.

The two men, one past sixty and the other around sixteen, shouldered the horses through the gate of the home pasture about dark, with lights beginning to shine out from the little freighting town across Three Notch Valley, and then they rode for the ranch house, knowing even before they drew up outside the yard that they had picked the wrong time to come. The house was too dark, and the corrals and outbuildings too still, for a place that anybody lived in.

There were sounds, but they were of shingles flapping in the wind, a windmill running loose and sucking noisily at a well that it had already pumped empty, a door that kept banging shut and dragging open again. The haystacks were gone, the stackyard fence had dwindled to a few naked posts, and the entire pasture was as bare and as hard as a floor all the way down into the valley.

The prospect looked so hopeless that the herd horses refused even to explore it, and merely stood with their tails turned to the wind, waiting to see what was to happen to them next.

Old Apling went poking inside the house, thinking somebody might have left a note or that the men might have run down to the saloon in town for an hour or two. He came back, having used up all his matches and stopped the door from banging, and said the place appeared to have been handed back to the Government, or maybe the mortgage company.

"You can trust old Ream Gervais not to be any place where anybody wants him," Beech said. He had hired out to herd for Ream Gervais over the winter. That entitled him to be more critical than old Apling, who had merely contracted to supply the horse herd with feed and pasture for the season at so much per head. "Well, my job was to help herd these steeds while you had 'em, and to help deliver 'em back when you got through with 'em, and here they are. I've put in a week on 'em that I won't ever git paid for, and it won't help anything to set around and watch 'em try to live on fence pickets. Let's git out."

Old Apling looked at the huddle of horses, at the naked slope with a glimmer of light still on it, and at the lights of the town twinkling in the wind. He said it wasn't his place to tell any man what to do, but that he wouldn't feel quite right to dump the horses and leave.

"I agreed to see that they got delivered back here, and I'd feel better about it if I could locate somebody to deliver 'em to," he said. "I'd like to ride across to town yonder, and see if there ain't somebody that knows something about 'em. You could hold 'em together here till I git back. We ought to look the fences over before we pull out, and you can wait here as well as anywhere else."

'I can't, but go ahead," Beech said, "I don't like to have 'em stand around and look at me when I can't do anything to help 'em out. They'd have been better off if we'd turned 'em out of your homestead and let 'em run loose on the country. There was more grass up there than there is here."

"There wasn't enough to feed 'em, and I'd have had all my neighbors down on me for it," old Apling said. "You'll find out one of these days that if a man aims to live in this world he's got to git along with the people in it. I'd start a fire and thaw out a little and git that pack horse unloaded, if I was you."

He rode down the slope, leaning low and forward to ease the drag of the wind on his tired horse. Beech heard the sound of the road gate being let down and put up again, the beat of hoofs in the hard road, and then nothing but the noises of easing down for the night to make room for the frost. Loose boards settled into place, the windmill clacked to a stop and began to drip water into a puddle, and the herd horses shifted around facing Beech, as if anxious not to miss anything he did.

He pulled off some fence pickets and built a fire, unsaddled his pony and unloaded the pack horse, and got out what was left of a sack of grain and fed them both, standing the herd horses off with a fence picket until they had finished eating.

That was strictly fair, for the pack horse and the saddle pony had worked harder and carried more weight than any of the herd animals, and the grain was little enough to even them up for it. Nevertheless, he felt mean at having to club animals away from food when they were hungry, and they crowded back and eyed the grain sack so wistfully that he carried it inside the yard and stored it down in the root cellar behind the house, so it wouldn't prey on their minds. Then he dumped another armload of fence pickets onto the fire and sat down to wait for old Apling.

The original mistake, he reflected, had been when old Apling took the Gervais horses to feed at the beginning of winter. Contracting to feed them had been well enough, for he had nursed up a stand of bunch grass on his homestead that would have carried an ordinary pack of horses with only a little extra feeding to help out in the roughest weather. But the Gervais horses were all big harness stock, they had pulled in half starved, and they had taken not much over three weeks to clean off the pasture that old Apling had expected would last them at least two months. Nobody would have blamed him for backing out on his agreement then, since he had only undertaken to feed the horses, not to treat them for malnutrition.

Beech wanted him to back out of it, but he refused to, said the stockmen had enough troubles without having that added to them, and started feeding out his hay and insisting that the dry wind couldn't possibly keep up much longer, because it wasn't in Nature.

By the time it became clear that Nature had decided to take in a little extra territory, the hay was all fed out, and, since there couldn't be any accommodation about letting the horses starve to death, he consented to throw the contract over and bring them back where they belonged.

The trouble with most of old Apling's efforts to be accommodating was that they did nobody any good. His neighbors would have been spared all their uneasiness if he had never brought in the horses to begin with. Gervais wouldn't have been any worse off, since he stood to lose them anyway; the horses could have starved to death as gracefully in November as in March, and old Apling would have been ahead a great deal of carefully accumulated bunch grass and two big stacks of extortionately valuable hay. Nobody had gained by his chivalrousness; he had lost by it, and yet he liked it so well that he couldn't stand to leave the horses until he had raked the country for somebody to hand the worthless brutes over to.

Beech fed sticks into the fire and felt out of patience with a man who could stick to his mistakes even after he had been cleaned out by them. He heard the road gate open and shut, and he knew by the draggy-sounding plod of old Apling's horse that the news from town was going to be bad.

Old Apling rode past the fire and over to the picket fence, got off as if he was trying to make it last, tied his horse carefully as if he expected the knot to last a month, and unsaddled and did up his latigo and folded his saddle blanket as if he was fixing them to put in a show window. He remarked that his horse had been given a bait of grain in town and wouldn't need feeding again, and then he began to work down to what he had found out.

"If you think things look bad along this road, you ought to see that town," he said. "All the sheep gone and all the ranches deserted and no trade to run on and their water threatenin' to give out. They've got a little herd of milk cows that they keep up for their children, and to hear 'em talk you'd think it was an ammunition supply that they expected to stand off hostile Indians with. They said Gervais pulled out of here around a month ago. All his men quit him, so he bunched his sheep and took 'em down to the railroad, where he could ship in hay for 'em. Sheep will be a price this year, and you won't be able to buy a lamb for under twelve dollars except at a fire sale. Horses ain't in much demand. There's been a lot of 'em turned out wild, and everybody wants to git rid of 'em"

'I didn't drive this bunch of pelters any eighty miles against the wind to git a market report," Beech said. "You didn't find anybody to turn 'em over to, and Gervais didn't leave any word about what he wanted done with 'em. You've probably got it figured out that you ought to trail 'em a hundred and eighty miles to the railroad, so his feelings won't be hurt, and you're probably tryin' to study how you can work me in on it, and you might as well save your time. I've helped you with your accommodation jobs long enough. I've quit, and it would have been a whole lot better for you if I'd quit sooner."

Old Apling said he could understand that state of feeling, which didn't mean that he shared it.

"It wouldn't be as much of a trick to trail down to the railroad as a man might think," he said, merely to settle a question of fact. "We couldn't make it by the road in a starve-out year like this, but there's old Indian trails back on the ridge where any man has got a right to take livestock whenever he feels like it. Still, as long as you're set against it, I'll meet you halfway. We'll trail these horses down the ridge to a grass patch where I used to corral cattle when I was in the business, and we'll leave 'em there. It'll be enough so they won't starve, and I'll ride on down and notify Gervais where they are, and you can go where you please. It wouldn't be fair to do less than that, to my notion."

"Ream Gervais triggered me out of a week's pay," Beech said. "It ain't much, but he swindled you on that pasture contract too. If you expect me to trail his broken-down horses ninety miles down this ridge when they ain't worth anything, you've turned in a poor guess. You'll have to think of a better argument than that if you aim to gain any ground with me."

"Ream Gervais don't count in this," old Apling said. "What does he care about these horses, when he ain't even left word what he wants done with 'em? What counts is you, and I don't have to think up any better argument, because I've already got one. You may not realize it, but you and me are responsible for these horses till they're delivered to their owner, and if we turn 'em loose here to bust fences and overrun that town and starve to death in the middle of it, we'll land in the pen. It's against the law to let horses starve to death, did you know that? If you pull out of here I'll pull out right along with you, and I'll have every man in that town after you before the week's out. You'll have a chance to git some action on that pistol of yours, if you're careful."

Beech said he wasn't intimidated by that kind of talk, and threw a couple of handfuls of dirt on the fire, so it wouldn't look so conspicuous. His pistol was an old single-action relic with its grips tied on with fish line and no trigger, so that it had to be operated by flipping the hammer. The spring was weak, so that sometimes it took several flips to get off one shot. Suggesting that he might use such a thing to stand off any pack of grim-faced pursuers was about the same as saying that he was simple-minded. As far as he could see, his stand was entirely sensible, and even humane.

"It ain't that I don't feel sorry for these horses, but they ain't fit to travel," he said. "They wouldn't last twenty miles. I don't see how it's any worse to let 'em stay here than to walk 'em to death down that ridge."

"They make less trouble for people if you keep 'em on the move," old Apling said. "It's something you can't be cinched for in court, and it makes you feel better afterwards to know that you tried everything you could. Suit your-self about it, though. I ain't beggin' you to do it. If you'd sooner pull out and stand the consequences, it's you for it. Before you go, what did you do with that sack of grain?"

Beech had half a notion to leave, just to see how much of that dark threatening would come to pass. He decided that it wouldn't be worth it. "I'll help you trail the blamed skates as far as they'll last, if you've got to be childish about it," he said. "I put the grain in a root cellar behind the house, so the rats wouldn't git into it. It looked like the only safe place around here. There was about a half a ton of old sprouted potatoes ricked up in it that didn't look like they'd been bothered for twenty years. They had sprouts on 'em—" He stopped, noticing that old Apling kept staring at him as if something was wrong. "Good Lord, potatoes ain't good for horse feed, are they?" They had sprouts on 'em a foot long!"

Old Apling shook his head resignedly and got up. "We wouldn't ever find anything if it wasn't for you," he said. "We wouldn't ever git any good out of it if it wasn't for me, so maybe we make a team. Show me where that root cellar is, and we'll pack them spuds out and spread 'em around so the horses can git started on 'em. We'll git this herd through to grassland yet, and it'll be something you'll never be ashamed of. It ain't everybody your age gits a chance to do a thing like this, and you'll thank me for holdin' you to it before you're through."

II

They climbed up by an Indian trail onto a high stretch of tableland, so stony and scored with rock breaks that nobody had ever tried to cultivate it, but so high that it sometimes caught moisture from the atmosphere that the lower elevations missed. Part of it had been doled out among the Indians as allot-ment lands, which none of them ever bothered to lay claim to, but the main spread of it belonged to the nation, which was too busy to notice it.

The pasture was thin, though reliable, and it was so scantily watered and so rough and broken that in ordinary years nobody bothered to bring stock onto it. The open winter had spoiled most of that seclusion. There was no part of the trail that didn't have at least a dozen new bed grounds for lambed ewes in plain view, easily picked out of the landscape because of the little white flags stuck up around them to keep sheep from straying out and coyotes from straying in during the night. The sheep were pasturing down the draws out of the wind, where they couldn't be seen. There were no herders visible, not any startling amount of grass, and no water except a mud tank thrown up to catch a little spring for one of the camps.

They tried to water the horses in it, but it had taken up the flavor of sheep, so that not a horse in the herd would touch it. It was too near dark to waste time reasoning with them about it, so old Apling headed them down into a long rock break and across it to a tangle of wild cherry and mountain mahogany that lasted for several miles and ended in a grass clearing among some dwarf cottonwoods with a mud puddle in the center of it.

The grass had been grazed over, though not closely, and there were sheep tracks around the puddle that seemed to be fresh, for the horses, after sniffing the water, decided that they could wait a while longer. They spread out to graze, and Beech remarked that he couldn't see where it was any improvement over the tickle-grass homesteads.

"The grass may be better, but there ain't as much of it, and the water ain't any good if they won't drink it," he said. "Well, do you intend to leave 'em here, or have you got some wrinkle figured out to make me help trail 'em on down to the railroad?"

Old Apling stood the sarcasm unresistingly. "It would be better to trail 'em to the railroad, now that we've got this far," he said. "I won't ask you to do that much, because it's outside of what you agreed to. This place has changed since I was here last, but we'll make it do, and that water ought to clear up fit to drink before long. You can settle down here for a few days while I ride around and fix it up with the sheep camps to let the horses stay here. We've got to do that, or they're liable to think it's some wild bunch and start shootin' 'em. Somebody's got to stay with 'em, and I can git along with these herders better than you can."

"If you've got any sense, you'll let them sheep outfits alone." Beech said. "They don't like tame horses on this grass any better than they do wild ones, and they won't make any more bones about shootin' 'em if they find out they're in here. It's a hard place to find, and they'll stay close on account of the water, and you'd better pull out and let 'em have it to themselves. That's what I aim to do."

"You've done what you agreed to, and I ain't got any right to hold you any longer," old Apling said. "I wish I could. You're wrong about them sheep outfits. I've got as much right to pasture this ridge as they have, and they know it, and nobody ever lost anything by actin' sociable with people."

"Somebody will before very long," Beech said. "I've got relatives in the sheep business, and I know what they're like. You'll land yourself in trouble, and I don't want to be around when you do it. I'm pulling out of here in the morning, and if you had any sense you'd pull out along with me."

There were several things that kept Beech from getting much sleep during the night. One was the attachment that the horses showed for his sleeping place; they stuck so close that he could almost feel their breath on him, could hear the soft breaking sound that the grass made as they pulled it, the sound of their swallowing, the jar of the ground under him when one of the horses changed ground, the peaceful regularity of their eating, as if they didn't have to bother about anything so long as they kept old Apling in sight.

Another irritating thing was old Apling's complete freedom from uneasiness. He ought by rights to have felt more worried about the future than Beech did, but he slept, with the hard ground for a bed and his hard saddle for a pillow and the horses almost stepping on him every minute or two, as soundly as if the entire trip had come out exactly to suit him and there was nothing ahead but plain sailing.

His restfulness was so heavy and so unjustifiable that Beech couldn't sleep for feeling indignant about it, and got up and left about daylight to keep from being exposed to any more of it. He left without waking old Apling, because he saw no sense in a leave-taking that would consist merely in repeating his common-sense warnings and having them ignored, and he was so anxious to get clear of the whole layout that he didn't even take along anything to eat. The only thing he took from the pack was his ramshackle old pistol; there was no holster for it, and in the hope that he might get a chance to use it on a loose quail or prairie chicken, he stowed it in an empty flour sack and hung it on his saddle horn, a good deal like an old squaw heading for the far blue distances with a bundle of diapers.

III

There was never anything recreational about traveling a rock desert at any season of the year, and the combination of spring gales, winter chilliness and summer drought all striking at once brought it fairly close to hard punishment. Beech's saddle pony, being jaded at the start with overwork and underfeeding and no water, broke down in the first couple of miles, and got so feeble and tottery that Beech had to climb off and lead him, searching likely-looking thickets all the way down the gully in the hope of finding some little trickle that he wouldn't be too finicky to drink.

The nearest he came to it was a fair-sized rock sink under some big half-budded cottonwoods that looked, by its dampness and the abundance of fresh animal tracks around it, as if it might have held water recently, but of water there was none, and even digging a hole in the center of the basin failed to fetch a drop.

The work of digging, hill climbing and scrambling through brush piles raised Beech's appetite so powerfully that he could scarcely hold up, and, a little above where the gully opened into the flat sagebrush plateau, he threw away his pride, pistoled himself a jack rabbit, and took it down into the sagebrush to cook, where his fire wouldn't give away which gully old Apling was camped in.

Jack rabbit didn't stand high as a food. It was considered an excellent thing to give men in the last stages of famine, because they weren't likely to injure themselves by eating too much of it, but for ordinary occasions it was looked down on, and Beech covered his trail out of the gully and built his cooking fire in the middle of a high stand of sagebrush, so as not to be embarrassed by inquisitive visitors.

The meat cooked up strong, as it always did, but he ate what he needed of it, and he was wrapping the remainder in his flour sack to take along with him when a couple of men rode past, saw his pony, and turned in to look him over.

They looked him over so closely and with so little concern for his privacy that he felt insulted before they even spoke.

He studied them less openly, judging by their big gallon canteens that they were out on some long scout.

One of them was some sort of hired hand, by his looks; he was broad-faced and gloomy-looking, with a fine white horse, a flower-stamped saddle, an expensive rifle scabbarded under his knee, and a fifteen-dollar saddle blanket, while his own manly form was set off by a yellow hotel blanket and a ninety-cent pair of overalls.

The other man had on a store suit, a plain black hat, fancy stitched boots, and a white shirt and necktie, and rode a burr-tailed Indian pony and an old wrangling saddle with a loose horn. He carried no weapons in sight, but there was a narrow strap across the lower spread of his necktie which indicated the presence of a shoulder holster somewhere within reach.

He opened the conversation by inquiring where Beech had come from, what his business was, where he was going and why he hadn't taken the country road to go there, and why he had to eat jack rabbit when the country was littered with sheep camps where he could get a decent meal by asking for it?

"I come from the upper country," Beech said, being purposely vague about it. "I'm travelin', and I stopped here because my horse give out. He won't drink out of any place that's had sheep in it, and he's gone short of water till he breaks down easy."

"There's a place corralled in for horses to drink at down at my lower camp," the man said, and studied Beech's pony. "There's no reason for you to bum through the country on jack rabbit in a time like this. My herder can take you down to our water hole and see that you get fed and put to work till you can make a stake for yourself. I'll give you a note. That pony looks like he had Ream Gervais' brand on him. Do you know anything about that herd of old work horses he's been pasturing around?"

"I don't know anything about him," Beech said, side-stepping the actual question while he thought over the offer of employment. He could have used a stake, but the location didn't strike him favorably. It was too close to old Apling's camp, he could see trouble ahead over the horse herd, and he didn't want to be around when it started. "If you'll direct me how to find your water, I'll ride on down there, but I don't need anybody to go with me, and I don't need any stake. I'm travelin'."

The man said there wasn't anybody so well off that he couldn't use a stake, and that it would be hardly any trouble at all for Beech to get one. "I want you to understand how we're situated around here, so you won't think we're any bunch of stranglers,' 'he said. "You can see what kind of a year this has been, when we have to run lambed ewes in a rock patch like this. We've got five thousand lambs in here that we're trying to bring through, and we've had to fight the blamed wild horses for this pasture since the day we moved in. A horse that ain't worth hell room will eat as much as two dozen sheep worth twenty dollars, with the lambs, so you can see how it figures out. We've got 'em pretty well thinned out, but one of my packers found a trail of a new bunch that came up from around Three Notch within the last day or two, and we don't want them to feel as if we'd neglected them. We'd like to find out where they lit. You wouldn't have any information about 'em?"

"None that would do you any good to know," Beech said. "I know the man with that horse herd, and it ain't any use to let on that I don't, but it wouldn't be any use to try to deal with him. He don't sell out on a man he works for."

"He might be induced to," the man said. "We'll find him anyhow, but I don't like to take too much time to it. Just for instance, now, suppose you knew that pony of yours would have to go thirsty till you give us a few directions about that horse herd? You'd be stuck here for quite a spell, wouldn't you?"

He was so pleasant about it that it took Beech a full minute to realize that he was being threatened. The heavyset herder brought that home to him by edging out into a flank position and hoisting his rifle scabbard so it could be reached in a hurry. Beech removed the cooked jack rabbit from his flour sack carefully, a piece at a time, and, with the same mechanical thoughtfulness, brought out his triggerless old pistol, cut down on the pleasant-spoken man, and hauled back on the hammer and held it poised.

"That herder of yours had better go easy on his rifle," he said, trying to keep his voice from trembling. "This pistol shoots if I don't hold back the hammer, and if he knocks me out I'll have to let go of it. You'd better watch him, if you don't want your tack drove. I won't give you no directions about that horse herd, and this pony of mine won't go thirsty for it, either. Loosen them canteens of yours and let 'em drop on the ground. Drop that rifle scabbard back where it belongs, and unbuckle the straps and let go of it. If either of you tries any funny business, there'll be one of you to pack home, heels first."

The quaver in his voice sounded childish and undignified to him, but it had a more businesslike ring to them than any amount of manly gruffness. The herder unbuckled his rifle scabbard, and they both cast loose their canteen straps, making it last as long as they could while they argued with him, not angrily, but as if he was a dull stripling whom they wanted to save from some foolishness that he was sure to regret. They argued ethics, justice, common sense, his future prospects, and the fact that what he was doing amounted to robbery by force and arms and that it was his first fatal step into a probably unsuccessful career of crime. They worried over him, they explained themselves to him, and they ridiculed him.

They managed to make him feel like several kinds of a fool, and they were so pleasant and concerned about it that they came close to breaking him down. What held him steady was the thought of old Apling waiting up the gully.

"That herder with the horses never sold out on any man, and I won't sell out on him," he said. "You've said your say and I'm tired of holdin' this pistol on cock for you, so move along out of here. Keep to open ground, so I can be sure you're gone, and don't be in too much of a hurry to come back. I've got a lot of things I want to think over, and I want to be let alone while I do it."

IV

He did have some thinking that needed tending to, but he didn't take time for it. When the men were well out of range, he emptied their canteens into his hat and let his pony drink. Then he hung the canteens and the scabbarded rifle on a bush and rode back up the gully where the horse camp was, keeping to shaly ground so as not to leave any tracks. It was harder going up than it had been coming down.

He had turned back from the scene of his run-in with the two sheepmen about noon, and he was still a good two miles from the camp when the sun went down, the wind lulled and the night frost began to bite at him so hard that he dismounted and walked to get warm. That raised his appetite again, and, as if by some special considerateness of Nature, the cottonwoods around him seemed to be alive with jack rabbits heading down into the pitch-dark gully where he had fooled away valuable time trying to find water that morning.

They didn't stimulate his hunger much; for a time they even made him feel less like eating anything. Then his pony gave out and had to rest, and, noticing that the cottonwoods around him were beginning to bud out, he remembered that peeling the bark off in the budding season would fetch out a foamy, sweet-tasting sap which, among children of the plateau country, was considered something of a delicacy.

He cut a blaze on a fair-sized sapling, waited ten minutes or so, and touched his finger to it to see how much sap had accumulated. None had; the blaze was moist to his touch, but scarcely more so than when he had whittled it.

It wasn't important enough to do any bothering about, and yet a whole set of observed things began to draw together in his mind and form themselves into an explanation of something he had puzzled over: the fresh animal tracks he had seen around the rock sink when there wasn't any water; the rabbits going down into the gully; the cottonwoods in which the sap rose enough during the day to produce buds and got driven back at night when the frost set in. During the day, the cottonwoods had drawn the water out of the ground for themselves; at night they stopped drawing it, and it drained out into the rock sink for the rabbits.

It all worked out so simply that he led his pony down into the gully to see how much there was in it, and, losing his footing on the steep slope, coasted down into the rock sink in the dark and landed in water and thin mud up to his knees. He led his pony down into it to drink, which seemed little enough to get back for the time he had fooled away on it, and then he headed for the horse camp, which was all too easily discernible by the plume of smoke rising, white and ostentatious, against the dark sky from old Apling's campfire.

He made the same kind of entrance that old Apling usually affected when bringing some important item of news. He rode past the campfire and pulled up at a tree, got off deliberately, knocked an accumulation of dead twigs from his hat, took off his saddle and bridle and balanced them painstakingly in the tree fork, and said it was affecting to see how widespread the shortage of pasture was.

"It generally is," old Apling said. "I had a kind of a notion you'd be back after you'd had time to study things over. I suppose you got into some kind of a rumpus with some of them sheep outfits. What was it? Couldn't you git along with them, or couldn't they hit it off with you?"

"There wasn't any trouble between them and me," Beech said. "The only point we had words over was you. They wanted to know where you was camped, so they could shoot you up, and I didn't think it was right to tell 'em. I had to put a gun on a couple of 'em before they'd believe I meant business, and that was all there was to it. They're out after you now, and they can see the smoke of this fire of yours for twenty miles, so they ought to be along almost any time now. I thought I'd come back and see you work your sociability on 'em."

"You probably kicked up a squabble with 'em yourself," old Apling said. He looked a little uneasy. "You talked right up to 'em, I'll bet, and slapped their noses with your hat to show 'em that they couldn't run over you. Well, what's done is done. You did come back, and maybe they'd have jumped us anyway. There ain't much that we can do. The horses have got to have water before they can travel, and they won't touch that seep. It ain't cleared up a particle."

"You can put that fire out, not but what the whole country has probably seen the smoke from it already," Beech said. "If you've got to tag after these horses, you can run 'em off down the draw and keep 'em to the brush where they won't leave a trail. There's some young cottonwood bark that they can eat if they have to, and there's water in a rock sink under some big cottonwood trees. I'll stay here and hold off anybody that shows up, so you'll have time to git your tracks covered."

Old Apling went over and untied the flour-sacked pistol from Beech's saddle, rolled it into his blankets, and sat down on it. "If there's any holdin' to be done, I'll do it," he said. "You're a little too high-spirited to suit me, and a little too hasty about your conclusions. I looked over that rock sink down the draw today, and there wasn't anything in it but mud, and blamed little of that. Somebody had dug for water, and there wasn't none."

"There is now," Beech said. He tugged off one of his wet boots and poured about a pint of the disputed fluid on the ground. "There wasn't any in the daytime because the cottonwoods took it all. They let up when it turns cold, and it runs back in. I waded in it."

He started to put his boot back on. Old Apling reached out and took it, felt of it inside and out, and handed it over as if performing some ceremonial presentation.

135

"I'd never have figured out a thing like that in this world," he said. "If we git them horses out of here, it'll be you that done it. We'll bunch 'em and work 'em down there. It won't be no picnic, but we'll make out to handle it somehow. We've got to, after a thing like this."

Beech remembered what had occasioned the discovery, and said he would have to have something to eat first. "I want you to keep in mind that it's you I'm doin' this for," he said. "I don't owe that old groundhog of a Ream Gervais anything. The only thing I hate about this is that it'll look like I'd done him a favor."

"He won't take it for one, I guess," old Apling said. "We've got to git these horses out because it'll be a favor to you. You wouldn't want to have it told around that you'd done a thing like findin' that water, and then have to admit that we'd lost all the horses anyhow. We can't lose 'em. You've acted like a man tonight, and I'll be blamed if I'll let you spoil it for any childish spite."

They got the horses out none too soon. Watering them took a long time, and when they finally did consent to call it enough and climb back up the side hill, Beech and old Apling heard a couple of signal shots from the direction of their old camping place, and saw a big glare mount up into the sky from it as the visitors built up their campfire to look the locality over. The sight was almost comforting; if they had to keep away from a pursuit, it was at least something to know where it was.

V

From then on they followed a grab-and-run policy, scouting ahead before they moved, holding to the draws by day and crossing open ground only after dark, never pasturing over a couple of hours in any one place, and discovering food value in outlandish substances—rock lichens, the sprouts of wild plum and serviceberry, the moss of old trees and the bark of some young ones—that neither they nor the horses had ever considered fit to eat before. When they struck Boulder River Canyon they dropped down and toenailed their way along one side of it where they could find grass and water with less likelihood of having trouble about it.

The breaks of the canyon were too rough to run new-lambed sheep in, and they met with so few signs of occupancy that old Apling got overconfident, neglected his scouting to tie back a break they had been obliged to make in a line fence, and ran the horse herd right over the top of a camp where some men were branding calves, tearing down a cook tent and part of a corral and scattering cattle and bedding from the river all the way to the top of the canyon.

By rights, they should have sustained some damage for that piece of carelessness, but they drove through fast, and they were out of sight around a shoulder of rimrock before any of the men could get themselves picked up. Somebody did throw a couple of shots after them as they were pulling into a thicket of mock orange and chokeberry, but it was only with a pistol, and he probably did it more to relieve his feelings than with any hope of hitting anything.

They were so far out of range that they couldn't even hear where the bullets landed.

Neither of them mentioned that unlucky run-in all the rest of that day. They drove hard, punished the horses savagely when they lagged, and kept them at it until, a long time after dark, they struck an old rope ferry that crossed Boulder River at a place called, in memory of its original founders, Robbers' Roost.

The ferry wasn't a public carrier, and there was not even any main road down to it. It was used by the ranches in the neighborhood as the only means of crossing the river for fifty miles in either direction, and it was tied in to a log with a good solid chain and padlock. It was a way to cross, and neither of them could see anything else but to take it.

Beech favored waiting for daylight for it, pointing out that there was a ranch light half a mile up the slope, and that if anybody caught them hustling a private ferry in the dead of night they would probably be taken for criminals on the dodge. Old Apling said it was altogether likely, and drew Beech's pistol and shot the padlock apart with it.

"They could hear that up at that ranch house," Beech said. "What if they come pokin' down here to see what we're up to?"

Old Apling tossed the fragments of padlock into the river and hung the pistol in the waistband of his trousers. "Let 'em come," he said. "They'll go back again with their fingers in their mouths. This is your trip, and you put in good work on it, and I like to ruined the whole thing stoppin' to patch an eighty-cent fence so some scissorbill wouldn't have his feelings hurt, and that's the last accommodation anybody gits out of me till this is over with. I can take about six horses at a trip, it looks like. Help me to bunch 'em."

Six horses at a trip proved to be an overestimate. The best they could do was five, and the boat rode so deep with them that Beech refused to risk handling it. He stayed with the herd, and old Apling cut it loose, let the current sweep it across into slack water, and hauled it in to the far bank by winding in its cable on an old homemade capstan. Then he turned the horses into a counting pen and came back for another load.

He worked at it fiercely, as if he had a bet up that he could wear the whole ferry rig out, but it went with infernal slowness, and when the wind began to move for daylight there were a dozen horses still to cross and no place to hide them in case the ferry had other customers.

Beech waited and fidgeted over small noises until, hearing voices and the clatter of hoofs on shale far up the canyon behind him, he gave way, drove the remaining horses into the river, and swam them across, letting himself be towed along by the saddle horn and floating his clothes ahead of him on a board.

He paid for that flurry of nervousness before he got out. The water was so cold it paralyzed him, and so swift it whisked him a mile downstream before he could get his pony turned to breast it. He grounded on a gravel bar in a thicket of dwarf willows, with numbness striking clear to the center of his diaphragm and deadening his arms so he couldn't pick his clothes loose from the bundle to put on. He managed it, by using his teeth and elbows, and warmed himself a little by driving the horses afoot through the brush till he struck the ferry landing.

It had got light enough to see things in outline, and old Apling was getting ready to shove off for another crossing when the procession came lumbering at him out of the shadows. He came ashore, counted the horses into the corral to make sure none had drowned, and laid Beech under the blankets and built up a fire to limber him out by. He got breakfast and got packed to leave, and he did some rapid expounding about the iniquity of risking the whole trip on such a wild piece of foolhardiness.

"That was the reason I wanted you to work this boat," he said. "I could have stood up to anybody that come projectin' around, and if they wanted trouble I could have filled their order for 'em. They won't bother us now, anyhow; it don't matter how bad they want to."

"I could have stood up to 'em if I'd had anything to do it with," Beech said. "You've got that pistol of mine, and I couldn't see to throw rocks. What makes you think they won't bother us? You know it was that brandin' crew comin' after us, don't you?"

"I expect that's who it was," old Apling agreed. "They ought to be out after the cattle we scattered, but you can trust a bunch of cowboys to pick out the most useless things to tend to first. I've got that pistol of yours because I don't aim for you to git in trouble with it while this trip is on. There won't anybody bother us because I've cut all the cables on the ferry, and it's lodged downstream on a gravel spit. If anybody crosses after us within fifty miles of here, he'll swim, and the people around here ain't as reckless around cold water as you are."

Beech sat up. "We got to git out of here," he said. "There's people on this side of the river that use that ferry, you old fool, and they'll have us up before every grand jury in the country from now on. The horses ain't worth it."

"What the horses is worth ain't everything," old Apling said. "There's a part of this trip ahead that you'll be glad you went through. You're entitled to that much out of it, after the work you've put in, and I aim to see that you git it. It ain't any use tryin' to explain to you what it is. You'll notice it when the time comes."

VI

They worked north, following the breaks of the river canyon, finding the rock breaks hard to travel, but easy to avoid observation in, and the grass fair in stand, but so poor and washy in body that the horses had to spend most of their time eating enough to keep up their strength so they could move.

They struck a series of gorges, too deep and precipitous to be crossed at all, and had to edge back into milder country where there were patches of plowed ground, some being harrowed over for summer fallow and others venturing out with a bright new stand of dark-green wheat.

The pasture was patchy and scoured by the wind, and all the best parts of it were under fence, which they didn't dare cut for fear of getting in trouble with the natives. Visibility was high in that section; the ground lay open to the north as far as they could see, the wind kept the air so clear that it hurt to look at the sky, and they were never out of sight of wheat ranchers harrowing down summer fallow.

A good many of the ranchers pulled up and started after the horse herd as it went past, and two or three times they waved and rode down toward the road, as if they wanted to make it an excuse for stopping work. Old Apling surmised that they had some warning they wanted to deliver against trespassing, and he drove on without waiting to hear it.

They were unable to find a camping place anywhere among those wheat fields, so they drove clear through to open country and spread down for the night alongside a shallow pond in the middle of some new grass not far enough along to be pastured, though the horses made what they could out of it. There were no trees or shrubs anywhere around, not even sagebrush. Lacking fuel for a fire, they camped without one, and since there was no grass anywhere except around the pond, they left the horses unguarded, rolled in to catch up sleep, and were awakened about daylight by the whole herd stampeding past them at a gallop.

They both got up and moved fast. Beech ran for his pony, which was trying to pull loose from its picket rope to go with the bunch. Old Apling ran out into the dust afoot, waggling the triggerless old pistol and trying to make out objects in the half-light by hard squinting. The herd horses fetched a long circle and came back past him, with a couple of riders clouting along behind trying to turn them back into open country. One of the riders opened up a rope and swung it, the other turned in and slapped the inside flankers with his hat, and old Apling hauled up the old pistol, flipped the hammer a couple of rounds to get it warmed up, and let go at them twice.

The half darkness held noise as if it had been a cellar. The two shots banged monstrously, Beech yelled to old Apling to be careful who he shot at, and the two men shied off sideways and rode away into the open country. One of them yelled something that sounded threatening in tone as they went out of sight, but neither of them seemed in the least inclined to bring on any general engagement. The dust blew clear, the herd horses came back to grass, old Apling looked at the pistol and punched the two exploded shells out of it, and Beech ordered him to hand it over before he got in trouble with it.

"How do you know but what them men had a right here?" he demanded sternly. "We'd be in a fine jack pot if you'd shot one of 'em and it turned out he owned this land we're on, wouldn't we?"

Old Apling looked at him, holding the old pistol poised as if he was getting ready to lead a band with it. The light strengthened and shed a rose-colored radiance over him, so he looked flushed and joyous and lifted up. With some of the dust knocked off him, he could have filled in easily as a day star and son of the morning, whiskers and all.

"I wouldn't have shot them men for anything you could buy me!" he said, and faced north to a blue line of bluffs that came up out of the shadows, a blue gleam of water that moved under them, a white steamboat that moved upstream, glittering as the first light struck it. "Them men wasn't here because we was trespassers. Them was horse thieves, boy! We've brought these horses to a place where they're worth stealin', and we've brought 'em through! The railroad is under them bluffs, and that water down there is the old Columbia River!"

They might have made it down to the river that day, but having it in sight and knowing that nothing could stop them from reaching it, there no longer seemed any object in driving so unsparingly. They ate breakfast and talked about starting, and they even got partly packed up for it. Then they got occupied with talking to a couple of wheat ranchers who pulled in to inquire about buying some of the horse herd; the drought had run up wheat prices at a time when the country's livestock had been allowed to run down, and so many horses had been shot and starved out that they were having to take pretty much anything they could get.

Old Apling swapped them a couple of the most jaded herd horses for part of a haystack, referred other applicants to Gervais down at the railroad, and spent the remainder of the day washing, patching clothes and saddlery, and watching the horses get acquainted once more with a conventional diet.

The next morning a rancher dropped off a note from Gervais urging them to come right on down, and adding a kind but firm admonition against running up any feed bills without his express permission. He made it sound as if there might be some hurry about catching the horse market on the rise, so they got ready to leave, and Beech looked back over the road they had come, thinking of all that had happened on it.

"I'd like it better if old Gervais didn't have to work himself in on the end of it," he said. "I'd like to step out on the whole business right now."

"You'd be a fool to do that," old Apling said. "This is outside your work contract, so we can make the old gopher pay you what it's worth. I'll want to go in ahead and see about that and about the money that he owes me and about corral space and feed and one thing and another, so I'll want you to bring 'em in alone. You ain't seen everything there is to a trip like this, and you won't unless you stay with it."

VII

There would be no ending to this story without an understanding of what that little river town looked like at the hour, a little before sundown of a windy spring day, when Beech brought the desert horse herd down into it. On the wharf below town, some men were unloading baled hay from a steamboat, with some passengers watching from the saloon deck, and the river beyond them hoisting into white-capped peaks that shone and shed dazzling spray over the darkening water.

A switch engine was handling stock cars on a spur track, and the brakeman flagged it to a stop and stood watching the horses, leaning into the wind to keep his balance while the engineer climbed out on the tender to see what was going on.

The street of the town was lined with big leafless poplars that looked as if they hadn't gone short of moisture a day of their lives; the grass under them was bright green, and there were women working around flower beds and pulling up weeds, enough of them so that a horse could have lived on them for two days.

There was a Chinaman clipping grass with a pair of sheep shears to keep it from growing too tall, and there were lawn sprinklers running clean water on the ground in streams. There were stores with windows full of new clothes, and stores with bright hardware, and stores with strings of bananas and piles of oranges, bread and crackers and candy and rows of hams, and there were groups of anxious-faced men sitting around stoves inside who came out to watch Beech pass and told one another hopefully that the back country might make a good year out of it yet, if a youngster could bring that herd of horses through it.

There were women who hauled back their children and cautioned them not to get in the man's way, and there were boys and girls, some near Beech's own age, who watched him and stood looking after him, knowing that he had been through more than they had ever seen and not suspecting that it had taught him something that they didn't know about the things they saw every day. None of them knew what it meant to be in a place where there were delicacies to eat and new clothes to wear and look at, what it meant to be warm and out of the wind for a change, what it could mean merely to have water enough to pour on the ground and grass enough to cut down and throw away.

For the first time, seeing how the youngsters looked at him, he understood what that amounted to. There wasn't a one of them who wouldn't have traded places with him. There wasn't one that he would have traded places with, for all the haberdashery and fancy groceries in town. He turned down to the corrals, and old Apling held the gate open for him and remarked that he hadn't taken much time to it.

"You're sure you had enough of that ridin' through town?" he said. "It ain't the same when you do it a second time, remember."

"It'll last me," Beech said. "I wouldn't have missed it, and I wouldn't want it to be the same again. I'd sooner have things the way they run with us out in the high country. I'd sooner not have anything be the same a second time."

Ursula K. Le Guin

GWILAN'S HARP

The harp had come to Gwilan from her mother, and so had her mastery of
it, people said. "Ah," they said when Gwilan played, "you can tell—that's Diera's
touch," just as their parents had said when Diera played, "Ah, that's the true
Penlin touch!" Gwilan's mother had had the harp from Penlin, a musician's
dying gift to his worthiest pupil. From a musician's hands Penlin too had re-
ceived it; never had the harp been sold or bartered for, nor had any value been
put upon it that can be said in numbers. A princely and most incredible instru-
ment it was for a poor harper to own. The shape of it was perfection and every
part was strong and fine: the wood as hard and smooth as bronze, the fittings
of ivory and silver. The grand curves of the frame bore silver mountings chased
with long, intertwining lines that became waves and the waves became leaves,
and the eyes of gods and stags looked out from the leaves that became waves
and the waves became lines again. It was the work of great craftsmen—you
could see that at a glance. But all this beauty was practical, obedient, shaped to
the service of sound. The sound of Gwilan's harp was water running and rain
and sunlight on the water, waves breaking and the foam on the brown sands. It
was forests, the leaves and branches of the forest and the shining eyes of gods
and stags among the leaves when the wind blows in the valleys. It was all that
and none of that. When Gwilan played, the harp made music—and what is
music but a little wrinkling of the air?

Play she did, wherever they wanted her. Her singing voice was true but
had no sweetness, so when it was songs and ballads they wanted, she accom-
panied the singers. Weak voices were borne up by her playing, fine voices
gained a glory from it; the loudest, proudest singers might keep still a verse to
hear her play alone. She played with flute and reed-flute and tabour and music
made for the harp to play alone, and the music that sprang up of itself when her
fingers touched the strings. At weddings and festivals it was: "Gwilan will be
here to play," and at music-day competitions: "When will Gwilan play?"

She was young; her hands were iron and her touch was silk. She could play
all night and the next day too. She traveled from valley to valley, from town to
town, stopping here and staying there and moving on again with other musi-
cians on their wanderings. They walked, or a wagon was sent for them, or they
got a ride on a farmer's cart. However they went, Gwilan carried her harp in its
silk-and-leather case at her back or in her hands. When she rode, she rode with
the harp; and when she walked, she walked with the harp; and when she slept—
no, she didn't sleep with the harp, but it was there where she could reach out and
touch it. She was not jealous of it, and could change instruments with another
harper gladly; it was a great pleasure to her when at last they gave her back

her own, saying with sober envy, "I never played so fine an instrument." She kept it clean, polished the mountings and strung it with the harp strings made by old Uliad, which cost as much apiece as a whole set of common harp strings. In the heat of summer she carried it in the shade of her body; in the bitter winter it shared her cloak. In a firelit hall she did not sit with it very near the fire, nor yet too far away, for changes of heat and cold would change the voice of it and perhaps harm the frame. She did not look after herself with half the care. Indeed, she saw no need to. She knew there were other harpers, and would be other harpers—most not as good, some better. But the harp was the best. There had not been and there would not be a better. Delight and service were due and fitting to it. She was not its owner but its player. It was her music, her joy, her life, the noble instrument.

She played "A Fine Long Life" at weddings and "The Green Leaves" at festivals. There were funerals, with the burial feast, the singing of elegies, and Gwilan to play "The Lament of Orioth," the music that crashes and cries out like the sea and the sea birds, bringing relief and a burst of tears to the grief-dried heart. There were music days, with a rivalry of harpers and a shrilling of fiddlers and a mighty outshouting of tenors. She went from town to town in sun and rain, the harp on her back or in her hands.

So she was going one day to the yearly music day at Comin, and the landowner of Torm Vale was giving her a ride—a man who so loved music that he had traded a good cow for a bad horse, since the cow would not take him where he could hear music played. It was he and Gwilan in a rickety cart, and the leannecked roan stepping out down the steep, sunlit road from Torm Vale.

Torm was discussing music deeply with Gwilan, waving his hands to conduct a choir of voices, when the reins went flipping out of those startled hands. It might have been a bear in the forest by the road or a bear's ghost or the shadow of a hawk; the horse shied half across the road, jumped like a cat and ran. At a sharp curve of the road the cart swung round and smashed against a rocky cutting. A wheel leaped free and rolled, rocking like a top, for a few yards. The roan went plunging and sliding down the road with half the wrecked cart dragging behind and was gone, and the road lay silent in the sunlight between the forest trees.

Torm had been thrown from the cart and lay stunned for a minute or two.

Gwilan had clutched the harp to her when the horse shied, but had lost hold of it in the crash. The cart had tipped over and dragged on it. It was in its case of leather and embroidered silk, but when, one-handed, Gwilan got the case out from under the wheel and opened it, she did not take out a harp but a piece of wood, and another piece, and a tangle of strings, and a sliver of ivory, and a twisted shell of silver chased with lines and leaves and eyes, held by a silver nail to a fragment of the frame.

It was six months without playing after that, since her arm had broken at the wrist. The wrist healed well enough, but there was no mending the harp, and by then the landowner of Torm Vale had asked if she would marry him and she had said yes. Sometimes she wondered why she had said yes, having never thought much of marriage before, but if she looked steadily into her own mind, she saw the reason why. She saw Torm on the road in the sunlight, kneeling by the broken harp, his face all blood and dust, and he was weeping. When she looked at that she saw that the time for rambling and roving was over and gone. One day is the day for moving on, and overnight, the next day, there is no more good in moving on because you have come to where you were going.

Gwilan brought to the marriage a gold piece that had been the prize last year at Four Valleys music day; she had sewed it to her bodice as a brooch, because where on earth could you spend a gold piece? She also had two silver pieces, five coppers and a good winter cloak. Torm contributed house and household, fields and forests, four tenant farmers even poorer than himself, twenty hens, five cows and forty sheep.

They married in the old way, by themselves, over the spring where the stream began, and came back and told the household. Torm had never suggested a wedding, with singing and harp playing—never a word of all that.

What began in pain, in tears, was never free from the fear of pain. The two of them were gentle with each other. Not that they lived together thirty years without some quarreling. Two rocks, sitting side by side would tire of each other in thirty years, and who knows what they might say now and then when nobody was listening? But if people trust each other, they can grumble, and a good bit of grumbling takes the fuel from wrath. Their quarrels went up and burned out like bits of paper, leaving nothing but a feather of ash, a laugh in bed in the dark. Torm's land never gave more than enough and there was no money saved. But it was a good house, and the sunlight was sweet on those high, stony fields. There were two sons, who grew up into cheerful, sensible men. One had a taste for roving and the other was a farmer born, but neither had any gift for music.

Gwilan never spoke of wanting another harp. But about the time her wrist was healed, old Uliad had a traveling musician bring her one on loan; later, when he had an offer to buy it at its worth, he sent for it back again. At that time Torm had it that there was money from selling three good heifers to the landowner of Comin High Farm and that the money should buy a harp, which it did. A year or two later an old friend, a flute player still on his travels and rambles, brought Gwilan another harp from the south as a present. The three-heifers harp was a common instrument, plain and heavy; the southern harp was delicately carved and gilt, but cranky to tune and thin of voice. Gwilan could draw strength from the one and sweetness from the other. When she picked up a harp, as when she spoke to a child, it obeyed her.

She played at all festivities and funerals in the neighborhood, and with the musician's fees she bought good strings—not Uliad's strings, though, for Uliad was in his grave before her second child was born. If there was a music day nearby, she went to it with Torm. She would not play in the competitions—not for fear of losing, but because she was not a harper now, and if they did not know it, she did. So they had her judge the competitions, which she did well and mercilessly. Often in the early years musicians would stop by on their travels and stay two or three nights at Torm Vale; with them she would play the Hunts of Orioth, the Dances of Cail, the difficult and venerable music of the north, and would learn from them the new songs. Even on winter evenings there was music in the house of Torm, with Gwilan playing the harp—usually the three-heifers one, sometimes the fretful southerner—and Torm's good tenor voice, and the boys' singing, first a sweet treble, later on a husky, unreliable baritone. One of the farm men was a lively fiddler, and the shepherd Keth, when he was there, played on the pipes, though he never could tune them to anyone else's note. "It's our own music day tonight," Gwilan would say. "Put another log on the fire, Torm, and sing 'The Green Leaves' with me, and the boys will take the descant."

Her wrist that had been broken grew a little stiff as the years went on; then arthritis came into her hands. The work she did in house and farm was not easy work. But then, who, looking at a hand, would say it was made to do easy work? You can see from the look of it that it is meant to do difficult things, that it is the noble, willing servant of the heart and mind. But the best servants get clumsy as the years go on. Gwilan could still play the harp, but not as well as she had played, and she did not like half measures. So the two harps hung on the wall, though she kept them tuned. About that time the younger son went wandering off to see what things looked like in the north, and the elder married and brought his bride to Torm Vale. Old Keth was found dead up on the mountain in the spring rain, his dog crouched silently by him and the sheep nearby. And the drouth came, and the good year and the poor year, and there was food to eat and to be cooked and clothes to wear and to be washed, poor year or good year. In the depth of a winter Torm took ill. He went from a cough to a high fever to quietness, and died while Gwilan sat beside him.

Thirty years—how can you say how long that is?—and yet no longer than the saying of it: thirty years. The years began in pain; they passed in peace, contentment. But they did not end that way. They ended as they began.

Gwilan got up from her chair beside Torm's bed and went into the hearth room. The rest of the household were asleep. In the light of her candle she saw the two harps hung against the wall: the three-heifers harp and the gilded southern harp; the dull music and the false music. She thought, I'll take them down at last and smash them on the hearthstone, crush them till they're only bits of wood and tangles of wire, like my harp. But she did not. She could not play them at all any more; her hands were far too stiff. It is silly to smash an instrument you cannot even play.

There is no instrument left that I can play, Gwilan thought, and the thought hung in her mind for a while like a long chord, until she knew the notes that made it: I thought my harp was myself, but it was not. It was destroyed, I was not. I thought Torm's wife was myself, but she was not. He is dead, I am not. I have nothing left at all now but myself. The wind blows from the valley,

145

and there's a voice on the wind, a bit of a tune. Then the wind falls or changes. The work had to be done, and we did the work. It's their turn now for that, the children. There's nothing left for me to do but sing. I never could sing. But you play the instrument you have.

So she stood by the cold hearth and sang the melody "The Lament of Orioth." The people of the houhehold wakened in their beds and heard her singing, all but Torm; but he knew that tune already. The untuned strings of the harps hung on the wall wakened and answered softly, voice to voice, like eyes that shine among the leaves when the wind is blowing.

Don Berry

from TO BUILD A SHIP

There is an art to cutting down a tree. Unfortunately, it is an art none of us had. One can, of course, simply cut through the trunk, which is more or less the way I had it in my mind. In that case the tree will probably fall down. However, it may not be for another twenty years, if it should hang up in other trees, and it is virtually certain not to fall in any desirable direction. After a lifetime which it sometimes seems I devoted to cutting down trees, I am convinced that they were not meant to be cut down. God intended forests to stand eternally, and He so constructed them. Then He gave man a fixed image of cleared land as Good, just for the hell of it.

Near the exact center of the land I had chosen was a small rise, on which I decided to build my cabin. The top of this tiny mound was strangely clear of timber, and this undoubtedly had something to do with my choice. It was not much in the way of a clearing—certainly too small for a cabin and garden. As though half a dozen trees had been plucked out of the forest. Still, it was something slightly different, a landmark of sorts, something that struck the eye. And as most major decisions are made on no more than that, I don't know why I should feel any need to justify my choice. I was still somewhat annoyed with all those future generations of Thalers riding on my back, and figured if they didn't like the spot they could damn well find land of their own.

Vaughn did come when the time arrived, bringing tools and help and, above all, his knowledge of woodsmanship. Sam Howard came with him, feeling responsible for me since he had seen me first, and also a huge, blondish giant with a perpetual sheepish smile, whom I had not yet met. The big man made me a little nervous at first. He said nothing at all. And when he was not actively engaged in *doing* something he had a disconcerting habit of putting his hands on top of his head and staring vaguely up at the sky with his mouth half open, as though waiting for something to fall. His elbows stuck out like great, angular ears.

Looking upward from my minuscule clearing was intimidating. Even above the tiny empty space the vast spreading limbs of surrounding trees formed a twisted and tangled web that was almost solid. It is one thing to see the forest as a mass, and quite another to consider it as individual trees to be cut down one at a time. All around us was a perfect infinity of darkly massed trunks stretching upward into the sky. You could see no more than twenty feet into the wall; after that, it was a solid substance several thousand miles thick. Rank after rank of deep gloomy firs that extended unbroken to the edge of the bay, and in the other direction to the edge of the world, as nearly as I could tell.

147

The vastness, the incredible complexity of number and density that was the forest, was terrifying. It was like contemplating the number of stars, or the grains of sand on the beach.

I think we all felt the same thing as we looked around us in silence, the same awe, tinged with desperation. It was like a nightmare of helplessness. There was a vast disproportion somewhere; the endless packed ranks of the forest, silent and eternal, being faced by—us. Four tiny men with three axes and a crosscut saw.

The mood deepened into a conviction that there was no question of doing this thing. When I was finally faced with it, I didn't think it was possible to begin, there was simply no place to start. And once started, it would never finish. You could go on and on cutting trees in this country, and raise your children and your grandchildren and your descendants to the twentieth generation to devote their lives to cutting trees and it would never end. To learn humility, a man must stand in the midst of the Oregon forest. I was caught in a kind of awful paralysis, brought on by the simple contemplation of this infinity and my relation to it.

It was Vaughn who finally broke the silence.

"Let's take this one," he said. "It's small."

I think, very frankly, that Vaughn was profiting from this magnificent opportunity to perfect his lumbering technique, or at least his theory of it. We worked hard, all of us, and by noon had felled half a dozen trees. Our control had not been up to the required standard. The fallen trunks were tangled in a hideous mess of intertwining branches, resembling nothing so much as a pile of jackstraws. Getting them disentangled and limbed and dragged to a safe place for burning was going to be—difficult. Still, they had been standing straight and eternal, and now they were lying on the ground, which was already saying much.

Vaughn had showed us how to notch the tree on the side we wished it to fall. This we did with the axes. Then we cut through from the other side with the big falling saw and, in theory, the tree tipped into the notch and fell directly on a line with it. As we worked at the notch, Vaughn would occasionally step up with his ax and thrust the head in crossways. The tree would fall, he told us, in the direction indicated by the handle. It was both an impressive and a reasonable demonstration, and we believed it.

In practice—I don't know exactly what went wrong. We were lucky to guess within 180 degrees where the damned thing was going to go. However, as none of them had actually fallen over backward, we still felt we were ahead of the game. It seems a little strange in retrospect, but in all this we never questioned Vaughn's skill; our own crude physical performance was simply not up to that level. Understand, Vaughn himself made no effort to shift the responsibility, or even to pretend to a competence he didn't have. He was as puzzled by it as we were. But it was clear to everyone that when something went wrong the fault was elsewhere. It simply never occurred to any of us that *he* might be doing something wrong. It was just a part of his personality, that no one ever doubted him.

In the early afternoon we reached a tricky problem. A fir that was visibly inclined in the wrong direction and, to boot, had a pronounced bend in the trunk. Also in the wrong direction. It was a sick tree, an abnormal tree, and it was a tree that intended to fall in its own way, which was directly across the clearing.

"Well, now," Vaughn said cheerfully. He held his ax up, dangling it head down with his thumb and forefinger and gauging vertical from this handy plumb. He knew more things to do with axes than anybody I ever met. He squinted with one eye along the shaft and came to the conclusion we all had; that the thing had a hell of a lean to it. However, it was now official.

"This here's going to be a wee bit harder, boys," Vaughn said.

There were other trees bunched around it, of course, thick as hair on the back of a dog. The likelihood of it hanging up seemed excellent, particularly with that nasty bend in the trunk. If that happened we'd be left with the job of cutting the tree on which it had caught. The combination of forces in the two trees was such that they might fall anywhere at all; there was no predicting what would happen. In discussing the problem Vaughn said the professional loggers called that kind of situation a "widow-maker," which had a rather discouraging ring. The longer I looked at that tree the more ominous it seemed to me. It was jammed from butt to tip with murderous possibilities.

"I'm going to leave that one," I said. "I like it."

"Nonesense," said Vaughn. "You can't leave it."

"Yes, I can. I like it. I'm going to look at it out my window. It has a variety to it, it isn't straight like all the rest."

"That's a sick tree, Ben."

"I'll take care of it."

Vaughn changed his tactic. "Where you say you were going to put the cabin?"

I showed him again, the place in the clearing. "See how nice that'll be?" I said. "I can see it right out the window there, it'll give me something interesting to look at."

Vaughn considered the cabin site silently. Then he considered the sick tree, looking it up and down and pulling at his nose. Finally he turned away with a sad shake of the head, and put his hand on my shoulder. "Well, it's up to you, Ben. It's your tree. It's been nice knowin' you, fellow. I'm sorry it had to end this way."

That threw me off balance right there. "End? What end?"

"You're a dead man, Ben," Vaughn said with infinite melancholy. "Just a matter of time. Look there for yourself. She wants to fall right down on your cabin."

I think there was something wrong about Vaughn when it came to trees falling down, I think it weighed on his mind or something. "Now listen, Vaughn," I started, "we can just—"

He wasn't listening, he was speaking thoughtfully and low. "You get your cabin built, Ben. It's warm and comfy, right? And the sun shines in your window, and you lean on your elbows and look at that tree. You get used to it. There you are, a month, two months. Pretty soon you take that tree for granted out there. 'My funny old tree,' you think to yourself. Maybe you wonder a little about it from time to time, but you tell yourself you're just imagining things. Then one night there's a storm. You got your fire up good, and you're warm and snug and happy, thinking how comfortable you are when there's all that terrible weather howlin' around outside. You're just snuggling down into your blankets. You hear a little 'crack,' but you say to yourself it's just the wind. You put your head down again. You're just dropping off, sleepy, sleepy, and—BANG!"

He slammed his hands together, making us jump, and destiny thundered through the roof of my cabin, crushing it into splinters and pinning the lifeless bloody corpse of me to the floor. It was a horrible way to go.

"Course, it's up to you, Ben," Vaughn said sincerely. "I mean, it's your tree, after all."

So, in spite of the fact that I have always been more frightened of the present than the future, we cut it down.

Vaughn looked triumphant as he sighted along his arm. "We'll lay her right down that little alley there. You're going to have to be careful with your notch on this'n, boys."

"That ain't where she wants to go," the blond giant said. I had not realized until this moment he could talk. He worked well, but the rest of the time, when Vaughn was explaining something, he just stood around with his hands on his head looking up at the sky. Now he felt he had said too much, and he blushed with embarrassment.

"That's where the *skill* comes in," Vaughn said. "Listen, I got a plan."

By his plan, we tied a line high up on the tree, and ran it out in the direction we wanted it to fall. We pegged it down, and cut our perfect notch. When she began to weaken, somebody jumped up on the line, tipping the tree in the right direction for a starter. After that she'd go right on her own. It seemed wholly unreasonable to me, but Vaughn said he'd seen professionals do it like that in difficult cases.

"Wait a minute," I said. "Then the tree falls right on the guy that's doing the pulling."

"He runs," Vaughn said. "Soon as he sees her coming, he runs. He's got plenty of time to get clear."

"Who's going to do it?" Little Sam said, obviously worried about the lack of precision in the whole operation.

"We'll worry about that later, first we got to get the line up there."

There was a stony silence from the crew. You could hear the breakers over the hill.

"Well, come on," Vaughan said impatiently. "I'm too heavy for climbing, I'd be better for pulling on the rope. Or—Sam, would you rather do the rope-pulling part?"

Sam shook his head miserably. "No, but I don't—"

"*Hup* we go, then," Vaughn said cheerfully. "Good boy, Sam." He had, with typical foresight, brought a coil of rope.

We tied one end of the rope to Sam's belt in the back. Then the big blond man and I hoisted him up on our shoulders, giving him enough height to reach the first branch. His foot was about six inches lower on my side, but there was no help for it.

He was shaking noticeably, Sam was, either from the uneven support or some inner disturbance. Finally he got a good grip on the first branch and hunched himself up to it. He turned around.

"Don't turn *around*, Sam," Vaughn encouraged him. "Climb!"

Sam climbed. He climbed very well and speedily, in fact, dragging the rope behind him and looking like a monkey on a string.

"*Don't go around branches!*" Vaughn called. "You get her tangled up."

"Well, I *got* to go around *some* of them," Sam hollered down. By this time he was about thirty feet up. After a moment he added, "Vaughn, I don't think you know what you're doing," I guessed that thirty feet must be the range of Vaughn's personality, and Sam had passed out of the magic circle.

"Don't grab the plow and look back!" Vaughn said. "Push on!" Turning to me he called confidentially, "Sam's got no confidence, is his trouble."

Finally Sam called, "I ain't goin' no higher, you guys." He was well up now, fifty feet or better.

"Ten more feet, Sam!"

"No."

Vaughn sighed and shrugged. "All right, tie her off, then."

Sam straddled a branch and began to untie the rope from the back of his belt, leaning his forehead against the trunk. He was very small, so high up, and we couldn't see what he was doing clearly. At last he finished, gave the line a couple of good yanks and called, "That's it."

For the first time he looked down at us. He poised that way for a long moment, straddling the limb, and suddenly grabbed the trunk with both arms.

"Sam," I called, "what's the matter?"

"Nothin'."

"Well, come on down, then," Vaughn said.

Sam didn't answer for a minute, and his voice sounded strangled when it filtered down to us. "I can't."

"Are you scared, Sam?" I asked him.

"No."

"COME ON DOWN, SAM!" the blond giant hollered in an enormous voice.

"I can't."

"He's froze," Vaughn said. "That's what they call it, froze. It's a kind of fear a guy gets up high. He's froze up there, he can't move."

"Well, that's all fine, what they call it," I said. "But what the hell are we going to *do?*"

Vaughn shrugged. "Nothin' *to* do. Case like that, you just wait till he thaws, is all. Have a bit of a smoke."

We hollered up to Sam that we were going to have a smoke and wait for him to thaw. We lit up and sat with our backs against trees, thinking it over. Sam perched over our heads like a ripe plum, which I suppose was how he felt. Once in a while somebody would call up, "How you feelin', Sam?" and he always said "All right," but he never started down.

"How long can he stay up there?" I asked. "I mean, when a man's froze like that, how long does it take to get un-froze?"

"Well, Vaughn said hesitantly, "that depends. But listen, I got a plan. *I* figure, only way to bust a scare like that is with a worse one."

It made me a little uneasy. "That don't sound right to me."

"Well, what have we got to lose?" Vaughn said reasonably.

"Little Sam," said the blond giant, almost under his breath.

"Now listen, Joe," Vaughn said. "Just you don't worry about a thing. Trust me, I got a plan."

"Joe?" I said, startled. I had not caught the big man's name before. "Are you Joe Champion?"

He seemed embarrassed, but nodded.

"God, I been *wanting to* meet you," I said. "Say, listen, do you—" I broke off sharply. Lord, I'd almost blurted out did he hang by his knees in his tree and look around, the way I had it in my mind.

"Do I what?"

"Do you, ah, do you like it around here?"

"Ben," Vaughn said impatiently, "what's the matter with your *mind?* You got a mind like a grasshopper."

"Yeah," Champion said thoughtfully. "I like it pretty well, I guess."

"I like it pretty well, too," I told him.

"Listen, you boys, I got a plan, and I'm going to give her a try, all right?"

Without waiting for an answer he picked up an ax and went to stand under the tree looking up at Sam.

"Sam!" he hollered. "I'm sorry, but we can't wait any more." He hefted back the ax and took a good swing. The bit thunked into the tree, making it quiver.

"VAUGHN!" Sam screamed.

"What?"

"DON'T CHOP ME DOWN!"

Vaughn took another swing, very well placed, and a little triangular chip came popping out of the cut.

"VAUGHN, JESUS, DON'T DO IT ANY MORE!" Sam's voice had a funny note in it, like he was crying.

Vaughn leaned over and picked up the chip, sniffing it appreciatively. He threw it over to us. "Smell that, boys, that's pretty." He looked up in the tree again. "Sam!" he hollered. "You better come down."

"I'M COMING!"

Unfortunately he didn't start fast enough to suit Vaughn, who swung the ax again determinedly.

"DON'T DO IT, I'M COMING! DON'T CHOP ME ANY MORE!"

And by God, Sam started down. We almost held our breath for him all the way. Vaughn walked back to Joe and myself and sat down, plunging the ax in the dirt. We were a little in awe, but Vaughn seemed to take it for granted that his plan would work; he was neither surprised nor particularly elated. He sighed contentedly and wriggled against a tree, scratching his back.

When Sam reached the ground he was pale and shaking. "Vaughn," he said, "Vaughn, you shouldn't of done that. God, you scared me so bad."

"Sam," Vaughn said patiently, "it was for your own good, now. You come down, didn't you? There's no telling how long you'd of been up there without that. I mean, maybe all night, even, you wouldn't want that. Cold, the rain comin' down. Gettin' hungry, holdin' on for dear life, just tryin' to keep your eyes open. Gettin' sleepier and sleepier, what with being so hungry and tired like that. And along about the middle of the night, you'd start drowsin' off. Just a little, maybe, you start drowsin' off and then—BANG!"

We jumped, Sam toppled off his branch and crashed down through the thick tangle of limbs, crushing his head on one, breaking an arm on another, until by the time he thumped into the ground with that terrible dull sound there was no more than a feeble spark of life to be extinguished. In the night small animals came to sniff the crumpled corpse.

You really had to hand it to Vaughn, the way he told you about things.

We cut the notch with special care, and when Vaughn's ax-trick showed it was going to fall in the right direction we ran the rope out and tied it to another tree just out of the line of fall.

I was not terribly surprised to find myself scheduled as line puller: Vaughn had, after all, only said he would be *better* at that than climbing. He hadn't actually said he'd *do* it. He and Joe Champion began hauling away at the big crosscut saw, gradually chewing their way into the opposite side.

"Now, wait a minute," I said. "Where'm I going to run?"

"Into the clearing, of course. You'll have lots of time. When she starts to come, you go, that's all. Ten yards and you're clear."

"Well, I'm going to practice once," I said.

"Go ahead and practice," Vaughn said, grunting over the saw.

"Well, dammit, let up on that *saw!* I don't want the thing falling on my head when I'm just *practicing.*"

Vaughn shrugged, but he was already a little tired, so they all gathered around me and watched me practice. I stood under the line and made believe I saw the tree start coming. I took off toward the clearing, and when I reached the edge I dove as far as I could, crumpling up into a little inconspicuous, unhittable ball.

"That's good," Vaughn said. "That's very good. You got to get out of the way of the branches."

I picked my route carefully, removing small branches I might trip on, and whacking out the more troublesome clumps of brush with an ax. By the time I had practiced three or four times my belly was sort of scraped, but I felt safer. When I was really confident I could get out of there fast enough, they started again on the saw work.

"Jump up on that line a bit, Ben," Vaughn said.

I jumped up, letting my weight dangle from the taut rope. The tree didn't budge. This happened a couple more times, until I finally decided he was just getting me to do it when he wanted a little rest.

At last, when nobody expected it, there was a little cracking sound and the top of the tree wobbled.

"All right, boys," Vaughn said. "You get back in the clearing and watch. This might be dangerous here, cutting. Ben, where the hell you going? This is your tree."

I came back.

"Get up on that line, now."

"It ain't ready yet."

"Less'n you hold 'er the saw jams up."

I sighed and jumped up to dangle from the line like a hunk of drying meat. Vaughn went to work with a will. The saw scraped back and forth raspingly. I couldn't stop the tree from wobbling. The line on which I hung tightened and loosened as the trunk swayed, clamping down on the saw blade from time to time. It finally got a rhythm, and Vaughn could RASP RASP RASP before the cut closed down on the blade. It went that way for a while. *RASP RASP RASP* pause *RASP RASP RASP* pause. Champion and Little Sam were standing in the middle of the clearing, watching. Champion had his hands on top of his head, but he was watching the sawing instead of the sky, which was a sort of tribute.

"Listen," I hollered. "You guys get the hell out of my way, now. When I come I'm going to be movin' like a—"

CRACK!

Ponderously the treetop leaned. With a lovely smooth motion the rope slackened, lowering me to the ground as gently as a cloud.

"Pull!" Vaughn hollered.

I pulled with all my strength.

"Here she comes! Run, Ben, run!"

I waited, watching the top. It was clearly coming now, gathering speed. And just as clearly moving in the wrong direction. The tip swung in a wide circle, and the rope picked up from the ground and tightened again. With huge majesty the trunk headed straight for the clearing, where it had intended to fall from the very beginnings of time. I caught just a glimpse of the two bystanders, their mouths dropping open with astonishment and fear. Joe still had his hands on his head.

I started to run in the opposite direction, straight into the mass of brush toward the interior of the forest. I plowed into it like a cannonball, trying to get out of range of the branches. Finally I plunged face first into a big manzanita that sprang back like a mattress and stopped me flat. I prayed fast, and turned to see if I was dead.

The enormous trunk hesitated briefly as it reached the restraining limit of the rope. The line snapped like a thread. Vaughn had been watching the frantic scramble of the others as they thundered out of the clearing, rushing open-armed into the impenetrable brush. Then penetrated it with amazing ease, just like diving into a lake.

For some reason this struck our lumberman so funny he started to laugh, and he was doubled over with glee when the trunk hit, shaking the clearing with the sound of thunder and earthquake. As the peak hit, the strains in the twisted trunk were discharged like an explosion. The trunk splintered like a gunshot and the base leaped off the stump as though it had been catapulted six feet in the air. The butt end swung over Vaughn's back and crushed into the earth on the other side of him, not a foot from his body.

He straightened up suddenly, all the glee gone and the color fading from his face, leaving it gray. He looked at the trunk on one side of him, the stump on the other, and then at the air over his head where a good ton of hurtling wood had passed a second before.

He blinked once, then sat on the stump, resting his back against the huge splinter of wood that remained standing vertically in the center. He pulled out his handkerchief and began to wipe his forehead. The rest of us emerged from our diverse prickly hideaways and ran over to him.

"It didn't hit you? You all right, Vaughn?"

He breathed heavily and he didn't answer, but he wasn't bleeding or anything. He wiped and wiped and wiped at his forehead with the handkerchief, as though there were a big indelible stain there. Gradually the color came back into his face, and his voice returned to him.

"By god," he said. "You boys were a sight, now. Just like a bunch of quail takin' to the brush. Never saw anything like it."

"Jesus, you almost killed us *all*, Vaughn. You damn near got every loving one of us."

"How come you run the wrong way, Ben?" he asked curiously. "You was supposed to run into the clearing."

"If I'd run there, I'd be *dead!*"

"Yeah, I know, but I just wondered. Because you was supposed to run there, the way the plan was."

He sighed deeply again and got up off the stump, taking long breaths. We were all sort of agitated, but Vaughn recovered first. He picked up the ax and wandered along the length of the fallen, split tree, poking casually at it with the ax blade from time to time. When he got out into the middle of the clearing he looked back around at the space where the tree had been.

"Well, hell," he said, looking at the ground again. "I expect this is as good a place to burn them logs as any."

He slung the ax one-handed at the trunk, burying the bit in the shattered wood with a lusty thunk.

"Boys," he said confidentially. "I don't mind telling you this is the toughest tree I *ever* cut down. It is, now. It was a real challenge to me."

Ken Kesey

from ONE FLEW OVER THE CUCKOO'S NEST

Two whores on their way down from Portland to take us deep-sea fishing in a boat! It made it tough to stay in bed until the dorm lights came on at six-thirty.

I was the first one up out of the dorm to look at the list posted on the board next to the Nurses' Station, check to see if my name was really signed there. SIGN UP FOR DEEP SEA FISHING was printed in big letters at the top, then McMurphy had signed first and Billy Bibbit was number one, right after McMurphy. Number three was Harding and number four was Fredrickson, and all the way down to number ten where nobody'd signed yet. My name was there, the last put down, across from the number nine. I was actually going out of the hospital with two whores on a fishing boat; I had to keep saying it over and over to myself to believe it.

The three black boys slipped up in front of me and read the list with gray fingers, found my name there and turned to grin at me.

"Why, who you s'pose signed Chief Bromden up for this foolishness? Inniuns ain't able to write."

"What makes you think Inniuns able to *read?*"

The starch was still fresh and stiff enough this early that their arms rustled in the white suits when they moved, like paper wings. I acted deaf to them laughing at me, like I didn't even know, but when they stuck a broom out for me to do their work up the hall, I turned around and walked back to the dorm, telling myself, The hell with that. A man goin' fishing with two whores from Portland don't have to take that crap.

It scared me some, walking off from them like that, because I never went against what the black boys ordered before. I looked back and saw them coming after me with the broom. They'd probably have come right on in the dorm and got me but for McMurphy; he was in there making such a fuss, roaring up and down between the beds, snapping a towel at the guys signed to go this morning, that the black boys decided maybe the dorm wasn't such safe territory to venture into for no more than somebody to sweep a little dab of hallway.

McMurphy had his motorcycle cap pulled way forward on his red hair to look like a boat captain, and the tattoos showing out from the sleeves of his T-shirt were done in Singapore. He was swaggering around the floor like it was the deck of a ship, whistling in his hand like a bosun's whistle.

"Hit the deck, mateys, *hit* the deck or I keelhaul the lot of ye from stock to stern!"

He rang the bedstand next to Harding's bed with his knuckles.

"*Six* bells and *all's* well. Steady as she goes. Hit the deck. Drop your cocks and grab your socks."

He noticed me standing just inside the doorway and came rushing over to thump my back like a drum.

"Look here at the Big Chief; here's an example of a good sailor and fisherman: up before day and out diggin' red worms for bait. The rest of you scurvy bunch o' lubbers'd do well to follow his lead. *Hit* the deck. Today's the day! Outa the sack and into the sea!"

The Acutes grumbled and griped at him and his towel, and the Chronics woke up to look around with heads blue from lack of blood cut off by sheets tied too tight across the chest, looking around the dorm till they finally centered on me with weak and watered-down old looks, faces wistful and curious. They lay there watching me pull on warm clothes for the trip, making me feel uneasy and a little guilty. They could sense I had been singled out as the only Chronic making the trip. They watched me—old guys welded in wheelchairs for years, with catheters down their legs like vines rooting them for the rest of their lives right where they are, they watched me and knew instinctively that I was going. And they could still be a little jealous it wasn't them. They could know because enough of the man in them had been damped out that the old animal instincts had taken over (old Chronics wake up sudden some nights, before anybody else knows a guy's died in the dorm, and throw back their heads and howl), and they could be jealous because there was enough man left to still remember.

McMurphy went out to look at the list and came back and tried to talk one more Acute into signing, going down the line kicking at the beds still had guys in them with sheets pulled over their heads, telling them what a great thing it was to be out there in the teeth of the gale with a he-man sea crackin' around and a goddam yo-heave-ho and a bottle of rum. "C'mon, loafers, I need one more mate to round out the crew, I need one more goddam volunteer. . . ."

But he couldn't talk anybody into it. The Big Nurse had the rest scared with her stories of how rough the sea'd been lately and how many boats'd sunk, and it didn't look like we'd get that last crew member till a half-hour later when George Sorensen came up to McMurphy in the breakfast line where we were waiting for the mess hall to be unlocked for breakfast.

Big toothless knotty old Swede the black called Rub-a-dub George, because of his thing about sanitation, came shuffling up the hall, listing well back so his feet went well out in front of his head (sways backward this way to keep his face as far away from the man he's talking to as he can), stopped in front of McMurphy, and mumbled something in his hand. George was very shy. You couldn't see his eyes because they were in so deep under his brow, and he cupped his big palm around most of the rest of his face. His head swayed like a crow's nest on top of his mastlike spine. He mumbled in his hand till McMurphy finally reached up and pulled the hand away so's the words could get out.

"Now, George, what is it you're sayin'."

"Red worms," he was saying. "I joost don't think they do you no good—not for the Chin-nook."

"Yeah?" McMurphy said. "Red worms? I might agree with you, George, if you let me know what about these red worms you're speaking of."

"I think joost a while ago I hear you say Mr. Bromden was out digging the red worms for bait."

"That's right, Pop, I remember."

"So I joost say you don't have you no good fortune with them worms. This here is the month with one big Chinook run—su-ure. Herring you need. Su-ure. You jig you some herring and use those fellows for bait, *then* you have some good fortune."

His voice went up at the end of every sentence—for-*chune*—like he was asking a question. His big chin, already scrubbed so much this morning he'd worn the hide off it, nodded up and down at McMurphy once or twice, then turned him around to lead him down the hall toward the end of the line. McMurphy called him back.

"Now, hold 'er a minute, George; you talk like you know something about this fishin' business."

George turned and shuffled back to McMurphy, listing back so far it looked like his feet had navigated right out from under him.

"You bet, su-ure. Twenty-five year I work the Chinook trollers, all the way from Half Moon Bay to Puget Sound. Twenty-five year I fish—before I get so dirty." He held out his hands for us to see the dirt on them. Everybody around leaned over and looked. I didn't see the dirt but I did see scars worn deep into the white palms from hauling a thousand miles of fishing line out of the sea. He let us look a minute, then rolled the hands shut and drew them away and hid them in his pajama shirt like we might dirty them looking, and stood grinning at McMurphy with gums like brine-bleached pork.

"I had a good troller boat, joost forty feet, but she drew twelve feet water and she was solid teak and solid oak." He rocked back and forth in a way to make you doubt that the floor was standing level. "She was one good troller boat, by golly!"

He started to turn, but McMurphy stopped him again.

"Hell, George, why didn't you say you were a fisherman? I been talking up this voyage like I was the Old Man of the Sea, but just between you an' me an' the wall there, the only boat I been on was the battleship *Missouri* and the only thing I know about fish is that I like eatin' 'em better than cleanin' 'em."

"Cleanin' is *easy*, somebody show you how."

"By God, you're gonna be our captain, George; we'll be your crew."

George tilted back, shaking his head. "Those boats awful *dirty* any more—everything *awful* dirty."

"The hell with that. We got a boat specially sterilized fore and aft, swabbed clean as a hound's tooth. You won't get dirty, George, 'cause you'll be the captain. Won't even have to bait a hook; just be our captain and give orders to us dumb landlubbers—how's that strike you?"

I could see George was temped by the way he wrung his hands under his shirt, but he still said he couldn't risk getting dirty. McMurphy did his best to talk him into it, but George was still shaking his head when the Big Nurse's key hit the lock of the mess hall and she came jangling out the door with her wicker bag of surprises, clicked down the line with automatic smile-and-good-morning for each man she passed. McMurphy noticed the way George leaned back from her and scowled. When she'd passed, McMurphy tilted back his head and gave George the one bright eye.

"George, that stuff the nurse has been saying about the bad sea, about how terrible dangerous this trip might be—what about that?"

"That ocean could be awful bad, sure, awful rough."

McMurphy looked down at the nurse disappearing into the station, then back at George. George started twisting his hands around in his shirt more than ever, looking around at the silent faces watching him.

"By golly!" he said suddenly. "You think I let her scare me about that ocean? You think *that?*"

"Ah, I guess not, George. I was thinking, though, that if you don't come along with us, and if there *is* some awful stormy calamity, we're every last one of us liable to be lost at sea, you know that? I said I didn't know nothin' about boating, and I'll tell you something else: these two women coming to get us, I told the doctor was my two aunts, two widows of fishermen. Well, the only cruisin' either one of them ever did was on solid cement. They won't be no more help in a fix than me. We *need* you, George." He took a pull on his cigarette and asked, "You got ten bucks, by the way?"

George shook his head.

"No, I wouldn't suppose so. Well, what the devil, I gave up the idea of comin' out ahead days ago. Here." He took a pencil out of the pocket of his green jacket and wiped it clean on his shirttail, held it out to George. "You captain us, and we'll let you come along for five."

George looked around at us again, working his big brow over the predicament. Finally his gums showed in a bleached smile and he reached for the pencil. "By golly!" he said and headed off with the pencil to sign the last place on the list. After breakfast, walking down the hall, McMurphy stopped and printed c-a-p-t behind George's name.

The whores were late. Everybody was beginning to think they weren't coming at all when McMurphy gave a yell from the window and we all went running to look. He said that was them, but we didn't see but one car, instead of the two we were counting on, and just one woman. McMurphy called to her through the screen when she stopped on the parking lot, and she came cutting straight across the grass toward our ward.

She was younger and prettier than any of us'd figured on. Everybody had found out that the girls were whores instead of aunts, and were expecting all sorts of things. Some of the religious guys weren't any too happy about it. But seeing her coming lightfooted across the grass with her eyes green all the way up to the ward, and her hair, roped in a long twist at the back of her head, jouncing up and down with every step like copper springs in the sun, all any of us could think of was that she was a girl, a female, who wasn't dressed white from head to foot like she'd been dipped in frost, and how she made her money didn't make any difference.

She ran right up against the screen where McMurphy was and hooked her fingers through the mesh, and pulled herself against it. She was panting from the run, and every breath looked like she might swell right through the mesh. She was crying a little.

"McMurphy, oh, you damned McMurphy . . ."

"Never mind that. Where's Sandra?"

"She got tied up, man, can't make it. But you, damn it, are you okay?"

"She got tied up!"

"To tell the truth"—the girl wiped her nose and giggled— "ol' Sandy got *married*. You remember Artie Gilfillian from Beaverton? Always used to show up at the parties with some gassy thing, a gopher snake or a white mouse or some gassy thing like that in his pocket? A real maniac—"

"Oh, sweet Jesus!" McMurphy groaned. "How'm I supposed to get ten guys in one stinkin' Ford, Candy sweetheart? How'd Sandra and her gopher snake from Beaverton figure on me swingin' *that?*"

The girl looked like she was in the process of thinking up an answer when the speaker in the ceiling clacked and the Big Nurse's voice told McMurphy if he wanted to talk with his lady friend it'd be better if she signed in properly at the main door instead of disturbing the whole hospital. The girl left the screen and started toward the main entrance, and McMurphy left the screen and flopped down in a chair in the corner, his head hanging. "Hell's *bells*," he said.

The least black boy let the girl onto the ward and forgot to lock the door behind her (caught hell for it later, I bet), and the girl came jouncing up the hall past the Nurses' Station, where all the nurses were trying to freeze her bounce with a united icy look, and into the day room just a few steps ahead of the doctor. He was going toward the Nurses' Station with some papers, looked at her, and back at the papers, and back at her again, and went to fumbling after his glasses with both hands.

She stopped when she got to the middle of the day-room floor and saw she was circled by forty staring men in green, and it was so quiet you could hear bellies growling, and, all along the Chronic row, hear catheters popping off.

She had to stand there a minute while she looked around to find McMurphy, so everybody got a long look at her. There was a blue smoke hung near the ceiling over her head; I think apparatus burned out all over the ward trying to adjust to her come busting in like she did—took electronic readings on her and calculated they weren't built to handle something like this on the ward, and just burned out, like machines committing suicide.

She had on a white T-shirt like McMurphy's only a lot smaller, white tennis shoes and Levi pants snipped off above her knees to give her feet circulation, and it didn't look like that was near enough material to go around, considering what it had to cover. She must've been seen with lots less by lots more men, but under the circumstances she began to fidget around self-consciously like a schoolgirl on a stage. Nobody spoke while they looked. Martini did whisper that you could read the dates of the coins in her Levi pockets, they were so tight, but he was closer and could see better'n the rest of us.

Billy Bibbit was the first one to say something out loud, not really a word, just a low, almost painful whistle that described how she looked better than anybody else could have. She laughed and thanked him very much and he blushed so red that she blushed with him and laughed again. This broke things into movement. All the Acutes were coming across the floor trying to talk to her at once. The doctor was pulling on Harding's coat, asking who *is* this. McMurphy got up out of his chair and walked through the crowd to her, and when she saw him she threw her arms around him and said, "You damned McMurphy," and then got embarrassed and blushed again. When she blushed she didn't look more than sixteen or seventeen, I swear she didn't.

McMurphy introduced her around and she shook everybody's hand. When she got to Billy she thanked him again for the whistle. The Big Nurse came sliding out of the station, smiling, and asked McMurphy how he intended to get all ten of us in one car, and he asked could he maybe *borrow* a staff car and drive a load himself, and the nurse cited a rule forbidding this, just like everyone knew she would. She said unless there was another driver to sign a Responsibility Slip that half of the crew would have to stay behind. McMurphy told her this'd cost him fifty goddam bucks to make up the difference; he'd have to pay the guys back who didn't get to go.

"Then it may be," the nurse said, "that the trip will have to be canceled—and *all* the money refunded."

"I've already rented the boat; the man's got seventy bucks of mine in his pocket right now!"

"Seventy dollars? So? I thought you told the patients you'd need to collect a hundred dollars plus ten of your own to finance the trip, Mr. McMurphy."

"I was putting gas in the cars over and back."

"That wouldn't amount to thirty dollars, though, would it?"

She smiled so nice at him, waiting. He threw his hands in the air and looked at the ceiling.

"Hoo *boy*, you don't miss a chance do you, Miss District Attorney. Sure; I was keepin' what was left over. I don't think any of the guys ever thought any different. I figured to make a little for the trouble I took get—"

"But your plans didn't work out," she said. She was still smiling at him, so full of sympathy. "Your little financial speculations can't *all* be successes, Randle, and, actually, as I think about it now, you've had more than your share of victories." She mused about this, thinking about something I knew we'd hear more about later. "Yes. Every Acute on the ward has written you an IOU for some 'deal' of yours at one time or another, so don't you think you can bear up under this one small defeat?"

Then she stopped. She saw McMurphy wasn't listening to her any more. He was watching the doctor. And the doctor was eying the blond girl's T-shirt like nothing else existed. McMurphy's loose smile spread out on his face as he watched the doctor's trance, and he pushed his cap to the back of his head and strolled to the doctor's side, startling him with a hand on the shoulder.

"By God, Doctor Spivey, you ever see a Chinook Salmon hit a line? One of the fiercest sights on the seven seas. Say, Candy honeybun, whyn't you tell the doctor here about deep-sea fishing and all like that. . . ."

Working together, it didn't take McMurphy and the girl but two minutes and the little doctor was down locking up his office and coming back up the hall, cramming papers in a brief case.

"Good deal of paper work I can get done on the boat," he explained to the nurse and went past her so fast she didn't have a chance to answer, and the rest of the crew followed, slower, grinning at her standing in the door of the Nurses' Station.

The Acutes who weren't going gathered at the day-room door, told us don't bring our catch back till it's cleaned, and Ellis pulled his hands down off the nails in the wall and squeezed Billy Bibbit's hand and told him to be a fisher of men.

And Billy, watching the brass brads on that woman's Levis wink at him as she walked out of the day room, told Ellis to hell with that fisher of *men* business. He joined us at the door, and the least black boy let us through and locked the door behind us, and we were out, outside.

The sun was prying up the clouds and lighting the brick front of the hospital rose bed. A thin breeze worked at sawing what leaves were left from the oak trees, stacking them neatly against the wire cyclone fence. There was little brown birds occasionally on the fence; when a puff of leaves would hit the fence the birds would fly off with the wind. It looked at first like the leaves were hitting the fence and turning into birds and flying away.

It was a fine woodsmoked autumn day, full of the sound of kids punting footballs and the putter of small airplanes, and everybody should've been happy just being outside in it. But we all stood in a silent bunch with our hands in our pockets while the doctor walked to get his car. A silent bunch, watching the townspeople who were driving past on their way to work slow down to gawk at all the loonies in green uniforms. McMurphy saw how uneasy we were and tried to work us into a better mood by joking and teasing the girl, but this made us feel worse somehow. Everybody was thinking how easy it would be to return to the ward, go back and say they decided the nurse had been right; with a wind like this the sea would've been just too rough.

The doctor arrived and we loaded up and headed off, me and George and Harding and Billy Bibbit in the car with McMurphy and the girl, Candy; and

Frederickson and Sefelt and Scanlon and Martini and Tadem and Gregory following in the doctor's car. Everyone was awfully quiet. We pulled into a gas station about a mile from the hospital; the doctor followed. He got out first, and the service-station man came bouncing out, grinning and wiping his hands on a rag. Then he stopped grinning and went past the doctor to see just what was *in* these cars. He backed off, wiping his hands on the oil rag, frowning. The doctor caught the man's sleeve nervously and took out a ten-dollar bill and tucked it down in the man's hands like setting out a tomato plant.

"Ah, would you fill both tanks with regular?" the doctor asked. He was acting just as uneasy about being out of the hospital as the rest of us were. "Ah, would you?"

"Those uniforms," the service-station man said, "they're from the hospital back up the road, aren't they?" He was looking around him to see if there was a wrench or something handy. He finally moved over near a stack of empty pop bottles. "You guys are from that *asylum.*"

The doctor fumbled for his glasses and looked at us too, like he'd just noticed the uniforms. "Yes. No, I mean. We, they *are* from the asylum, but they are a work crew, not inmates, of course not. A work crew."

The man squinted at the doctor and at us and went off to whisper to his partner, who was back among the machinery. They talked a minute, and the second guy hollered and asked the doctor who we were and the doctor repeated that we were a work crew, and both of the guys laughed. I could tell by the laugh that they'd decided to sell us the gas—probably it would be weak and dirty and watered down and cost twice the usual price—but it didn't make me feel any better. I could see everybody was feeling pretty bad. The doctor's lying made us feel worse than ever—not because of the lie, so much, but because of the truth.

The second guy came over to the doctor, grinning. "You said you wanted the Soo-preme, sir? You bet. And how about us checking those oil filters and windshield wipes?" He was bigger than his friend. He leaned down on the doctor like he was sharing a secret. "Would you believe it: eighty-eight per cent of the cars show by the figures on the road today that they need new oil filters and windshield wipes?"

His grin was coated with carbon from years of taking out spark plugs with his teeth. He kept leaning down on the doctor, making him squirm with that grin and waiting for him to admit he was over a barrel. "Also, how's your work crew fixed for sunglasses? We got some good Polaroids." The doctor knew he had him. But just the instant he opened his mouth, about to give in and say Yes, anything, there was a whirring noise and the top of our car was folding back. McMurphy was fighting and cursing the accordion-pleated top, trying to force it back faster than the machinery could handle it. Everybody could see how mad he was by the way he thrashed and beat at that slowly rising top; when he got it cussed and hammered and wrestled down into place he climbed right out over the girl and over the side of the car and walked up between the doctor and the service station guy and looked up into the black mouth with one eye.

"Okay now, Hank, we'll take regular, just like the doctor ordered. Two tanks of regular. That's all. The hell with that other slum. And we'll take it at three cents off because we're a goddamned government-sponsored expedition."

The guy didn't budge. "Yeah? I thought the professor here said you weren't patients?"

"Now Hank, don't you see that was just a kindly precaution to keep from *startlin'* you folks with the truth? The doc wouldn't lie like that about just *any* patients, but we ain't ordinary nuts; we're every bloody one of us hot off the criminal-insane ward, on our way to San Quentin where they got better facilities to handle us. You see that freckle-faced kid there? Now he might look like he's right off a *Saturday Evening Post* cover, but he's a insane knife artist that killed three men. The man beside him is known as the Bull Goose Loony, unpredictable as a wild hog. You see that big guy? He's an Indian and he beat six white men to death with a pick handle when they tried to cheat him trading muskrat hides. Stand up where they can get a look at you, Chief."

Harding goosed me with his thumb, and I stood up on the floor of the car. The guy shaded his eyes and looked up at me and didn't say anything.

"Oh, it's a bad group, I admit," McMurphy said, "but it's a planned, authorized, legal government-sponsored excursion, and we're entitled to a legal discount just the same as if we was the FBI."

The guy looked back at McMurphy, and McMurphy hooked his thumbs in his pockets and rocked back and looked up at him across the scar on his nose. The guy turned to check if his buddy was still stationed at the case of empty pop bottles, then grinned back down on McMurphy.

"Pretty tough customers, is that what you're saying, Red? So much we better toe the line and do what we're told, is that what you're saying? Well, tell me, Red, what is it *you're* in for? Trying to assassinate the President?"

"Nobody could *prove* that, Hank. They got me on a bum rap. I killed a man in the ring, ya see, and sorta got *taken* with the kick."

"One of these killers with boxing gloves, is that what you're telling me, Red?"

"Now, I didn't say that, did I? I never could get used to those pillows you wore. No, this wasn't no televised main event from the Cow Palace; I'm more what you call a back-lot boxer."

The guy hooked his thumbs in his pockets to mock McMurphy. "You are more what I call a back-lot bull-thrower."

"Now I didn't say that bull-throwing wasn't also one of my abilities, did I? But I want you to look here." He put his hands up in the guy's face, real close, turning them over slowly, palm and knuckle. "You ever see a man get his poor old meat-hooks so pitiful chewed up from just throwin' the *bull?* Did you, Hank?"

He held those hands in the guy's face a long time, waiting to see if the guy had anything else to say. The guy looked at the hands, and at me, and back at the hands. When it was clear he didn't have anything else real pressing to say, McMurphy walked away from him to the other guy leaning against the pop cooler and plucked the doctor's ten-dollar bill out of his fist and started for the grocery store next to the station.

"You boys tally what the gas comes to and send the bill to the hospital," he called back. "I intend to use the cash to pick up some refreshments for the men. I believe we'll get that in place of windshield wipes and eighty-eight per cent oil filters."

By the time he got back everybody was feeling cocky as fighting roosters and calling orders to the service-station guys to check the air in the spare and wipe the windows and scratch that bird drooping off the hood if you please, just like we owned the show. When the big guy didn't get the windshield to suit Billy, Billy called him right back.

"You'd didn't get this sp-spot here where the bug h-h-hit."

"That wasn't a bug," the guy said sullenly, scratching at it with his fingernail, "that was a bird."

Martini called all the way from the other car that it couldn't of been a bird. "There'd be feathers and bones if it was a bird."

A man riding a bicycle stopped to ask what was the idea of all the green uniforms; some kind of club? Harding popped right up and answered him.

"No, my friend. We are lunatics from the hospital up the highway, psychoceramics, the cracked pots of mankind. Would you like me to decipher a Rorschach for you? No? You must hurry on? Ah, he's gone. Pity." He turned to McMurphy. "Never before did I realize that mental illness could have the aspect of power, *power*. Think of it: perhaps the more insane a man is, the more powerful he could become. Hitler an example. Fair makes the old brain reel, doesn't it? Food for thought here."

Billy punched a beer can for the girl, and she flustered him so with her bright smile and her "Thank you, Billy," that he took to opening cans for all of us.

While the pigeons fretted up and down the sidewalk with their hands folded behind their backs.

I sat there, feeling whole and good, sipping at a beer; I could hear the beer all the way down me—zzzth zzzth, like that. I had forgotten that there can be good sounds and tastes like the sound and taste of a beer going down. I took another big drink and started looking around me to see what else I had forgotten in twenty years.

"Man!" McMurphy said as he scooted the girl out from under the wheel and tight over against Billy. "Will you just look at the Big Chief slug down on that firewater!"—and slammed the car out into traffic with the doctor squealing behind to keep up.

He'd shown us what a little bravado and courage could accomplish, and we thought he'd taught us how to use it. All the way to the coast we had fun pretending to be brave. When people at a stop light would stare at us and our green uniforms we'd do just like he did, sit up straight and strong and tough-looking and put a grin on our face and stare straight back at them till their motors died and their windows sunstreaked and they were left sitting when the light changed, upset bad by what a tough bunch of monkeys was just now not three feet from them, and help nowhere in sight.

As McMurphy led the twelve of us toward the ocean.

I think McMurphy knew better than we did that our tough looks were all show, because he still wasn't able to get a real laugh out of anybody. Maybe he couldn't understand why we weren't able to laugh yet, but he knew you can't really be strong until you can see a funny side to things. In fact, he worked so hard at pointing out the funny side of things that I was wondering a little if maybe he was blind to the other side, if maybe he wasn't able to see what it was that parched laughter deep inside your stomach. Maybe the guys weren't able to see it either, just feel the pressures of the different beams and frequencies coming from all directions, working to push and bend you one way or another, feel the Combine at work—but I was able to *see* it.

The way you see the change in a person you've been away from for a long time, where somebody who sees him every day, day in, day out, wouldn't notice because the change is gradual. All up the coast I could see the signs of what the Combine had accomplished since I was last through this country, things like, for example—a *train* stopping at a station and laying a string of full-grown men in mirrored suits and machined hats, laying them like a hatch of identical insects, half-life things coming pht-pht-pht out of the last car, then hooting its electric whistle and moving on down the spoiled land to deposit another hatch.

Or things like five thousand houses punched out identical by a machine and strung across the hills outside of town, so fresh from the factory they're still linked together like sausages, a sign saying "NEST IN THE WEST HOMES—NO DWN. PAYMENT FOR VETS," a playground down the hill from the houses, behind a checker-wire fence and another sign that read "ST. LUKE'S SCHOOL FOR BOYS"— there were five thousand kids in green corduroy pants and white shirts under green pullover sweaters playing crack-the-whip across an acre of crushed gravel. The line popped and twisted and jerked like a snake, and every crack popped a little kid off the end, sent him rolling up against the fence like a tumbleweed. Every crack. And it was always the same little kid, over and over.

All that five thousand kids lived in those five thousand houses, owned by those guys that got off the train. The houses looked so much alike that, time and time again, the kids went home by mistake to different houses and different families. Nobody ever noticed. They ate and went to bed. The only one they noticed was the little kid at the end of the whip. He'd always be so scuffed and bruised that he'd show up out of place wherever he went. He wasn't able to open up and laugh either. It's a hard thing to laugh if you can feel the pressure of those beams coming from every new car that passes, or every new house you pass.

"We can even have a lobby in Washington," Harding was saying, "an organization NAAIP. Pressure groups. Big billboards along the highway showing a babbling schizophrenic running a wrecking machine, bold, red and green type: 'Hire the Insane.' We've got a rosy future, gentlemen."

We crossed a bridge over the Siuslaw. There was just enough mist in the air that I could lick out my tongue to the wind and taste the ocean before we could see it. Everyone knew we were getting close and didn't speak all the way to the docks.

The captain who was supposed to take us out had a bald gray metal head set in a black turtleneck like a gun turret on a U-boat; the cold cigar sticking from his mouth swept over us. He stood beside McMurphy on the wooden pier and looked out to sea as he talked. Behind him and up a bunch of steps, six or eight men in windbreakers were sitting on a bench along the front of the bait shop. The captain talked loudly, half to the loafers on his side and half to McMurphy on the other side, firing his copper-jacket voice someplace in between.

"Don't care. Told you specifically in the letter. You don't have a signed waiver clearing me with proper authorities, I don't go out." The round head swiveled in the turret of his sweater, beading down that cigar at the lot of us. "Look there. Bunch like that at sea, could go to diving overboard like rats. Relatives could sue me for everything I own. I can't risk it."

McMurphy explained how the other girl was supposed to get all those papers up in Portland. One of the guys leaning against the bait shop called, "What other girl? Couldn't Blondie there handle the lot of you?" McMurphy didn't pay the guy any mind and went on arguing with the captain, but you could see how it bothered the girl. Those men against the shop kept leering at her and leaning close together to whisper things. All our crew, even the doctor, saw this and got to feeling ashamed that we didn't do something. We weren't the cocky bunch that was back at the service station.

McMurphy stopped arguing when he saw he wasn't getting any place with the captain and turned around a couple of times, running his hand through his hair.

"Which boat have we got rented?"

"That's it there. The *Lark*. Not a man sets foot on her till I have a signed waiver clearing me. Not a man."

"I don't intend to rent a boat so we can sit all day and watch it bob up and down at the dock," McMurphy said. "Don't you have a phone up there in your bait shack? Let's go get this cleared up."

They thumped up the steps onto the level with the bait shop and went inside, leaving us clustered up by ourselves, with that bunch of loafers up there watching us and making comments and sniggering and goosing one another in the ribs. The wind was blowing the boats at their moorings, nuzzling them up against the wet rubber tires along the dock so they made a sound like they were laughing at us. The water was giggling under the boards, and the sign hanging over the door to the bait shack that read "SEAMAN'S SERVICE—CAPT BLOCK, PROP" was squeaking and scratching as the wind rocked it on rusty hooks. The mussels that clung to the pilings, four feet out of water marking the tide line, whistled and clicked in the sun.

The wind had turned cold and mean, and Billy Bibbit took off his green coat and gave it to the girl, and she put it on over her thin little T-shirt. One of the loafers kept calling down, "Hey you, Blondie, you like fruitcake kids like that?" The man's lips were kidney-colored and he was purple under his eyes where the wind'd mashed the veins to the surface. "Hey you, Blondie," he called over and over in a high, tired voice, "hey you, Blondie . . . hey you, Blondie . . . hey you, Blondie . . ."

We bunched up closer together against the wind.

"Tell me, Blondie, what've they got *you* committed for?"

"Ahr, she ain't committed, Perce, she's part of the *cure!*"

"Is that right, Blondie? You hired as part of the *cure?* Hey you, Blondie."

She lifted her head and gave us a look that asked where was that hard-boiled bunch she'd seen and why weren't they saying something to defend her? Nobody would answer the look. All our hard-boiled strength had just walked up those steps with his arm around the shoulders of the bald-headed captain.

She pulled the collar of the jacket high around her neck and hugged her elbows and strolled as far away from us down the dock as she could go. Nobody went after her. Billy Bibbit shivered in the cold and bit his lip. The guys at the bait shack whispered something else and whooped out laughing again.

"Ask 'er, Perce—go on."

"Hey, Blondie, did you get 'em to sign a waiver clearing you with proper authorities? Relatives could sue, they tell me, if one of the boys fell in and drown while he was on board. Did you ever think of that? Maybe you'd better stay here with us, Blondie."

"Yeah, Blondie; my relatives wouldn't sue. I promise. Stay here with us fellows, Blondie."

I imagined I could feel my feet getting wet as the dock sank with shame into the bay. We weren't fit to be out here with people. I wished McMurphy would come back out and cuss these guys good and then drive us back where we belonged.

The man with the kidney lips folded his knife and stood up and brushed the whittle shavings out of his lap. He started walking toward the steps. "C'mon, now, Blondie, what you want to mess with these bozos for?"

She turned and looked at him from the end of the dock, then back at us, and you could tell she was thinking his proposition over when the door of the bait shop opened and McMurphy came shoving out past the bunch of them, down the steps.

"Pile in, crew, it's all set! Gassed and ready and there's bait and beer on board."

He slapped Billy on the rear and did a little hornpipe and commenced slinging ropes from their snubs.

"Ol' Cap'n Block's still on the phone, but we'll be pulling off as quick as he comes out. George, let's see if you can get that motor warmed up. Scanlon, you and Harding untie that rope there. Candy! What are you doing off down there? Let's get with it, honey, we're shoving off."

We swarmed into the boat, glad for anything that would take us away from those guys standing in a row at the bait shop. Billy took the girl by the hand and helped her on board. George hummed over the dashboard up on the bridge, pointing out buttons for McMurphy to twist or push.

"Yeah, these pukers, puke boats, we call them," he said to McMurphy, "they joost as easy like driving ottomobile."

The doctor hesitated before climbing aboard and looked toward the shop where all the loafers stood milling toward the steps.

"Don't you think, Randle, we'd better wait . . . until the captain—"

McMurphy caught him by the lapels and lifted him clear of the dock into the boat like he was a small boy. "Yeah, Doc," he said, "wait till the captain *what?*" He commenced to laugh like he was drunk, talking in an excited, nervous way. "Wait till the captain comes out an tells us that the phone number I gave him is a flophouse up in Portland? You bet. Here, George, damn your eyes; take hold of this thing and get us out of here! Sefelt! Get that rope loose and get on. George, come *on.*"

The motor chugged and died, chugged again like it was clearing its throat, then roared full on.

"*Hoowee!* There she goes. Pour the coal to 'er, George, and all hands stand by to repel boarders!"

A white gorge of smoke and water roared from the back of the boat, and the door of the bait shop crashed open and the captain's head came booming out and down the steps like it was not only dragging his body behind it but the bodies of the eight other guys as well. They came thundering down the dock and stopped right at the boil of foam washing over their feet as George swung the big boat out and away from the docks and we had the sea to ourselves.

A sudden turn of the boat had thrown Candy to her knees, and Billy was helping her up and trying to apologize for the way he'd acted on the dock at the same time. McMurphy came down from the bridge and asked if the two of them would like to be alone so they could talk over old times, and Candy looked at Billy and all he could do was shake his head and stutter. McMurphy said in that case he and Candy'd better go below and check for leaks and the rest of us could make do for a while. He stood at the door down to the cabin and saluted and winked and appointed George captain and Harding second in command and said, "Carry on, mates," and followed the girl out of sight into the cabin.

The wind lay down and the sun got higher, chrome-plating the east side of the deep green swells. George aimed the boat straight out to sea, full throttle, putting the docks and that bait shop farther and farther behind us. When we passed the last point of the jetty and the last black rock, I could feel a great calmness creep over me, a calmness that increased the farther we left land behind us.

The guys talked excitedly for a few minutes about our piracy of the boat, but now they were quiet. The cabin door opened once long enough for a hand to shove out a case of beer, and Billy opened us each one with an opener he found in the tackle box, and passed them around. We drank and watched the land sinking in our wake.

A mile or so out George cut the speed to what he called a trolling idle, put four guys to the four poles in the back of the boat, and the rest of us sprawled in the sun on top of the cabin or up on the bow and took off our shirts and watched the guys trying to rig their poles. Harding said the rule was a guy got to hold the pole till he got one strike, then he had to change off with a man who hadn't had a chance. George stood at the wheel, squinting out through the salt-caked windshield, and hollered instructions back how to fix up the reels and lines and how to tie a herring into the herring harness and how far back to fish and how deep:

"And take that number *four* pole and you put you twelve ounces on him on a rope with a breakaway rig—I show you how in joost a minute—and we go after that *big* fella down on the bottom with that pole, by golly!"

Martini ran to the edge and leaned over the side and stared down into the water in the direction of his line. "Oh. Oh, my God," he said, but whatever he saw was too deep down for the rest of us.

There were other sports boats trolling up and down the coast, but George didn't make any attempt to join them; he kept pushing steadily straight on out past them, toward the open sea. "You bet," he said. "We go out with the commercial boats, where the real *fish* is."

The swells slid by, deep emerald on one side, chrome on the other. The only noise was the engine sputtering and humming, off and on, as the swells dipped the exhaust in and out of the water, and the funny, lost cry of the raggedy little black birds swimming around asking one another directions. Everything else was quiet. Some of the guys slept, and the others watched the water. We'd been trolling close to an hour when the tip of Sefelt's pole arched and dived into the water.

"George! Jesus, George, give us a hand!"

George wouldn't have a thing to do with the pole; he grinned and told Sefelt to ease up on the star drag, keep the tip pointed up, *up*, and work hell outa that fella!

"But what if I have a seizure?" Sefelt hollered.

"Why, we'll simply put hook and line on you and use you for a lure," Harding said. "Now work that fella, as the captain ordered, and quit worrying about a seizure."

171

Thirty yards back of the boat the fish broke into the sun in a shower of silver scales, and Sefelt's eyes popped and he got so excited watching the fish he let the end of his pole go down, and the line snapped into the boat like a rubber band.

"*Up*, I told you! You let him get a straight pull, don't you see? Keep that tip *up* . . . *up!* You had you one big silver there, by golly."

Sefelt's jaw was white and shaking when he finally gave up the pole to Fredrickson. "Okay—but if you get a fish with a hook in his mouth, that's my godblessed fish!"

I was as excited as the rest. I hadn't planned on fishing, but after seeing that steel power a salmon has at the end of a line I got off the cabin top and put on my shirt to wait my turn at a pole.

Scanlon got up a pool for the biggest fish and another for the first fish landed, four bits from everybody that wanted in it, and he'd no more'n got his money in his pocket than Billy drug in some awful thing that looked like a ten-pound toad with spines on it like a porcupine.

"That's no fish," Scanlon said. "You can't win on that."

"It isn't a b-b-bird."

"That there, he's a *ling* cod," George told us. "He's one good eating fish you get all his warts off."

"See there. He is too a fish, P-p-pay up."

Billy gave me his pole and took his money and went to sit up close to the cabin where McMurphy and the girl were, looking at the closed door forlornly. "I wu-wu-wu-wish we had enough poles to go around," he said, leaning back against the side of the cabin.

I sat down and held the pole and watched the line swoop out into the wake. I smelt the air and felt the four cans of beer I'd drunk shorting out dozens of control leads down inside me: all around, the chrome sides of the swells flickered and flashed in the sun.

George sang out for us to look up ahead, that here come just what we been looking for. I leaned around to look, but all I saw was a big drifting log and those black seagulls circling and diving around the log, like black leaves caught up in a dust devil. George speeded up some, heading into the place where the birds circled, and the speed of the boat dragged my line until I couldn't see how you'd be able to tell if you did get a bite.

"Those fellas, those cormorants, they go after a school of *candle* fishes," George told us as he drove. "Little white fishes the size of your finger. You dry them and they burn joost like a candle. They are *food* fish, chum fish. And you bet where there's a big school of them candle fish you find the silver salmon feeding."

He drove into the birds, missing the floating log, and suddenly all around me the smooth slopes of chrome were shattered by diving birds and churning minnows, and the sleek silver-blue torpedo backs of the salmon slicing through it all. I saw one of the backs check its direction and turn and set course for a spot thirty yards behind the end of my pole, where my herring would be. I braced, my heart ringing, and then felt a jolt up both arms as if somebody'd hit the pole with a ball bat, and my line went burning off the reel from under my thumb, red as blood. "Use the star drag!" George yelled at me, but what I knew about star drags you could put in your eye so I just mashed harder with my thumb until the line turned back to yellow, then slowed and stopped. I looked around, and there were all three of the other poles whipping around just like mine, and the rest of the guys scrambling down off the cabin at the excitement and doing everything in their power to get underfoot.

"Up! Up! Keep the tip up!" George was yelling.

"McMurphy! Get out here and look at this."

"Godbless you, Fred, you got my blessed fish!"

"McMurphy, we need some help!"

I heard McMurphy laughing and saw him out of the corner of my eye, just standing at the cabin door, not even making a move to do anything, and I was too busy cranking at my fish to ask him for help. Everyone was shouting at him to do something, but he wasn't moving. Even the doctor, who had the deep pole, was asking McMurphy for assistance. And McMurphy was just laughing. Harding finally saw McMurphy wasn't going to do anything, so he got the gaff and jerked my fish into the boat with a clean, graceful motion like he's been boating fish all his life. He's big as my leg, I thought, big as a fence post! I thought, He's bigger'n any fish we ever got at the falls. He's springing all over the bottom of the boat like a rainbow gone wild! Smearing blood and scattering scales like little silver dimes, and I'm scared he's gonna flop overboard. McMurphy won't make a move to help. Scanlon grabs the fish and wrestles it down to keep it from flopping over the side. The girl comes running up from below, yelling it's her turn, dang it, grabs my pole, and jerks the hook into me three times while I'm trying to tie on a herring for her.

"Chief, I'll be damned if I ever saw anything so *slow!* Ugh, your thumb's bleeding. Did that monster bite you? Somebody fix the Chief's thumb—hurry!"

"Here we go into them again," George yells, and I drop the line off the back of the boat and see the flash of the herring vanish in the dark blue-gray charge of a salmon and the line go sizzling down into the water. The girl wraps both arms around the pole and grits her teeth. "*Oh* no you don't, dang you! *Oh* no . . .!"

She's on her feet, got the butt of the pole scissored in her crotch and both arms wrapped below the reel and the reel crank knocking against her as the line spins out: "*Oh* no you don't!" She's still got on Billy's green jacket, but that reel's whipped it open and everybody on board sees the T-shirt she had on is gone—everybody gawking, trying to play his own fish, dodge mine slamming around the boat bottom, with the crank of that reel fluttering her breast at such a speed the nipple's just a red blur!

Billy jumps to help. All he can think to do is reach around from behind and help her squeeze the pole tighter in between her breasts until the reel's finally stopped by nothing more than the pressure of her flesh. By this time she's flexed so taut and her breasts look so firm I think she and Billy could both turn loose with their hands and arms and she'd *still* keep hold of that pole.

This scramble of action holds for a space, a second there on the sea—the men yammering and struggling and cussing and trying to tend their poles while watching the girl; the bleeding, crashing battle between Scanlon and my fish at everybody's feet; the lines all tangled and shooting every which way with the doctor's glasses-on-a-string tangled and dangling from one line ten feet off the back of the boat, fish striking at the flash of the lens, and the girl cussing for all she's worth and looking now at her bare breasts, one white and one smarting red—and George takes his eye off where he's going and runs the boat into that log and kills the engine.

While McMurphy laughs. Rocking farther and farther backward against the cabin top, spreading his laugh out across the water—laughing at the girl, at the guys, at George, at me sucking my bleeding thumb, at the captain back at the pier and the bicycle rider and the service-station guys and the five thousand houses and the Big Nurse and all of it. Because he knows you have to laugh at the things that hurt you just to keep yourself in balance, just to keep the world from running you plumb crazy. He knows there's a painful side; he knows my thumb smarts and his girl friend has a bruised breast and the doctor is losing his glasses, but he won't let the pain blot out the humor no more'n he'll let the humor blot out the pain.

I notice Harding is collapsed beside McMurphy and is laughing too. And Scanlon from the bottom of the boat. At their own selves as well as at the rest of us. And the girl, with her eyes still smarting as she looks from her white breast to her red one, she starts laughing. And Sefelt and the doctor, and all.

It started slow and pumped itself full, swelling the men bigger and bigger. I watched, part of them, laughing with them—and somehow not with them. I was off the boat, blown up off the water and skating the wind with those black birds, high above myself, and I could look down and see myself and the rest of the guys, see the boat rocking there in the middle of those diving birds, see McMurphy surrounded by his dozen people, and watch them, us, swinging a laughter that rang out on the water in ever-widening circles, farther and farther, until it crashed up on beaches all over the coast, on beaches all over all coasts, in wave after wave after wave.

The doctor had hooked something off the bottom on the deep hole, and everybody else on board except George had caught and landed a fish by the time he lifted it up to where we could even see it—just a whitish shape appearing, then diving for the bottom in spite of everything the doctor tried to do to hold it. As soon as he'd get it up near the top again, lifting and reeling it in with tight, stubborn little grunts and refusing any help the guys might offer, it would see the light and down it would go.

George didn't bother starting the boat again, but came down to show us how to clean the fish over the side and rip the gills out so the meat would stay sweeter. McMurphy tied a chunk of meat to each end of a four-foot string, tossed it in the air, and sent two squawking birds wheeling off, "Till death do them part."

The whole back of the boat and most of the people in it were dappled with red and silver. Some of us took our shirts off and dipped them over the side and tried to clean them. We fiddled around this way, fishing a little, drinking the other case of beer, and feeding the birds till afternoon, while the boat rolled lazily around the swells and the doctor worked with his monster from the deep. A wind came up and broke the sea into green and silver chunks, like a field of glass and chrome, and the boat began to rock and pitch about more. George told the doctor he'd have to land his fish or cut it loose because there was a bad sky coming down on us. The doctor didn't answer. He just heaved harder on the pole, bent forward and reeled the slack, and heaved again.

Billy and the girl had climbed around to the bow and were talking and looking down in the water. Billy hollered that he saw something, and we all rushed to that side, and a shape broad and white was becoming solid some ten or fifteen feet down. It was strange watching it rise, first just a light coloring, then a white form like fog under water, becoming solid, alive. . . .

"Jesus God," Scanlon cried, "that's the doc's fish!"

It was on the side opposite the doctor, but we could see by the direction of his line that it led to the shape under the water.

"We'll never get it in the boat," Sefelt said. "And the wind's getting stronger."

"He's a big flounder," George said. " Sometimes they weigh two, three hundred. You got to lift them in with the winch."

"We'll have to cut him loose, Doc," Selelt said and put his arm across the doctor's shoulders. The doctor didn't say anything; he had sweated clear through his suit between his shoulders, and his eyes were bright red from going so long without glasses. He kept heaving until the fish appeared on his side of the boat. We watched it near the surface for a few minutes longer, then started getting the rope and gaff ready.

Even with the gaff in it, it took another hour to drag the fish into the back of the boat. We had to hook him with all three other poles, and McMurphy leaned down and got a hand in his gills, and with a heave he slid in, transparent white and flat, and flopped down to the bottom of the boat with the doctor.

"That was something." The doctor panted from the floor, not enough strength left to push the huge fish off him. "That was . . . certainly something."

The boat pitched and cracked all the way to shore, with McMurphy telling grim tales about shipwrecks and sharks. The waves got bigger as we got closer to shore, and from the crests clots of white foam blew swirling up in the wind to join the gulls. The swells at the mouth of the jetty were combing higher than the boat, and George had us all put on life jackets. I noticed all the other sports boats were in.

We were three jackets short, and there was a fuss as to who'd be the three that braved that bar without jackets. It finally turned out to be Billy Bibbit and Harding and George, who wouldn't wear one anyway on account of the dirt. Everybody was kind of surprised that Billy had volunteered, took his life jacket off right away when we found we were short, and helped the girl into it, but everybody was even more surprised that McMurphy hadn't insisted that he be one of the heroes; all during the fuss he'd stood with his back against the cabin, bracing against the pitch of the boat, and watched the guys without saying a word. Just grinning and watching.

We hit the bar and dropped into a canyon of water, the bow of the boat pointing up the hissing crest of the wave going before us, and the rear down in the trough in the shadow of the wave looming behind us, and everybody in the back hanging on the rail and looking from the mountain that chased behind to the streaming black rocks of the jetty forty feet to the left, to George at the wheel. He stood there like a mast. He kept turning his head from the front to the back, gunning the throttle, easing off, gunning again, holding us steady riding the uphill slant of that wave in front. He'd told us before we started the run that if we went over the crest in *front*, we'd surfboard out of control as soon as the prop and rudder broke water, and if we slowed down to where that wave *behind* caught up it would break over the stern and dump ten tons of water into the boat. Nobody joked or said anything funny about the way he kept turning his head back and forth like it was mounted up there on a swivel.

Inside the mooring the water calmed to a choppy surface again, and at our dock, by the bait shop, we could see the captain waiting with two cops at the water's edge. All the loafers were gathered behind them. George headed at them full throttle, booming down on them till the captain went to waving and yelling and the cops headed up the steps with the loafers. Just before the prow of the boat tore out the whole dock, George swung the wheel, threw the prop into reverse, and with a powerful roar snuggled the boat in against the rubber tires like he was easing it into bed. We were already out tying up by the time our wake caught up; it pitched all the boats around and slopped over the dock and whitecapped around the docks like we'd brought the sea home with us.

The captain and the cops and the loafers came tromping back down the steps to us. The doctor carried the fight to them by first off telling the cops they didn't have any jurisdiction over us, as we were a legal, government-sponsored expedition, and if there was anyone to take the matter up with it would have to be a federal agency. Also, there might be some investigation into the number of life jackets that the boat held if the captain really planned to make trouble. Wasn't there supposed to be a life jacket for every man on board, according to the law? When the captain didn't say anything the cops took some names and left, mumbling and confused, and as soon as they were off the pier McMurphy and the captain went to arguing and shoving each other around. McMurphy was drunk enough he was still trying to rock with the roll of the boat and he slipped on the wet wood and fell in the ocean twice before he got his footing sufficient to hit the captain one up alongside of his bald head and settle the fuss. Everybody felt better that that was out of the way, and the captain and McMurphy both went to the bait shop to get more beer while the rest of us worked at hauling our fish out of the hold. The loafers stood on that upper dock, watching and smoking pipes they'd carved themselves. We were waiting for them to say something about the girl again, hoping for it, to tell the truth, but when one of them finally did say something it wasn't about the girl but about our fish being the biggest halibut he'd ever seen brought in on the Oregon coast. All the rest nodded that that was sure the truth. They came edging down to look it over. They asked George where he learned to dock a boat that way, and we found out George'd not just run fishing boats but he'd also been captain of a PT boat in the Pacific and got the Navy Cross. "Shoulda gone into public office," one of the loafers said, "Too dirty," George told him.

They could sense the change that most of us were only suspecting; these weren't the same bunch of weak-knees from a nuthouse that they'd watched take their insults on the dock this morning. They didn't exactly apologize to the girl for the things they'd said, but when they asked to see the fish she'd caught they were just as polite as pie. And when McMurphy and the captain came back out of the bait shop we all shared a beer together before we drove away.

Tom Robbins

from ANOTHER ROADSIDE ATTRACTION*

Puget Sound may be the most rained-on body of water on earth. Cold, deep, steep-shored, home to salmon and lipstick-orange starfish, the Sound lies between the Cascades and the Olympics. The Skagit Valley lies between the Cascades and the Sound—sixty miles north of Seattle, an equal distance south of Canada. The Skagit River, which formed the valley, begins up in British Columbia, leaps and splashes southwestward through the high Cascade wilderness, absorbing glaciers and sipping alpine lakes, running two hundred miles in total before all fish-green, driftwood-cluttered and silty, it spreads its double mouth like suckers against the upper body of Puget Sound. Toward the Sound end of the valley, the fields are rich with river silt, the soil ranging from black velvet to a blond sandy loam. Although the area receives little unfiltered sunlight, peas and strawberries grow lustily in Skagit fields, and more than half the world's supply of beet seed and cabbage seed is harvested here. Like Holland, which it in some ways resembles, it supports a thriving bulb industry: in spring its lowland acres vibrate with tulips, iris and daffodils; no bashful hues. At any season, it is a dry duck's dream. The forks of the river are connected by a network of sloughs, bedded with ancient mud and lined with cattail, tules, eelgrass and sedge. The fields, though diked, are often flooded; there are puddles by the hundreds and the roadside ditches could be successfully navigated by midget submarines.

It is a landscape in a minor key. A sketchy panorama where objects, both organic and inorganic, lack well-defined edges and tend to melt together in a silver-green blur. Great islands of craggy rock arch abruptly up out of the flats, and at sunrise and moonrise these outcroppings are frequently tangled in mist. Eagles nest on the island crowns and blue herons flap through the veils from slough to slough. It is a poetic setting, one which suggests inner meanings and invisible connections. The effect is distinctly Chinese. A visitor experiences the feeling that he has been pulled into a Sung dynasty painting, perhaps before the intense wisps of mineral pigment have dried upon the silk. From almost any vantage point, there are expanses of monochrome worthy of the brushes of Mi Fei or Kuo Hsi.

The Skagit Valley, in fact, inspired a school of neo-Chinese painters. In the Forties, Mark Tobey, Morris Graves and their gray-on-gray disciples turned their backs on cubist composition and European color and using the shapes and shades of this misty terrain as a springboard, began to paint the visions of the inner eye. A school of sodden, contemplative poets emerged here, too. Even the original inhabitants were an introspective breed. Unlike the Plains Indians, who enjoyed mobility and open spaces and sunny skies, the Northwest coastal tribes were caught between the dark waters to the west, the heavily forested foothills and towering Cascade peaks to the east; forced by the lavish rains to spend weeks on end confined to their longhouses. Consequently, they turned inward, evolving religious and mythological patterns that are startling in their complexity and intensity, developing an artistic idiom that for aesthetic weight and psychological depth was unequaled among all primitive races. Even today, after the intrusion of neon signs and supermarkets and aircraft industries and sports cars, a hushed but heavy force hangs in the Northwest air: it defies flamboyance, deflates extroversion and muffles the most exultant cry.

°Editors note: Our selections from *Another Roadside Attraction* are unified only in that they describe rain and the Northwest countryside. Perhaps it would have been fitting to publish them in the poetry section of this collection rather than with the fiction.

¤ ¤ ¤ ¤ ¤ ¤ ¤ ¤

Autumn does not come to the Skagit Valley in sweet-apple chomps, in blasts of blue sky and painted leaves, with crisp football afternoons and squirrel chatter and bourbon and lap robes under a harvest moon. The East and Midwest have their autumns, and the Skagit Valley has another.

October lies on the Skagit like a wet rag on a salad. Trapped beneath low clouds, the valley is damp and green and full of sad memories. The people of the valley have far less to be unhappy about than many who live elsewhere in America, but, still, an aboriginal sadness clings like the dew to their region; their land has a blurry beauty (as if the Creator started to erase it but had second thoughts), it has dignity, fertility and hints of inner meaning—but nothing can seem to make it laugh.

The short summer is finished, it is October again, and Sung dynasty mists swirl across the fields where seed cabbages, like gangrened jack-o'-lanterns, have been left to rot. The ghost-light of old photographs floods the tide flats, the island outcroppings, the salt marshes, the dikes and the sloughs. The frozen-food plants have closed for the season. A trombone of geese slides southward between the overcast and the barns. Upriver, there is a chill in the weeds. Old trucks and tractors rusting among the stumps seem in autumn especially forlorn.

October scenes:

At the dog-bitten Swinomish Indian Center near La Conner, there is a forty-foot totem pole the top figure of which is Franklin Delano Roosevelt. One of the queerer projects of the WPA Roosevelt's Harvard grin is faded and wooden in the reservation mist.

Outside of Concrete, boys have thrown crab apples through the colored glass windows of an abandoned church. Crows carry the bright fragments away to their nests.

On the Freeway south of Mount Vernon, watched over by a hovering sausage, surrounded by a ring of prophecy, an audacious roadside zoo rages against the multiplying green damp chill as if it were a spell cast upon the valley by

179

gypsy friends of the sun. Events transpire within that zoo which must be re-
corded immediately and correctly if they are to pass into history undeformed.
Things rot with a terrible swiftness in the Northwest rains. A century from now,
the ruins of the Capt. Kendrick Memorial Hot Dog Wildlife Preserve will offer
precious little to reimburse archaeologists for their time. No Dead Sea Scrolls
will ever be found in the Skagit Valley. It's now or never for *this* bible.

*   *   *   *   *   *   *   *

The afternoon sky looked like a brain. Moist. Gray. Convoluted. A mad-
scientist breeze probed at the brain, causing it to bob and quiver as if it were
immersed in a tank of strange liquids. The Skagit Valley was the residue at the
bottom of the tank. Toward dusk, the wind flagged, the big brain stiffened
(mad doctor's experiment a failure), and ragged ribbons of Chinese mist un-
furled in the valley. The blaring cries of ducks and geese and the popping of
hunters' guns echoed over the sloughs. During the waning Sung dynasty mo-
ments of the day, Ziller cooked up his first batch of sausages. A trial run at the
Capt. Kendrick Memorial Hot Dog Wildlife Preserve.

*   *   *   *   *   *   *   *

A trailer of rain fell for an hour at sunrise, but the afternoon was dry. The
hot dog was erected on the roof of the cafe. It looked good. It could be seen for
miles.

Ziller's magnificent sausage became a landmark in Skagit County. Direc-
tions were given in relation to it. "Turn right a couple hundred yards past the
big weenie," some helpful farmer might say. From that time on, Mount Vernon
school children would be obliged to compose annual essays on "The Sausage:
Its Origin, Its Meaning and Its Cure."

To this day it hovers in plump passivity above the fertile fields. It is a per-
fect emblem for the people and the land.

A sausage is an image of rest, peace and tranquility in stark contrast to the
destruction and chaos of everyday life.

Consider the peaceful repose of the sausage compared with the aggres-
siveness and violence of bacon.

*   *   *   *   *   *   *   *

Rain fell on Skagit Valley.

It fell in sweeps and it fell in drones. It fell in unending cascades of cheap
Zen jewelry. It fell on the dikes. It fell on the firs. It fell on the downcast necks
of the mallards.

And it rained a fever. And it rained a silence. And it rained a sacrifice. And
it rained a miracle. And it rained sorceries and saturnine eyes of the totem.

Rain drenched the chilly green tidelands. The river swelled. The sloughs
fermented. Vapors rose from black stumps on the hillsides. Spirit canoes pad-
dled in the mists of the islands. Legends were washed from desecrated burial
grounds. (The Skagit Indians, too, have a tradition of a Great Flood. The flood,
they say, caused a big change in the world. Another big change is yet to occur.

The world will change again. The Skagit don't know when. "When we can converse with the animals, we will know the change is half-way here. When we can converse with the forest, we will know the change has come.") Water spilled off the roofs and the rain hats. It took on the colors of neon and head lamps. It glistened on the claws of nighttime animals.

And it rained a screaming. And it rained a rawness. And it rained a plasma. And it rained a disorder.

The rain erased the prints of the sasquatch. It beat the last withered fruit from the orchard trees. It soaked the knotted fans who gathered to watch high-school boys play football in the mud. It hammered the steamed-up windshields of lover's lane Chevvies, hammered the larger windshields of hunters' pickups, hammered, upriver, the still larger windshields of logging trucks. And it hammered the windowpane through which I gazed at the Freeway reflection of Ziller's huge innocent weenie, finding in its gentle repose precious few parallels with my own condition.

o o o o o o o o

And then the rains came.

They came down from the hills and up from the Sound.

And it rained a sickness. And it rained a fear. And it rained an odor. And it rained a murder. And it rained dangers and pale eggs of the beast.

Rain fell on the towns and the fields. It fell on the tractor sheds and the labyrinth of sloughs. Rain fell on toadstools and ferns and bridges. It fell on the head of John Paul Ziller.

Rain poured for days, unceasing. Flooding occurred. The wells filled with reptiles. The basements filled with fossils. Mossy-haired lunatics roamed the dripping peninsulas. Moisture gleamed on the beak of the Raven. Ancient shamans, rained from their homes in dead tree trunks, clacked their clam-shell teeth in the drowned doorways of forests. Rain hissed on the Freeway. It hissed at the prows of fishing boats. It ate the old warpaths, spilled the huckle-berries, ran in the ditches. Soaking. Spreading. Penetrating.

And it rained an omen. And it rained a poison. And it rained a pigment. And it rained a seizure.

Notes on Contributors

Beth Bentley (1928), who was born in St. Paul, Minnesota, received her B.A. from the University of Minnesota in 1948. Her M.A. was awarded by the University of Michigan in 1950. She has taught at all levels, including to gifted children. In 1978 she and her husband, the respected teacher and poet Nelson Bentley, read their poetry at the Library of Congress. Following her study of French on a writer's grant in France, she is currently translating French women poets. She lives in Seattle.

Honors and Awards

Borestone Mountain Poetry Awards, 1967, for "Changing a Diaper on Chuckanut Drive" and "The Lesson"; 1968, for "The Birthing: Eve"

Pacific Northwest Booksellers Regional Authors Award, 1971, for *Phone Calls from the Dead*

Governor's Writers' Day Award, State of Washington, 1972, for *Phone Calls from the Dead;* 1976, for *Country of Resemblances*

National Endowment for the Arts Poetry Grant, 1976

National Endowment for the Arts Administrative Internship, 1978

Gertrude Clarke Whittall Series, Library of Congress, 1978

Books

Country of Resemblances. Athens, Ohio: Ohio University Press, 1976.

Field of Snow. Seattle: Madrona Press, 1973.

Philosophical Investigations. Seattle: Sea Pen Press, 1977.

Phone Calls from the Dead. Athens, Ohio: Ohio University Press, 1970.

Don Berry (1932) is a versatile man: novelist, poet, historian, musician, and sculptor are a part of his list of accomplishments. Among the places he has lived are France, Vienna, New Zealand, Hong Kong, Martinique, and the British West Indies. For several years, he also lived on a classic fifty-four foot wooden sailboat. His home is now on Vashon Island near Seattle.

Honors and Awards

Western Writers of America Awards, 1963, for *Moon Trap*

Books

A Majority of Scoundrels: An Informal History of the Rocky Mountain Fur Company. New York: Harper & Row, 1961.

Moontrap, New York: Viking Press, 1962.

Mountain Men. New York: Macmillan, 1966.

To Build a Ship. New York: Viking Press, 1963.

Trask. New York: Viking Press, 1960.

Olga Broumas (1949) came into national prominence in 1977 when she received the Yale Series of Younger Poets Award. She was born on Syros, a Cyclades island, in Greece. Architecture was her major at the University of Pennsylvania, where she took her B.A. She received an M.F.A. in writing from the University of Oregon.

Honors and Awards

Fulbright Travel Grant, 1967

Oregon Arts Commission Grant, 1977

Yale Series of Younger Poets Award, 1977, for *Beginning with O*

National Endowment for the Arts Grant, 1978

Books

Beginning with O. New Haven: Yale University Press, 1977.

Caritas. Eugene, Oregon: Jackrabbit Press, 1976.

Namaste. Port Townsend, Washington: Copper Canyon Press, 1978.

Soie Sauvage. Port Townsend, Washington: Copper Canyon Press, forthcoming.

H. L. Davis (1896-1960), one of the Northwest's best known novelists, realized his first success as a poet. Astonishingly, the first nine poems he sent out were published in *Poetry* magazine, and in that same year, 1919, he received the magazine's highest award, the Levinson Prize. In 1936, his reputation as a novelist was firmly established when he was awarded the Pulitzer Prize for *Honey in the Horn.* Born near Yoncalla in southwestern Oregon, he worked as a cowboy, sheepherder, deputy sheriff, packer, and typesetter before he became a writer.

Honors and Awards

Levinson Prize, *Poetry* magazine, 1919, for "Primapara" (group of poems)

Guggenheim Fellowship, 1932

Harper Prize, 1935, for *Honey in the Horn*

Pulitzer Prize, 1936, for *Honey in the Horn*

Silver Medal, California Literature Medal Award, 1943, for *Proud Riders*

Gold Medal for Fiction, Commonwealth Club of California, 1953, for *Winds of Morning*

Books

Beulah Land. New York: William Morrow, 1949.

The Distant Music. New York: William Morrow, 1957.

Harp of a Thousand Strings. New York: William Morrow, 1947.

Honey in the Horn. New York: Harper and Brothers, 1935.

Kettle of Fire. New York: William Morrow, 1959.

Proud Riders, and Other Poems. New York: Harper & Brothers, 1942.

Status Rerum: A Manifesto upon the Present Condition of Northwestern Literature Containing Several Near-Libelous Utterances upon Persons in the Public Eye, with James Stevens. The Dalles, Oregon: privately printed, 1927.

Team Bells Woke Me, and Other Stories. New York: William Morrow, 1953.

Winds of Morning. New York: William Morrow, 1952.

Madeline DeFrees (1919) is a native of eastern Oregon. She received her B.A. in English literature from Marylhurst College in 1948. In 1951, she took an M.A. at the University of Oregon. She also attended the University of Washington and Indiana University. During her years as a nun, she lived in virtually every part of the Northwest. She now resides in Missoula, Montana, where she teaches at the University of Montana.

Honors and Awards

Honorary Litt. D., Gonzaga University, 1959

Borestone Mountain Poetry Awards, 1961, for "Requiem Mass: Convent Cemetery"; 1966, for From "A Catch of Summer"

Poetry Prize, Indiana University Writers Conference, 1961

Short story ("The Model Chapel") in *Best American Short Stories of 1962,* Martha Foley, ed.

Visiting Lecturer, Writer in Residence, Seattle University, 1965

Governor's Writers' Day Award, State of Washington, 1966

Abbie M. Copps Award, Olivet College, 1973

Books

From the Darkroom. Indianapolis: Bobbs-Merrill, 1962.

Imaginary Ancestors. Missoula, Montana: CutBank/SmokeRoot Press, 1978.

Later Thoughts from the Springs of Silence. Indianapolis: Bobbs-Merrill, 1962.

Springs of Silence: An Autobiographical Account of Convent Life. Englewood Cliffs, New Jersey: Prentice-Hall, 1953.

When Sky Lets Go. New York: Braziller, 1978.

Vardis Fisher (1895-1968) was born in the pioneer Mormon settlement of Annis, Idaho. In 1925, he received his Ph.D., magna cum laude, from the University of Chicago. The suicide of his first wife during his pressure-filled graduate school years turned him in the direction of introspective fiction. After a brief career in university teaching, he devoted the rest of his life to farming and writing. Ironically, he returned to the isolated Antelope Hills region on the Snake River he had hated as a child to experience the life of hardship his parents had endured. His best known novel, *The Children of God,* is a balanced account of the history of the Mormon church that he rejected before he was twenty. During the course of his extremely productive career, he was consistently passed over for grants and awards.

Honors and Awards

Harper Prize Novel Award, 1939, for *The Children of God*

Western Heritage Award, 1966, for *Mountain Man*

Western Writers of America Award, 1966, for *Mountain Man*

Books

Adam and the Serpent. New York: Vanguard Press, 1948.

April: A Fable of Love. Garden City, New York: Doubleday, Doran; Caldwell, Idaho: Caxton, 1937.

The Caxton Printers in Idaho: A Short History. Cincinnati, Ohio: Society of Bibliosophers, 1944.

Children of God; An American Epic. New York: Harper, 1939.

City of Illusion, A Novel. New York: Harper, 1941.

Dark Bridwell. Boston: Houghton Mifflin; Cambridge: Riverside Press, 1931.

Darkness and the Deep. New York: Vanguard Press, 1943.

The Divine Passion. New York: Vanguard Press, 1948.

Forgive Us Our Virtues: A Comedy of Evasions. Caldwell, Idaho: Caxton, 1938.

A Goat for Azael. Denver: Alan Swallow, 1956.

God or Caesar: The Writing of Fiction for Beginners. Caldwell, Idaho: Caxton, 1953.

Gold Rushes and Mining Camps of the Early American West. Caldwell, Idaho: Caxton, 1968. With Opal Laurel Holmes.

The Golden Rooms. New York: Vanguard Press, 1944.

In Tragic Life. Garden City, New York: Doubleday, Dorn; Caldwell, Idaho: Caxton, 1932.

Intimations of Eve. New York: Vanguard Press, 1946.

The Island of the Innocent. New York: Abelard Press, 1952.

Jesus Came Again. Denver: Alan Swallow, 1956.

Love and Death: The Complete Stories of Vardis Fisher. Garden City, New York: Doubleday, 1959.

The Mothers: An American Saga of Courage. New York: Vanguard, 1943.

Mountain Man: A Novel of Male and Female in the Early American West. New York: William Morrow, 1965.

My Holy Satan. Denver: Alan Swallow, 1958.

The Neurotic Nightingale. Milwaukee: Casanova Press, 1935.

No Villain Need Be. Garden City, New York: Doubleday, Doran; Caldwell, Idaho: Caxton, 1936.

Odyssey of a Hero. Philadelphia: Ritten House, 1937.

Orphans in Gethsemane. Denver: Alan Swallow, 1960.

Peace Like a River. Denver: Alan Swallow, 1957.

Passions Spin the Plot. Garden City, New York: Doubleday, Doran; Caldwell, Idaho: Caxton, 1934.

Pemmican: A Novel of the Hudson's Bay Company. Garden City, New York: Doubleday, 1956.

Suicide or Murder? The Strange Death of Governor Meriwether Lewis. Denver: Alan Swallow, 1962.

A Tale of Valor: A Novel of the Lewis and Clark Expedition. Garden City, New York: Doubleday, 1958.

Thomas Wolfe as I Knew Him, and Other Essays. Denver: Alan Swallow, 1963.

Toilers of the Hills. Caldwell, Idaho: Caxton, 1945.

The Valley of Vision. New York: Abelard Press, 1951.

We Are Betrayed. Garden City, New York: Doubleday, Doran; Caldwell, Idaho: Caxton, 1937.

John Haines (1929), who homesteaded in Alaska from 1954 to 1969, was named poet laureate of Alaska in 1969. He was educated at American University in Washington, D.C., and the Hans Hoffmann School of Fine Arts in New York City. He has taught at the University of Washington. His home is now in Pacific Grove, California.

Honors and Awards

Jennie Tane Award for Poetry, *Massachusetts Review*, 1964, for "The Traveller" and "A Winter Light"

Guggenheim Fellowship, 1965

National Endowment for the Arts Grant, 1967

Poet Laureate of Alaska, 1969

Poet in Residence, University of Alaska, 1972

Books

Cicada. Middletown, Connecticut: Wesleyan University Press, 1971.

The Mirror. Santa Barbara: Unicorn Press, 1971.

The Stone Harp. Middletown, Connecticut: Wesleyan University Press, 1964.

Twenty Poems. Santa Barbara, California: Unicorn Press, 1971.

Winter News. Middletown, Connecticut: Wesleyan University Press, 1962.

Robert Huff (1924) was the first recipient of the University of Virginia Poetry Prize in 1976 for his book, *The Ventriloquist.* He teaches at Western Washington University and is poetry editor for *Concerning Poetry.* He was born in Evanston, Illinois, and received both his B.A. and M.A. from Wayne State University in Detroit.

Honors and Awards

Writing Scholarship, Breadloaf Writers' Conference, 1961

Writing Fellowship, The MacDowell Colony, 1963

Honorary Trustee, Theodore Roethke Memorial Foundation, 1968

First Prize, University of Virginia Series for Contemporary Poetry, 1976, for the *Ventriloquist*

Books

Colonel Johnson's Ride. Detroit: Wayne State University Press, 1959.

The Course: One, Two, Three Now! Detroit: Wayne State University Press, 1966.

The Ventriloquist: New and Selected Poems. Charlottesville: University Press of Virginia, 1977.

Richard Hugo (1923) was named judge of the Yale Series of Younger Poets in 1977. Born in Seattle, he served in the Air Force during World War II and was awarded the Air Medal and the Distinguished Flying Cross. He received a B.A. from the University of Washington in 1948 and an M.A. in 1952. Hugo worked at Boeing Aircraft from 1951 to 1963 before becoming a faculty member at the University of Montana in 1964, where he continues to teach and direct the creative writing program.

Honors and Awards

Northwest Writers Book of the Year Award, 1965, for *Death of the Kapowsin Tavern*

Pacific Northwest Booksellers Regional Authors Award, 1965, for *Death of the Kapowsin Tavern*

Governor's Writer's Day Award, State of Washington, 1966

Rockefeller Foundation Creative Writing Fellowship, 1967

Theodore Roethke Memorial Poetry Prize, *Poetry Northwest*, 1976

Guggenheim Fellowship, 1977

Books

Death of the Kapowsin Tavern. New York: Harcourt, Brace, and World, 1965.

Duwamish Head. Port Townsend, Washington: Cooperhead, 1976.

Good Luck in Cracked Italian. New York: World Publishing Company, 1969.

The Lady in Kicking Horse Reservoir. New York: W. W. Norton, 1973.

A Run of Jacks. Minneapolis: University of Minnesota Press, 1961.

31 Letters and 13 Dreams. New York: W. W. Norton, 1977.

What Thou Lovest Well Remains American. New York: W. W. Norton, 1975.

Ken Kesey (1935), who was born in La Junta, California, moved with his parents to Pleasant Hill, Oregon, in 1944, where he still lives with his wife and family. He took his B.S. at the University of Oregon in 1957, where he was an All American in wrestling. Kesey's growing interest in religion recently prompted him to describe himself as a "revelationary revolutionary."

Honors and Awards

Woodrow Wilson Fellowship, 1958

Eugene F. Saxton Memorial Trust Award, 1959, for "Zoo"

Certificate of Achievement, University of Oregon, 1978.

Books

Kesey, edited by Michael Strelow and staff of *Northwest Review.* Eugene, Oregon: Northwest Review Books, 1977.

Kesey's Garage Sale. New York: Viking Press, 1973.

One Flew Over the Cuckoo's Nest. New York: Viking Press, 1962.

Sometimes a Great Notion. New York: Viking Press, 1964.

Carolyn Kizer (1925) was born in Spokane, Washington. She took her B.A. at Sarah Lawrence College in 1945 and was a Chinese Government Fellow in comparative literature at Columbia University in 1946-1947. In 1953 and 1954, she studied poetry with Theodore Roethke at the University of Washington. Kizer was Specialist in Literature in Pakistan for the State Department in 1964, and from 1966 through 1970, she was the first Director of the Literature Program for the National Endowment for the Arts. She is the founder of *Poetry Northwest* and was editor from 1959 to 1965. She now lives in Berkeley, California.

Honors and Awards

Governor's Writers' Day Award, State of Washington, 1966

Poet in Residence, University of North Carolina, 1970-1974

Hurst Professor, Washington University, St. Louis, 1971

Acting Director, Graduate Writing Program, Columbia University, 1972

Lecturer, Spring Lecture Series, Barnard College, 1972

McGuffey Lecturer, Poet in Residence, Ohio University, 1975

Visiting Professor of Poetry, Iowa Writers' Workshop, 1976

Books

Knock upon Silence. Garden City, New York: Doubleday, 1965.

Midnight was My Cry: New and Selected Poems. Garden City, New York: Doubleday, 1971.

The Ungrateful Garden. Bloomington: Indiana University Press, 1961.

Ursula K. Le Guin (1929) lives and writes in Portland, Oregon. She received her B.A. from Radcliffe College in 1951 and her M.A. from Columbia University in French and Italian Renaissance literature in 1952. In 1953, she lived in France as a Fulbright student. She has taught and participated in writers workshops at many universities. While she is best known as a writer of science fiction, she has also published poetry and conventional fiction.

Honors and Awards

Boston Globe/Hornbook Award, 1968, for *A Wizard of Earthsea*

Nebula Award, 1969, for *The Left Hand of Darkness*

Hugo Award, 1969, for *The Left Hand of Darkness*

Hugo Award, 1972, for "The Word for World is Forest"

National Book Award, 1972, for *The Farthest Shore*

Hugo Award, 1973, for "The Ones Who Walk Away from Omelas"

Hugo Award, 1974, for *The Dispossessed*

Nebula Award, 1974, for *The Dispossessed*

Nebula Award, 1975, for "The Day Before the Revolution"

Resident Writer, Australian Workshop in Speculative Fiction, 1975

Books

City of Illusions. New York: Ace Books, 1966.

The Dispossessed. New York: Harper & Row, 1974.

Dreams Must Explain Themselves. New York: Algol Press, 1975.

The Eye of the Heron. In *Millennial Women: Tales for Tomorrow*, edited by Virginia Kidd. New York: Delacorte/Dell, 1978.

The Farthest Shore. New York: Atheneum, 1972.

From Elfland to Poughkeepsie. Portland, Oregon: Pendragon Press, 1973.

The Lathe of Heaven. New York: Charles Schribner's Sons, 1971.

Leese Webster. New York: Atheneum, forthcoming.

The Left Hand of Darkness. New York: Ace Books, 1969.

Orsinian Tales. New York: Harper & Row, 1976.

Planet of Exile. New York: Ace Books, 1966.

Rocannon's World. New York: Ace Books, 1966.

The Tombs of Atuan. New York: Atheneum, 1970.

Very Far Away from Anywhere Else. New York: Atheneum, 1976.

The Water Is Wide. Portland, Oregon: Pendragon Press, 1976.

Wild Angels. Santa Barbara, California: Capra Press, 1974.

The Wind's Twelve Quarters. New York: Harper & Row, 1976.

A Wizard of Earthsea. Emeryville, California: Parnassus Press, 1968.

The Word for World is Forest. New York: G. P. Putnam's Sons, 1976.

Sandra McPherson (1943) taught for two years in the University of Iowa Writers' Workshop. She was born and educated in California and also attended the University of Washington. She now lives with her husband, the equally well known poet, Henry Carlile, in Portland, Oregon, where she conducts workshops and poetry readings.

Honors and Awards

Helen Bullis Prize, *Poetry Northwest*, 1968

Borestone Mountain Poetry Awards, 1969, for "View from Observatory Hill"

Ingram Merrill Foundation Grant, 1972

Bess Hokin Prize, *Poetry* magazine, 1972

Emily Dickinson Award, Poetry Society of America, 1973

Pacific Northwest Booksellers Regional Authors Award, 1973, for *Radiation*

National Endowment for the Arts Grant, 1974

Faculty Member, Iowa Writers' Workshop, 1974-1976, 1978-1979

Blumenthal-Leviton-Blonder Prize, *Poetry* magazine, 1975

Guggenheim Fellowship, 1976

Books

Elegies for the Hot Season. Bloomington: University of Indiana Press, 1974.

Radiation. New York: Ecco Press, 1973.

The Year of Our Birth. New York: Ecco Press, 1978.

Tom Robbins (1936) has been called "the prince of the paperback literate" by the *New York Times Magazine*. Without question he is the leading counterculture writer of the moment. The fact that his two novels have sold over two million copies and that films are being made from them is proof that he has captured the youth market. Of his life he says, "I was born in 1936 in Blowing Rock, N.C. So what?" He attended Washington and Lee and was expelled from his fraternity for pelting the housemother with biscuits. He was formerly a copy editor and art critic, but now lives in the small town of La Connor, Washington, and devotes himself to writing.

Honors and Awards

Governor's Writers' Day Award, State of Washington, 1972, for *Another Roadside Attraction*

Pacific Northwest Booksellers Regional Authors Award, 1977, for *Even Cowgirls Get the Blues*

Books

Another Roadside Attraction. Garden City, New York: Doubleday, 1971.

Even Cowgirls Get the Blues. Boston: Houghton Mifflin, 1976.

Theodore Roethke (1908-1963) was without question the most influential poet to write in the Pacific Northwest. His work is known and appreciated throughout the literary world. He was educated at the University of Michigan where he took his B.A. in 1929 and, after a short stay in law school and study at Harvard, completed his M.A. in 1936. A question that interested and troubled him throughout his adult life was the relationship between his recurrent mental illness and his creativity. He died of a coronary occlusion while swimming in a friend's pool on Bainbridge Island.

Honors and Awards

Guggenheim Fellowship, 1945

Eunice Tietjens Memorial Prize, *Poetry* magazine, 1947, for "Long Alley"

Levinson Prize, *Poetry* magazine, 1951, for "Sensibility! O La!" and "O Lull Me, Lull Me"

Fellowship, Fund for the Advancement of Education, 1952

National Institute and American Academy Awards in Literature, 1952

Pulitzer Prize for Poetry, 1954, for *The Waking*

Bollingen Prize in Poetry, 1959, for *Words in the Wind*

Edna St. Vincent Millay Memorial Award, 1959, for *Words in the Wind*

Books

The Collected Poems of Theodore Roethke. Garden City, New York: Doubleday, 1966.

Dirty Dinky and Other Creatures: Poems for Children. Selected by Beatrice Roethke and Stephen Lushington. Garden City, New York: Doubleday, 1973.

The Exorcism: A Portfolio of Poems. San Francisco: Mallette Dean, 1957.

The Far Field. Garden City, New York: Doubleday, 1964.

I Am! Says the Lamb. Garden City, New York: Doubleday, 1961.

The Lost Son and Other Poems. Garden City, New York: Doubleday, 1948.

On the Poet and His Craft: Selected Prose of Theodore Roethke. Edited by Ralph J. Mills, Jr. Seattle: University of Washington Press, 1965.

Open House. New York: Alfred A. Knopf, 1941.

Party at the Zoo. New York: Crowell-Collier, Modern Masters Book for Children, 1963.

Praise to the End! Garden City, New York: Doubleday, 1951.

Selected Letters of Theodore Roethke. Edited by Ralph J. Mills, Jr. Seattle: University of Washington Press, 1968.

Selected Poems of Theodore Roethke. Edited by Beatrice Roethke. London: Faber, 1969.

Sequence, Sometimes Metaphysical. Iowa City, Iowa: Stone Wall Press, 1963.

Straw for the Fire: From the Notebooks of Theodore Roethke, 1943-1963. Garden City, New York: Doubleday, 1972.

The Waking: Poems 1933-1953. Garden City, New York: Doubleday, 1954.

Words for the Wind. London: Secker & Warburg, 1957.

Gary Snyder (1930) was born in San Francisco but spent most of his youth on his parents' farm north of Seattle. He graduated from Reed College in 1951 and attended Indiana University and the University of California at Berkeley from 1951 to 1956. He spent most of the period from 1956 to 1968 studying in Japan. He is a Buddhist of the Mahayana-Vajrayana line. Snyder, along with Jack Kerouac and Allen Ginsberg, was one of the initiators of "beat" movement in literature. He has made his home at Kitkitdizze in Nevada City, California, since 1970.

Honors and Awards

Scholarship to Japan, First Zen Institute of America, 1956

Bess Hokin Prize, *Poetry* magazine, 1964, for "Four from Six Years"

Bollingen Fellow, 1966

National Institute and American Academy Awards in Literature, 1966

Levinson Prize, *Poetry* magazine, 1968, for "Eight Songs of Clouds and Water"

Guggenheim Fellow, 1968

Pulitzer Prize for Poetry, 1974, for *Turtle Island*

Books

The Blue Sky. New York: Phoenix Book Shop, 1969.

The Back Country. New York: New Directions, 1968.

Earth House Hold: technical notes & queries to fellow dharma revolutionaries. New York: New Directions, 1969.

The Fudo Trilogy: Spel Against Demons. Smokey the Bear Sutra. The California Water Plan. Berkeley: Shaman Drum, 1973.

"In Transit: The Gary Snyder Issue." Eugene, Oregon: Toad Press, 1969.

Manzanita. Bolinas, California: Four Seasons Foundation, 1972.

Myths and Texts. New Haven: Totem Press, 1960.

The Old Ways. New York: New Directions, 1977.

A Range of Poems. London: Fulcrum Press, 1966.

Regarding Wave. New York: New Directions, 1970.

Riprap, & Cold Mountain Poems. San Francisco: Four Seasons Foundation, 1965.

Six Selections from Mountains and Rivers Without End, Plus One. San Francisco: Four Seasons Foundations, 1965.

Sours of the Hills. (n. p.) Samuel Charters, 1969.

Three Worlds, Three Realms, Three Roads. Marlboro, Vermont: Griffin Press, 1966.

Turtle Island. New York: New Directions, 1973.

William Stafford (1914) is one of the most widely published poets in America. His work is regularly included in the most prestigious collections of American poetry and the most authoritative surveys of American literature. He is poet laureate of the state of Oregon. Stafford teaches at Lewis and Clark College and has homes in Lake Oswego and Sisters, Oregon.

Honors and Awards

Yaddo Foundation Fellow, 1956

Union League Civic and Arts Foundation Prize, *Poetry* magazine, 1959

First Prize, Oregon Centennial Exposition, Poetry Contest for the General Public, 1959, for "Memorials of a Tour Around Mt. Hood"

First Prize, Oregon Centennial Exposition, Short Story Contest for the General Public, 1959, for "The Osage Orange"

National Book Award, 1963, for *Traveling Through the Dark*

Shelley Memorial Award, 1964

Honorary Litt. D., Ripon College, 1965; Linfield College, 1970

Guggenheim Fellowship, 1966

National Endowment for the Arts Grant, 1966

Consultant in Poetry, Library of Congress, 1970

U.S. Information Agency Lecturer in Egypt, Iran, Pakistan, India, Nepal, and Bangladesh, 1972

Melville Cane Award, 1974, for *Someday, Maybe*

Books

Allegiances. New York: Harper and Row, 1970.

Down in My Heart. Elgin, Illinois: Brethren Press, 1947.

The Rescued Year. New York: Harper and Row, 1966.

Someday, Maybe. New York: Harper and Row, 1973.

Stories That Could Be True. New York: Harper and Row, 1977.

Traveling Through the Dark. New York: Harper and Row, 1962.

West of Your City. Lincoln, Nebraska: Talisman Press, 1960.

David Wagoner (1926) was born in Massillon, Ohio. He received a B.A. from Pennsylvania State University in 1947 and an M.A. from Indiana University in 1949. Theodore Roethke persuaded the English department at the University of Washington to hire Wagoner in 1954, where he continues to teach. He has been editor of *Poetry Northwest* since 1966. Although we have chosen to represent him in this collection with a selection of his poetry, he is also an accomplished novelist, having published nine novels since 1954.

Honors and Awards

Guggenheim Fellowship, 1956

Indiana Authors' Day Awards, 1959, for *A Place to Stand*

Ford Fellowship in Drama, 1964

Governor's Writers' Day Award, State of Washington, 1966

Morton Dauwen Zabel Prize, *Poetry* magazine, 1967, for "Four Poems"

National Institute and American Academy Awards in Literature, 1967

Elliston Lecturer in Modern Poetry, University of Cincinnati, 1968

National Endowment for the Arts Grant, 1969

Editor, *Poetry Northwest*, 1969

Blumenthal-Leviton-Blonder Prize, *Poetry* magazine, 1974

Fels Prize for Poetry, Coordinating Council of Literary Magazines, 1975

Eunice Tietjens Memorial Prize, *Poetry* magazine, 1977

Member, Board of Chancellors, Academy of American Poets, 1978

Books

Baby, Come on Inside. New York: Farrar, Straus & Giroux, 1965.

Collected Poems. Bloomington: Indiana University Press, 1976.

Dry Sun, Dry Wind. Bloomington: Indiana University Press, 1953.

The Escape Artist. New York: Farrar, Straus & Giroux, 1965.

The Man in the Middle. New York: Harcourt, Brace, 1954.

Money Money Money. New York: Harcourt, Brace, 1955.

The Nesting Ground. Bloomington: Indiana University Press, 1963.

New and Selected Poems. Bloomington: Indiana University Press, 1963.

A Place to Stand. Bloomington: Indiana University Press, 1958.

Riverbed. Bloomington: Indiana University Press, 1972.

The Road to Many a Wonder. New York: Farrar, Straus & Giroux, 1974.

Rock. New York: Viking Press, 1958.

Sleeping in the Woods. Bloomington: Indiana University Press, 1974.

Staying Alive. Bloomington: Indiana University Press, 1966.

Tracker. Boston: Atlantic-Little, Brown, 1976.

Where is My Wandering Boy Tonight? New York: Farrar, Straus & Giroux, 1970.

Whole Hog. Boston: Atlantic-Little, Brown, 1976.

Who Shall Be the Sun? Bloomington: Indiana University Press, 1978.

Selected Bibliography

Bakeless, John E. *Lewis and Clark: Partners in Discovery.* New York: William Morrow, 1947.

Bede, Elbert. *Fabulous Opal Whiteley: From Logging Camp to Princess of India.* Portland: Binfords and Mort, 1954.

Bertolino, James, ed. *Northwest Poets.* Madison, Wisconsin: Quixote Press, 1968.

Blessing, Richard A. *Theodore Roethke's Dynamic Vision.* Bloomington: Indiana University Press, 1974.

Boulton, Jane. *Opal/Opal Whiteley.* Arranged and adapted by Jane Boulton. New York: Macmillan, 1976.

Bradburne, E. S. *Opal Whiteley: The Unsolved Mystery.* London: Putnam, 1962.

Brand, Max. *The Notebooks and Poems of Max Brand.* Edited by John Schoolcroft. New York: Dodd Mead, 1957.

Brandon, William. *The Magic World: American Indian Songs and Poems.* New York: William Morrow, 1971.

Brown, Robert D., Thomas Kranidas, and Faith G. Norris, eds. *Oregon Signatures.* Corvallis: Oregon State University, 1959.

Chatterton, Wayne. *Vardis Fisher: The Frontier and Regional Works.* Idaho: Boise State College, 1972.

Chittick, V. L. O., ed. *Northwest Harvest: A Regional Stock-taking.* New York: Macmillan, 1948.

Crandall, Allen. *Fisher of the Antelope Hills.* Manhattan, Kansas: Crandall Press, 1949.

Criswell, Elijah H. *Lewis and Clark: Linguistic Pioneers.* Columbia: University of Missouri Press, 1940.

Day, George F. *The Uses of History in the Novels of Vardis Fisher.* New York: Revisionist Press, 1974.

DeVoto, Bernard, ed. *The Journals of Lewis and Clark.* Boston: Houghton Mifflin, 1953.

Dillon, Richard. *Meriwether Lewis: A Biography.* New York: Coward-McCann, 1965.

Easton, Robert. *Max Brand: The Big Westerner.* Norman: University of Oklahoma Press, 1970.

Etalain, Richard W. *Western American Literature: A Bibliography of Interpretive Books and Articles.* Vermillion, South Dakota: Dakota Press, 1972.

Fiedler, Leslie. *The Return of the Vanishing American*. New York: Stein and Day, 1968.

Flora, Joseph M. *Vardis Fisher*. New York: Twayne Publishers, 1965.

Frost, O. W. *Joaquin Miller*. New York: Twayne Publishers, 1967.

Holbrook, Stewart H. *Far Corner: A Personal View of the Pacific Northwest*. New York: Macmillan, 1952.

Holbrook, Stewart H., ed. *Promised Land: A Collection of Northwest Writing*. New York: McGraw-Hill; London: Whittlesey House, 1945.

Holden, Jonathan. *The Mark to Turn: A Reading of William Stafford's Poetry*. Lawrence: University Press of Kansas, 1976.

Horner, John B. *Oregon Literature*. Portland: J. K. Gill, 1902.

Howard, Richard. *Alone with America: Essays on the Art of Poetry in the United States since 1950*. New York: Atheneum, 1969.

Jackson, Donald Dean, ed. *Letters of the Lewis and Clark Expedition with Related Documents, 1783-1859*. Urbana: University of Illinois Press, 1962.

Kellogg, George. "Vardis Fisher: A Bibliography." *Western American Literature* 5 (Spring 1970): 45-64.

Kesey, Ken. "Letters from Mexico." In *The Single Voice: An Anthology of Contemporary Fiction*, edited by Jerome Charyn. London: Collier-MacMillan, 1969, pp. 417-426.

Larson, Clinton F. and William Stafford. *Modern Poetry of Western America*. Provo, Utah: Brigham Young University Press, 1975.

Lee, W. Storrs, ed. *Washington State: A Literary Chronicle*. New York: Funk and Wagnalls, 1969.

Lensing, George and Ronald Moran. *Four Poets and the Emotive Imagination*. Baton Rouge: Louisiana State University Press, 1977.

Levin, Jeff. "Ursula K. Le Guin: A Selected Bibliography." *Science Fiction Studies* 2 (1975): 204-208.

Lucia, Ellis, ed. *This Land Around Us: A Treasury of Pacific Northwest Writing*. New York: Doubleday, 1969.

Malkoff, Karl. *Theodore Roethke: An Introduction to the Poetry*. New York: Columbia University Press, 1966.

Mayberry, M. Marion. *Splendid Poseur: Joaquin Miller—American Poet*. New York: Thomas Y. Crowell, 1953.

McCole, C. John. *Lucifer at Large*. New York: Longmans, 1937.

McLeod, James R. *Theodore Roethke: A Bibliography*. Kent, Ohio: Kent State University Press, 1973.

McMillan, Sammuel H. "On William Stafford and His Poems: A Selected Bibliography." *Tennessee Poetry Journal* 2 (Spring 1969): 21-22.

Merriam, Harold G, ed. *Northwest Verse, An Anthology.* Caldwell, Idaho: Caxton, 1931.

Miller, Joaquin. *The Poetical Works of Joaquin Miller.* Edited by Stewart Sherman. New York: G. P. Putnam, 1923.

Mills, Ralph J. *Theodore Roethke.* Minneapolis: University of Minnesota Press, 1963.

Moul, Keith R. *Theodore Roethke's Career: An Annotated Bibliography.* Boston: G. K. Hall, 1977.

Nelson, Herbert B. *The Literary Impulse in Pioneer Oregon.* Corvallis: Oregon State College Press, 1948.

Newman, Mrs. Mary Wentworth (pseudonymn May Wentworth), ed. *Poetry of the Pacific: Selections and Original Poems from the Poets of the Pacific States.* San Francisco: Pacific, 1867.

Niatum, Duane, ed. *Carriers of the Dream Wheel: Contemporary Native American Poetry.* New York: Harper and Row, 1975.

Peterson, Martin Severin. *Joaquin Miller: Literary Frontiersman.* Palo Alto, California: Stanford University Press, 1937.

Powers, Alfred. *History of Oregon Literature.* Portland: Metropolitan Press, 1935.

Pratt, John C. *One Flew Over the Cuckoo's Nest: Text and Criticism.* New York: Viking, 1973.

Rein, David. *Vardis Fisher: Challenge to Evasion.* Chicago: Black Cat, 1937.

Richards, John S., ed. *Joaquin Miller: His California Diary.* Seattle: F. McCaffrey, 1936.

Richardson, Darrell C. *Max Brand, The Man and His Work: Critical Appreciations and Bibliography.* Los Angeles: Fantasy, 1952.

Roethke, Theodore. *On the Poet and His Craft: Selected Prose of Theodore Roethke.* Edited by Ralph Mills, Jr. Seattle: University of Washington Press, 1965.

Roethke, Theodore. *Straw for the Fire: From the Notebooks of Theodore Roethke, 1943-63.* Selected and arranged by David Wagoner. Garden City, New York: Doubleday, 1972.

Scott, Nathan A., Jr. *The Wild Prayer of Longing: Poetry and the Sacred.* New Haven: Yale University Press, 1971.

Seager, Allen. *The Glass House: The Life of Theodore Roethke.* New York: McGraw-Hill, 1968.

Skelton, Robin, ed. *Five Poets of the Pacific Northwest: Kenneth O. Hanson, Richard Hugo, Carolyn Kizer, William Stafford, David Wagoner.* Seattle: University of Washington Press, 1964.

Slasser, George Edgar. *The Farthest Shores of Ursula K. Le Guin.* San Bernadino, California: Borgo, 1976.

Stein, Arnold, ed. *Theodore Roethke: Essays on the Poetry.* Seattle: University of Washington Press, 1965.

Steuding, Bob. *Gary Snyder.* Boston: Twayne, 1976.

Sullivan, Rosemary. *Theodore Roethke: The Garden Master.* Seattle: University of Washington Press, 1976.

Swan, James G. *The Northwest Coast, or Three Years' Residence in Washington Territory.* Seattle: University of Washington Press, 1972.

Thwaites, Reuben Gold, ed. *Original Journals of the Lewis and Clark Expedition, 1804-1806.* 8 vols. New York: Dodd, Mead and Company, 1904-1905.

Wagner, Harr. *Joaquin Miller and His Other Self.* San Francisco: Harr Wagner, 1929.

Weixlmann, Joseph. "Ken Kesey: A Bibliography." *Western American Literature* 10 (1975): 219-231.

Wolfe, Tom. *The Electric Kool-Aid Acid Test.* New York: Farrar, Straus and Giroux, 1968.